WOLF

THE WILL SLATER SERIES BOOK ONE

MATT ROGERS

Join the Reader's Group and get a free 200-page book by Matt Rogers!

Sign up for a free copy of '**HARD IMPACT**'.
Meet Jason King — another member of Black Force, the shadowy organisation that Slater dedicated his career to.

Experience King's most dangerous mission — action-packed insanity in the heart of the Amazon Rainforest.

No spam guaranteed.

Just click here.

BOOKS BY MATT ROGERS

THE JASON KING SERIES

Isolated (Book 1)

Imprisoned (Book 2)

Reloaded (Book 3)

Betrayed (Book 4)

Corrupted (Book 5)

Hunted (Book 6)

THE JASON KING FILES

Cartel (Book 1)

THE WILL SLATER SERIES

Wolf (Book 1)

"I, William J. Clinton, President of the United States of America, find that the proliferation of nuclear, biological, and chemical weapons and of the means of delivering such weapons, constitutes an unusual and extraordinary threat to the national security, foreign policy, and economy of the United States, and hereby declare a national emergency to deal with that threat."

— EXECUTIVE ORDER 12938

WOLF

PART ONE

1

The lab reeked of disinfectant, an artificial stench that permeated throughout the steel room — a half-hearted attempt to overpower the smell of the dead.

The three occupants couldn't smell a thing. They wore protective rubber hazmat suits, covered head to toe in vapour-tight material to prevent a single viral particle from making contact with their skin. A hushed silence had fallen over the lab as they observed the grisly results of their experiment, the only noise coming from the distinct rasping of their self-contained breathing apparatus.

The scene in front of them was ordinarily reserved for bad science fiction movies.

Years ago, the trio would have turned away in disgust at the body on the steel gurney in the centre of the room. They would have lost the contents of their stomachs, unable to help themselves as natural instincts took over.

Now, they stood silent, watching and analysing in clinical fashion.

The world was a harsh, unforgiving place.

They had come to learn that.

'Take samples,' the man in the middle said in his native tongue.

His voice came out wrong, muffled by the face mask hanging over his features. It filtered out through the sides of his mouthpiece — the device that separated him from a fate worse than death itself.

The men on either side stepped forward, approaching the corpse without hesitation. They knew the consequences of displeasing their boss. The rivers of blood dripping out of the body's every orifice did little to deter them.

They worked methodically, collecting DNA samples and slotting them into pre-arranged storage containers. The leader hung back, letting his underlings carry out the dirty work. He had no qualms about doing everything himself, but over the years he'd made a pointed attempt to delegate tasks more often.

Trying to handle it all on his own had almost cost him his life six years ago.

In this world, there was no margin for error.

Once the necessary samples had been collected from the grotesque, misshapen corpse on the table, the trio set about running them through a complicated web of machinery and lab equipment that had set their financier back well over a million USD.

The price would be worth it, though.

It took just over an hour to confirm their rudimentary theory. Weeks of further testing and analysing and tweaking would be required, but for now they had the answer they'd been looking for.

The pair of underlings turned to the leader.

'You were right,' one of them said.

'It's different to the original strain?' the leader said.

The other man nodded. 'Ever so slightly. We don't know what that means yet, but it could very well align with what you thought.'

The leader turned to look at the horrifying sight of the body they had extracted the samples from. He couldn't imagine the extent of the suffering the man had gone through before he finally succumbed to the virus. They had patiently observed every second of the three weeks it had taken the guy to finally reach breaking point and fade away into oblivion.

It had tested all their resolves, but the leader had made it explicitly clear that if any of them had second thoughts about their involvement in the experiment, they would be silenced and thrown in a ditch for the wolves to pick at.

Freeze-frames of horrific memories had etched into the leader's brain, and he couldn't see them ever going away. He remembered locking eyes with the test subject as the man spasmed in his death throes, bleeding out of his eyes and nostrils and mouth all at once.

He remembered a hell of a lot more, but he tried not to dwell on it.

Not yet.

The operation was still live.

Emotion had to be forced to the side.

'It can't be anything else,' he said. 'An incubator can turn any lab-forged virus into something more powerful. You know that.'

'We're not certain yet. We need to run further testing.'

'Do it. But I'll make the call. I'll tell them we have a weaponised variant.'

'What does this mean?' one of the men said. 'Is our work done?'

'Almost. Everything's going according to plan.'

The leader stepped out of the workstation, slipping silently through an adjoining door with a digital keypad built into the wall alongside it. He closed and locked the door behind him, just to be safe, and pressed on into a small office. The space was indistinguishable from a retail store's backroom. The operation's budget had been reserved exclusively for the testing facilities — anything else was spartan in comparison.

The leader sat down on a rickety wooden chair, peeled his face mask off, and reached for the landline phone on the desk. He punched in a long string of digits and waited for the call to be received.

'Yes?' a low voice said after a single second of ringing.

'It's done.'

'You have the variant?'

'We believe so. Further testing is required.'

'Run the tests. There's no rush. Make sure it's airtight.'

'You still haven't told me what you need it for.'

'And I never will. You'll see it in the news, though. Get back to work.'

The call disconnected abruptly, without a word of farewell.

The man stared at the phone in his hand for a significant length of time, twirling the device in his fingers, deep in thought. He glanced sideways at the tiered trays of empty round steel containers resting in orderly rows against the far wall of the office.

Bomblets, ready to be filled with enough weaponised bacteria to cause unimaginable devastation.

Especially given the nature of the virus they had bioengineered.

The memories of the man who had succumbed to the infection came rolling back into the forefront of his mind.

The skin turning a dark shade of horrifying blue. The uncontrollable bleeding, which had subsequently turned him entirely crimson by the end of the descent into madness. The loss of control of his bowels. The distinct screeches of agony as his organs failed and melted away inside of him.

The leader pictured a populated city square inhaling the contents of the bomblets, trekking back to their apartment complexes to spread the virus to their loved ones and anyone who so much as stepped foot in the same room as them.

He found himself disgusted by what he had become.

But he wasn't being paid to sit around and ponder the morality of his choices. He had made them, and now he was stuck fulfilling the wishes of a man who wanted nothing more than to see raw suffering on a global scale.

He didn't know the reasons for his financier's deep-seated hatred.

He only saw the wire transfers materialise in his account.

He rose off the chair with enough speed for the legs to creak underneath him and — just as his financier had instructed — got back to work.

2

Diana Edwards tucked her tiny fingers inside the ribbed cuffs of her raincoat as the sky darkened and the first of the day's sleet began to fall from the sky.

Because it was her sixth birthday, her mother had finally allowed her to make the short trek home from school on her own. When the bell finally rang and she gathered her tattered beige backpack off its hook in the corridor and stepped out into the overcast afternoon, muscle memory had kicked in. She'd searched the faces of the hordes of parents bunched up around the school gates for her mother. She was accustomed to seeing the scrunched-up face with heavy bags under the eyes and heavily-chapped lips.

It took her a moment to remember that today was her special day.

Maybe her mother had taken the opportunity to start drinking a little earlier than usual.

Diana didn't really want to go home all that much.

She trotted animatedly along the sidewalk, taking her time with her newfound freedom, staring at the familiar sights of Kingston upon Thames as she passed them by. She had never been able to take it slow along these streets. Her afternoons usually consisted of her mother holding a vice-like grip around her little wrist, tugging her along without much concern for how Diana felt about the whole thing. She didn't appreciate it when her mother was in a rush. It was only ever to get to her favourite bottles, anyway.

Sometimes the skin around Diana's wrist changed colour, when her mother was unusually desperate to get home.

She stopped by the familiar sight of the most well-known sculpture in the suburb of Kingston, an enormous row of twelve red post boxes all leaning on each other. She stood still on the cobbled path and spent a drawn-out minute admiring the strange sight. She only ever caught glimpses of it, usually.

Now, she could take her time.

She felt like she was doing something wrong by lingering.

Mother was always in a hurry, after all.

Maybe it's normal to always be in a hurry.

Pouting with uncertainty, she set off along the typical route, suddenly nervous. Passers-by noticed her trotting by and smiled as she went past.

Diana smiled back.

She felt the downpour starting to fall across her upper back and ducked her head, pulling the raincoat's hood over her golden locks. She allowed herself a cheeky smile as she did so. When her mother wasn't around, she had all the time in the world.

Sometimes Diana got in trouble for wanting to pull her hood up. She didn't like to slow her mother down. It was usually met with a verbal tirade.

Never physical.

Steve was the only one who was allowed to hit her.

She didn't much like it when that happened.

Diana found her building and hurried undercover as the afternoon sky went entirely dark and the sheets of rain began to intensify. She scurried into reception, which consisted of nothing more than a small room with plaster walls and a shadowy staircase in the far corner.

London had a limited amount of space, after all.

'Diana!' a voice cried. 'Where's your mother, dear?'

Diana recognised the tone and smiled up at Beryl, the kind-faced elderly woman who manned the reception desk at all hours of the day. 'I'm a big girl now!'

'I'm sure you are,' Beryl said, smiling warmly back. 'You shouldn't be walking home on your own though, my love.'

'Mummy said it's okay.'

'I might need to talk to Mummy about that. Will you tell her to come down later?'

Diana shrugged, even though she knew it would be impossible to drag her mother off the couch after six in the evening. Something in the bottles she drank from made her hard to understand in the evenings. 'Okay.'

'Go on now, dear. Get upstairs.'

Diana smiled and nodded and hurried up the stairwell, a twisting cylinder permanently plagued by a strong, musty aroma — the scent of damp boots leaving imprints on the carpeted stairs, which no-one ever bothered to wash off. She hummed softly to herself as she made the journey up to the fourth floor, where her home was tucked into a cramped corner of the apartment complex.

They didn't have much room, but it seemed like no-one in London did.

There were two people in the narrow fourth floor corridor when Diana stepped out of the stairwell and began the trek down to the other side of the complex. She recognised both of them — she always seemed to pass them by at roughly the same time each afternoon. She'd never spoken to them. Her mother didn't like hanging around in public unnecessarily.

Maybe today would be the start of a new pattern in her life.

She skipped along the carpet, ignoring the make-up stains and crusty remnants of God-knows-what caked into the floor. The first person she passed refused to look at her — an elderly woman who lived three doors down, sporting a permanent scowl across her features at all times.

Diana smiled as she passed her by.

The woman brushed crumbs off the shoulder of her faded overcoat and bustled straight past, ignoring Diana entirely.

Diana frowned, and continued.

The second person seemingly kept to himself just as much as the elderly woman did, but his demeanour seemed warmer. He appeared to be in his early twenties, with dark skin and a mop of unkempt brown hair atop his head. Diana decided to attempt her pleasantries again and smiled up at the man as he strode toward her.

He returned the smile, nodding imperceptibly.

As Diana shuffled past him, her insides warmed.

It wasn't important in the grand scheme of things, but it provided an effective rebound from the harshness of the first passer-by.

She found the panelled black door to her apartment and

pushed it open. It was unlocked. She stepped through into a tiny entrance hallway with a cluster of open doorways bunched tightly together along the walls, leading into a smattering of different rooms with just as little space as the one she currently stood in.

Already, she could hear the raised voices resonating through the apartment.

A deep knot formed in the pit of her stomach. Diana physically grimaced as she heard the vile insults being thrown back and forth.

'You were probably off fucking some cheap whore!' a female voice roared.

Mummy.

'It's none of your business where I fuckin' was, bitch!' a deep voice returned, sharp enough to cut through the air and make Diana jolt in alarm. 'I pay most of the rent, so shut your mouth.'

Steve.

Diana bowed her head and moped into her room, trying not to disturb them. Steve hadn't been around for long, but during the short stint he'd spent with them, he'd been awfully mean to her mother. Diana hated the way he treated her.

But there was nothing she could do about it.

She'd spoken up once.

Steve had taught her a lesson to never interfere again.

She dropped her schoolbag on the floor and leapt onto her bed. The usual routine took over. She operated out of instinct whenever she heard Mummy and Steve arguing. The automated actions unfolded without a hitch.

She slotted her head between the two pillows resting against her bedhead and pressed down over her ears with the fluffy material. The biting voices became muffled, drowned out by the thick pillow over her head.

Silently, dejectedly, she sobbed into the pillowcase.

3

Hadhramaut Valley
Yemen

The sun beat down relentlessly, scorching the baked earth.

The plain stretched for thousands of miles in every direction, dotted intermittently with dry rocky mountain ranges spearing into the sky, blocking the view of the land beyond. A narrow, two-lane dirt road twisted along the plateau, the only sign of civilisation amidst the deserted valley.

A newcomer with no knowledge of the geographical location would have assumed they had reached the edge of the earth itself, where most ordinary life shrank away, replaced by something more intense and primal.

There were no rules out here.

For Will Slater, it was temporarily home.

He strode with measured paces along the side of the dirt track, littered with potholes and only traversable by four-wheel-drives and other heavy-duty vehicles. Archaic Toyota

Land Cruisers made up ninety percent of the vehicles that had roared past over the last few days. They seemed to be all that anyone drove out here, most of them beat to shit and barely functioning.

Slater had been subconsciously hoping that one of the speeding pick-up trucks would slow down to enquire what he was doing out here.

But it seemed that nobody cared.

They went about their lives, keeping their noses out of other people's business, avoiding any kind of confrontation with strangers.

Over the course of his time in Yemen, he had come to learn that nearly everyone he'd stumbled across was plagued by a certain reservedness, a suspicion that carried through into their mannerisms.

Out here, everyone was scared.

Slater wondered exactly what they were tense about.

He'd caught broader flashes of what might be troubling them. The poverty. The isolation. The rampant unemployment. The civil war that occasionally roared into fruition all around him, whether that presented itself through a bloody close-quarters skirmish or the distant crack of gunshots resonating around the outskirts of the villages he'd passed through.

But so far, the language barrier had prevented him from holding any kind of meaningful conversation. He'd only managed to observe from a distance.

That suited him just fine.

He'd been observing from a distance his whole life.

When the opportunity presented itself, he was happy to dive into conversation. He didn't shy away from it. But solitude didn't bother him.

It never had.

He wouldn't have lasted a day in his previous occupation if it did.

For what felt like the first time in weeks — despite the fact that he'd set off from the village of Fughmah earlier that morning — a roadblock materialised down the road. In the shimmering heat that seemed to waft off everything in sight, Slater found it hard to make out exactly what lay ahead.

It seemed to be a single hut, thrown together haphazardly with the scrap materials that lay on hand at the time. He recognised it as a security checkpoint, seeing as he'd strolled past many similar abandoned structures over the course of the day.

This one, however, was occupied.

The tiny blip of humanity in the middle of the desolate valley accentuated the toll that the civil war had dealt on Yemen. As Slater got closer to the security checkpoint he made out a trio of individuals, all dressed in identical uniforms. It made him realise how alien this area of the planet was. It felt strange to lay eyes on a group of people so far out from the towns and villages scattered throughout the Hadhramaut Valley.

They were equally shocked by his appearance on the horizon.

Slater saw them reaching for the battered old rifles hanging by their side. He froze in his tracks, kicking up twin clouds of orange dust as the soles of his boots ground to a halt on the uneven valley floor. He sized up the distance between himself and the checkpoint — close to a hundred feet.

They would need to have expert weapons training to hit him with their first volley of shots. He might be able to avoid the initial barrage, but a quick glance in either direction revealed that he had nowhere to go. The only cover for dozens of miles in any direction was the guards' hut itself. It would only be a waiting game before he caught a cluster of lead and it put him down for good.

He knew what that felt like.

An ancient instinct speared through him, recalling the sensation of twisted flesh and the sight of arterial blood.

Then the trio of militants relaxed as they saw that Slater was unarmed.

He stayed put for a long, drawn-out minute, sizing up their mannerisms.

Satisfied of no immediate threat, he continued toward the checkpoint.

The document in his back pocket would hopefully see him through to the road beyond without incident. The *tasrih* — written entirely in Arabic, indecipherable to Slater — had been acquired from a policeman stationed along the eastern border of Yemen. It had required a sizeable cash payment.

Slater had crossed into Yemen from Oman three weeks earlier.

When the policeman asked — using the limited English skills he possessed — what Slater had been doing in Oman, he'd found himself at a loss for words.

He'd clammed up and offered more money in exchange for the policeman's discretion.

The man had obliged.

Now, Slater opted not to reach for the *tasrih*.

Not just yet.

The policeman had promised it would see him through almost any roadblocks while moving between Yemen's occupied territories.

So far, it had worked three out of three times.

He wondered if it would make it through a fourth inspection.

Upon handing over the document back in the east, the policeman had advised him to turn around and head back to Oman. Apparently, due to a number of reasons — the intense civil war and unrest one of the major factors — soldiers at security checkpoints could opt to deny a *tasrih* on a whim and throw him into a lawless Yemen jail without reason.

Slater had nodded politely and assured the man that he would be able to handle any problems that came his way.

Now, he wasn't so sure.

He drew closer to the trio, keeping his arms by his sides, refusing to reach back for the *tasrih* or even reach up to wipe the thin sheen of sweat off his forehead, drawn out of his pores by the stifling heat. The plastic water bottle tucked into his other back pocket was nearly empty — he had been on the road for three and a half hours, now.

In his old life, a cakewalk.

But not in these conditions.

He drew to a stop in front of the three men, all regarding him with unrestrained surprise.

'Afternoon,' he said, which made them recoil even further at the sound of his accent.

He wondered how long it had been since they'd met an African-American man out here in the Hadhramaut Valley.

If ever.

None of them responded. They didn't speak English.

Slater hadn't expected anything else.

He lifted a finger in a non-threatening manner, keeping his expression placid, and gestured behind him at his rear pocket.

'*Tasrih,*' he said slowly.

They stared back, uniformly mute.

He repeated the word.

One of the men nodded, as if to say *go ahead*, but touched a hand to his Kalashnikov rifle.

Just in case.

Slater reached back tentatively as the wind howled across the flat valley floor and slid the single sheet of faded paper out of the back of his jeans.

He handed it over.

The trio of guards crowded around the *tasrih*, studying it all too intently. Slater guessed that this would be the most exciting interaction they would have in months. The beat-up old Toyotas trundling through the checkpoint every day would be as familiar to these men as their own families.

Slater imagined he might be the first tourist in these parts in years.

He dropped his guard, ever so slightly. It wasn't a conscious decision, simply a response to the muted silence of the three soldiers and their prolonged scrutiny of the document in their hands. It had been nearly a month since Slater had seen conflict — and he quickly realised that it had dulled his instincts.

By the time he started to suspect that these three men might not be as accommodating as the other militants he'd encountered throughout Yemen, the man on the left had seized his Kalashnikov and swung the barrel up to point directly between Slater's eyes.

'No,' the man said, teeth bared.

A single syllable that spelled disaster for anyone in the immediate vicinity.

4

N ever had Slater seen such a sudden shift into mob mentality.

The other two soldiers kept their eyes firmly planted on the document before them while the first man reached for his weapon. When the motionless pair looked up and noticed the shift in atmosphere, it charged their adrenalin levels like a super-drug.

Slater watched the pair mask twin smiles of glee. They reached for their own weapons, hurling the *tasrih* away into the wind like a useless coupon. Slater's stomach sank at the sight of the document drifting away across the baked earth. It meant that there was only one way the following confrontation would go down.

Instantly, the trio fell on him, jabbing him in the ribs and between the shoulder blades with the scratched barrels of their Kalashnikovs. Slater's eyes instinctively darted to each weapon's safety — all were switched on.

The guns — in their present state — were useless.

The three men didn't know he was aware of that. They were using their automatic weapons as a group intimidation tactic, designed to send bolts of crippling fear through the hearts of the victims they prodded.

Slater's resting heart rate barely shifted, but he acted like it did.

He started to breathe heavily.

One of the trio cackled and turned to his two comrades, chattering away in Arabic and gesticulating wildly at Slater. Spurred on by the heightened tension, one of the others stepped forward and planted two hands on Slater's shoulders, shoving him with enough force to send him sprawling back into the dirt.

He got to his feet, brushed off his clothes, and let a hint of fear sparkle across his eyes.

He'd been warned about groups like this. Soldiers who reacted off their gut instincts rather than any kind of official procedure. The policeman who had gifted him the *tasrih* had explicitly told him as much.

Somehow, he thought he might have been able to reason with those types of men when he encountered them.

That would not be the case.

Their tempers started to rise exponentially. The trio fed off each other, shouting obscenities at Slater, shooing him back the way he had come.

Slater pointed at the *tasrih,* which had blown a few dozen feet off the trail, skittering wildly along the plain. 'That's mine. Go get that.'

The three of them stared blankly at him, frankly surprised that he had even bothered to retort. Machismo dripped off them, palpable in the air. They didn't get many opportunities to stick their chests out and parade their authority around, so now they were taking every opportunity to do so.

None of them budged an inch.

Slater stared at the *tasrih* and sighed. 'Okay — well, that's gone. How about you three just let me through?'

He was met with absolute silence.

Then the man on the left — the soldier who had first kicked off the egotistical display of dominance by snatching for his gun — strode fast at Slater, unleashing a tirade of abuse in his direction. Flecks of spit arced from the corners of his mouth.

Up close, Slater could see the wavering of his gaze, the slight lack of spatial awareness that brought him to within half a foot of Slater's own face. He stared past the soldier to the pair behind him, noting the similar expressions on their faces.

They were high on khat, a drug that Slater hadn't known existed before he stepped foot in Yemen. Over the course of his time in-country, he'd come to learn that nearly three-quarters of the population munched on the leaves, which had a similar effect to marijuana.

With the three of them spaced out ever so slightly, Slater realised he could take them all at once.

As that thought entered his mind, he burst off the mark in the blink of an eye.

The soldier in his face hadn't been prepared for anything close to what unfolded. He stood completely still as Slater shouldered straight *through* him, charging into his chest with enough force to send him sprawling back onto the trail. The guy's head followed the same trajectory as his falling body, meeting the hard, crusty earth with enough force to knock him senseless.

The back of the man's skull whiplashed off the ground, accompanied by a hollow *thud*. He'd be fine in the long run, but Slater wouldn't be surprised if he had dealt out a concussion.

Never slowing or hesitating, he scooped up the Kalash-nikov that the man had dropped and spun it around in his hands, locking a firm grip around the weapon's barrel. He took three bounding steps into the range of the other pair and swung the rifle in one scything motion like a baseball bat, smashing the stock into the closest soldier's ribs.

The guy buckled, and Slater swung again into the back of his neck, hard enough to send him face-first into the dusty earth but with enough restraint to prevent lasting neurological damage.

He twisted on the spot fast enough to catch the last man fumbling with his rifle, pawing at the safety with meaty fingers. Slater could see the confusion spreading across the man's face as he struggled to work the tiny switch. His senses and reflexes had been dulled by the fat ball of khat residue lodged inside his left cheek.

'Goddamnit,' Slater muttered to himself as he witnessed the pathetic sight.

He would have much rather been on his way, leaving the third guy to tend to his beaten comrades. But this man was unrelenting, determinedly trying to make his weapon oper-ational despite his adversary staring him in the face from two feet away.

Slater recognised the gun barrel swinging in his direc-tion and opted to put his foot down. He would not take it easy on the man in front of him. It was an undeniable truth that if Slater hadn't possessed the ability to act, he would have been gunned down where he stood.

And no-one would have been any the wiser.

He would have been buried in a hot ditch and all record of his existence would have faded away into nothingness.

Thankfully, Will Slater lived and breathed combat.

He shot into range, ducking underneath the Kalashnikov while the man carried on fumbling with the safety catch. He activated his glutes and hamstrings, pushing off the dusty track with enough explosive power to knock all the breath out of the man's lungs. The point of his shoulder sunk deep into the guy's exposed stomach, taking him off his feet.

Together, the pair sprawled into the dirt.

The sun had scorched the track over the course of the morning, turning the dirt impossibly hot. Slater winced as he went through the practiced motions of flattening out an inexperienced adversary. The man had zero jiu-jitsu training based off his panicked reaction, something that proved disastrous ten times out of ten when up against a black belt. He flapped around on the ground like a wounded hamster.

Slater sliced one leg over the guy's mid-section, sliding into a position known as full-mount. Helpless to resist, the man panicked and rolled onto his front, a natural reaction when someone was unable to buck the weight of an enemy off them.

Instinctively turning away from the punches that would inevitably follow suit.

It played directly into Slater's skill set.

He looped an arm around the man's throat from behind, almost lackadaisical in his approach. The Kalashnikov had skittered across the track moments earlier and come to rest well out of reach, coated in dust and desert sand. With the fatal threat eliminated, now he could nullify the man underneath him.

A rear-naked-choke took, on average, less than five seconds to choke a man into temporary unconsciousness. Cut off the blood supply to the brain and all sorts of neurological systems shut down instantly. In mixed martial arts, opponents tapped in the space of seconds to prevent unnecessary damage.

Out here, there was no referee to pull Slater off.

He unleashed maximum exertion, tightening a muscular forearm around the guy's neck. It happened so fast that the man wouldn't have realised what hit him. He struggled feebly for a brief moment, then his brain responded to the choke by shutting itself down all at once.

He went limp.

Slater released the hold as soon as he felt the man's limbs turn to jelly, and slid off the unconscious mass. Within the span of a few seconds, the guy spluttered awake, staring at his surroundings with dilated pupils. It would take him a few minutes to get his bearings.

Until then, Slater had rendered him useless.

He was in no state to mount any kind of resistance.

Slater kicked the three Kalashnikov rifles off the side of the track, watching them tumble down the side of a craggy valley dotted with rock formations and overgrown patches of weeds. Satisfied with where the weapons finally tumbled to a halt, well off the beaten path, he nodded to himself and strode quickly through the checkpoint.

It would take the three policemen at least ten minutes to retrieve their weapons. By then, Slater would be long gone. He had briefly considered taking one of the rifles with him for reassurance's sake, but it would spell nothing but disaster if he strolled into the next town wielding an automatic weapon.

He preferred to avoid that kind of reaction.

The trail twisted and turned ahead, weaving through a complex maze of rocky outcrops and vast sloping hills, all covered in the same barren sand and bleak stone.

Slater took one look back at the trio of whimpering

checkpoint guards lying in the dust behind him. He imagined that — even if they managed to recuperate from their injuries and fetch their weapons from the treacherous valley slope — Slater's outburst would have intimidated them into submission.

At least, he hoped so.

He wouldn't take their lives while they lay there, helpless.

He had caused enough pain over the last ten years.

And — despite their attitudes — none of them deserved it.

He pressed on into the Hadhramaut Valley, letting all thoughts of the confrontation pass from his mind.

To an inexperienced combatant, the encounter would have affected their psyche for months, plagued by the memories of a life-or-death situation in which they could have caught a stray bullet at any moment.

To Slater, it was Tuesday.

By the time he made it to the first bend in the road and strode purposefully out of sight of the security checkpoint, all recollections of the fight had blended into the thousands of other echoes he'd rather forget.

5

The road provided Slater ample time for solitude.

Out here, at the edge of the earth, he could reflect.

The trail turned to a blur after twenty minutes of uninterrupted hiking. Every now and then he slid a thin plastic bottle out of the back of his jeans and took a long swig from the neck, but other than keeping hydrated he had nothing else to concern himself with.

He didn't quite know exactly what he was doing in Yemen. It had been a simple-enough journey, crossing the border from Oman after trawling uneventfully through the neighbouring country as slow as he pleased.

How he had ended up in Oman was a tale that he almost didn't believe himself.

It involved a man by the name of Jason King who used to work for the same highly-classified special-operations division as Slater. The pair had become acquainted in Corsica of all places, and since then Slater's entire life had been flipped on its head.

King did that to people.

Now King had retreated to parts unknown to live out the rest of his days in privacy, and Slater was out of a job. Not long ago, he'd spent a relaxing week at a private luxury resort in Antigua in a hopeless attempt to wind down from a career of madness. That period of his life had taught him little, except for the fact that he wasn't wired to stay in one place.

He was a wanderer, through and through.

And he didn't mind wandering through the most dangerous places on the planet.

In fact, he welcomed it.

He shouldn't have been expecting any less than what had resulted at the security checkpoint. The policeman who had sold him the tasrih had warned him of the confrontational nature of Northern Yemenis. Slater had sensed that the man had something against the Northerners, judging by the level of disdain in his voice when he'd described them as barbarians.

Slater chalked the aggression of the checkpoint guards up to a mixture of boredom and a lack of foreigners, and pressed on further into the Hadhramaut Valley.

A town appeared on the horizon, most of it shimmering through the haze of sunshine battering the desert plains from above. Slater had been expecting to come across civilisation at some point in the near future — the rudimentary map he'd perused at the beginning of the day had told him that a remote mountain town called Qasam rested past the security checkpoint he'd come through earlier.

He made for the collection of buildings, passing a pair of khat farms on either side of the trail. The tall trees rested still in the middle of the sweeping plateau, soon to be harvested for a sizeable profit. Slater kept a lookout for any sign of life amidst the plantations, but found nothing.

He continued.

The rumbling of an engine behind him caused him to grimace in anticipation. He tensed up like a coiled spring and turned on his heel, ready for a fight. If the trio of checkpoint guards had piled into a vehicle and set off in pursuit of their foe, Slater would have trouble dealing with them this time.

He had caught them off-guard initially.

It wouldn't happen again.

Thankfully, the source of the noise turned out to be another beat-up Land Cruiser, lacking registration plates or a windshield. A pair of Yemeni men sat in the cabin, guiding the old truck along the winding trail towards Qasam. The vehicle rumbled past, and Slater exchanged a nod with the pair. As it trawled further along the track and reached Qasam's limits, Slater eyed the flapping tarpaulin sheet draped across the rear tray. For a moment the tarp lifted in the wind, revealing bundles of khat lined along the metal in orderly rows.

Slater shook his head, flabbergasted.

From an outsider's perspective, it seemed like the entire Yemeni economy revolved around the drug.

Gradually, more signs of life presented themselves. The monotonous view of sweeping plains and rocky outcrops for as far as the eye could see was replaced with the odd local administration building, set apart from the rest of the mountain town.

Slater passed by a couple of men dressed in official uniform sitting at a rickety table out the front of a broad three-storey brick building, chewing absent-mindedly on khat and talking in hushed voices as they gazed at the arid mountains all around them.

He nodded politely to them.

They nodded back, unable to hide their surprise at seeing a man in the region who wasn't of Middle-Eastern origin.

Slater continued up into the centre of Qasam. He concluded the policeman who had given him the *tasrih* had been making a simple generalisation when he had warned of the northerners' hostility.

People in this region seemed pleasant enough.

For the most part.

Artificial noise materialised for the first time in what felt like an eternity. Slater had become so accustomed to the quiet drone of the wind howling across the valley floor that he found himself shocked by a foreign sound. He identified it as the harsh, discordant blare of loudspeakers all across the town. He checked his watch and chalked the commotion up to one of the daily prayers that often tore through small towns such as these.

Every single person he strode past as he made his way into Qasam stared at him unashamedly, none of them bothering to mask their shock. He could only imagine what they were thinking.

A foreigner — *out here?*

He nodded and smiled warmly at each civilian in turn, electing not to linger in one place for too long. There was plenty of commotion outside the mosque as a group of townspeople dispersed from the entrance, draped in simple clothing, many of them sporting towels hanging off their shoulders. Slater moved along and strolled slowly through streets packed with merchants and khat-sellers, listening to the hiss of meat on makeshift grilles and the braying of animals in neighbouring alleys.

It contrasted sharply with the barren desolation of the plateau.

Despite everything, he smiled.

He had no place to stay, no personal belongings to speak of, nowhere in the world to be. He didn't speak the native language, which had made communication next to impossible throughout his entire time in Yemen.

But he wouldn't have traded it for anything else.

It was a welcome relief from a typical day in his life just a few short months ago.

He appreciated the unknown.

It was preferable to always having a task to complete, always having someone to rescue or someone that needed eliminating.

His worries were nothing in comparison.

He found a lookout on the outskirts of the town and opted to rest for a while, soaking in the sights for as long as he could. Despite all of Yemen's dangers, he made sure to take the time to admire the beauty of the landscape. For as long as he could remember, he had been thrust from location to location, travelling the world in service to his country but never spending enough time in one place to truly appreciate it.

It helped that no-one was looking to murder him out here.

Not yet, he thought.

The lookout consisted of a tiny gravel courtyard sandwiched between a pair of archaic residential buildings overlooking the plateau. This portion of the town was positioned atop a rocky outcrop. It provided a view of all the khat farms surrounding the mountains, as well as the valley floor stretching for thousands of miles in any direction. Behind the lookout, past Qasam, the rocky promontory rose sharply into the jagged mountains. The cliffs stretched well into the distance, an imposing backdrop.

Slater sat down on an unoccupied bench, alone at the lookout. All the faint sounds of civilian life echoed up through the narrow laneways. After close to ten miles of travel on foot, the sweat ran freely from his pores. He let it come. Ordinarily the perspiration would cause discomfort, but comfort was something he hadn't experienced in quite some time.

He wasn't sure if he liked being comfortable, anyway.

That was no way to live.

He turned his gaze outward, across the plateau. The policeman who had provided him with the tasrih had described the vast valleys as wadis, most of them half a mile wide and over a hundred miles long. From the outpost, Slater could almost make out the dimensions of one of the great gorges dotting the plateau. It was an impressive sight, to say the least.

'Don't get many tourists out here,' a voice said from behind.

English.

Slater turned, startled, to lay eyes on the man who had stepped into the lookout.

6

The man appeared to be in his mid-forties, dressed in a strange combination of formal and tribal attire. Slater recognised the white *futa* that the majority of Yemeni civilians wore around their waists — a plain white cloth that wrapped around one's mid-section to cover the legs, like a skirt of sorts. Yet there was a collared business shirt draped over the man's shoulders, hanging open and unbuttoned to compensate for the intense heat. His head was wrapped in a tribal cloth and his face was surprisingly smooth, lacking the weather-beaten lines that so many civilians out here possessed.

'You speak English,' Slater stated, taken aback by the revelation. He certainly hadn't been expecting it.

'Quite well,' the man said, nodding. 'I am almost fluent. A rarity out here — I know.'

'I guess I'm something of a rarity out here too,' Slater said, gesturing to his skin tone.

He wondered who had been the last African-American to wander through Qasam.

The man across from Slater smiled warmly and clasped

his hands together in front of his waist. 'Then we have some-thing in common, my friend. We are unique.'

'Can I help you with anything?'

The man shrugged. 'Not particularly. My name is Abu.'

'I'm Will.'

'Pleasure to meet you, Will. Do you mind if I sit?'

Slater shrugged. 'Be my guest.'

Abu crossed to the bench and sat down across from Slater. Together they stared out at the Hadhramaut Valley, soaking in the sights. Despite knowing almost nothing about each other, neither man felt it necessary to speak. The setting was too tranquil. Too calm.

Finally, Abu piped up.

'Some people in these parts believe that the wadis in this valley were created by an ancient tribe of great beings known as the Ad. Allah removed the giants from the valley after they infuriated him, and all that is left of them is these valleys. They are the footprints of the Ad.'

Slater paused, soaking in the story. 'Do you believe it?'

'That's quite a personal question.'

'Sorry. May I ask how you know English so well?'

'I think you have some explaining to do first, my friend.'

'Do I?'

'An American out here is a little rarer than my ability to speak a second language. If you don't mind, I'd like to know a little more about you.'

'And why's that?'

Abu shrugged. 'I like to know things. Otherwise — why bother?'

'Why is it so strange to see an American in these parts?' Slater said.

Abu looked across at Slater, staring at him like he was foolish. 'You cannot be serious.'

'I'm curious as to why everyone I make eye contact with looks like they've seen a ghost.'

'You do not come here unless you were born here,' Abu said. 'Not by choice. Especially not now.'

'Why?'

'You know why.'

'I know partially why. Lay it out for me.'

'The oversupply of weapons. The civil war. The corruption. It is the poorest and most tribal state in the Middle East, my friend. You do not come here for leisure.'

'I did.'

'Which is why I'd like you to enlighten me as to your reasons.'

'Do I need a reason?'

'I think you do.'

'I don't have to explain myself to you.'

Abu bowed his head. 'I mean no disrespect. I am always curious about these things.'

Slater paused, gathering his thoughts. 'I was in a routine. My life was a hard one, but I was used to luxury. My job put me up in the most lavish hotels, the most opulent corners of the earth. I got stagnant. Then shit hit the fan at my workplace, which I won't go into detail about, and I found myself out of a job. I was already in Oman, so I decided to shake things up a bit.'

'You are not scared of what might happen? Some people in these parts do not like outsiders. Many are pleasant, but there are always a certain few.'

'I've already run into a couple.'

'And?'

'They don't bother me.'

'What is it you used to do?' Abu said, perhaps wising up to the fact that Slater wasn't troubled by confrontation.

'A lot of things,' Slater said.

'Any of them pleasant?'

'Not really.'

'I understand.'

'I'm not sure if you do.'

'I've met men like you. You don't say much, but what you do say speaks volumes. You are haunted by your past.'

'Am I?'

'Well, I can't speak for you. Most are.'

Slater paused. 'I don't think that kind of stuff has hit me yet. Maybe it will now that I have nothing to do.'

'When's the last time you had nothing to do?'

'Childhood.'

Abu paused and nodded solemnly. 'You think that what you've done might catch up to you?'

'Who knows, Abu,' Slater said. 'Who knows.'

Abu reached into the pocket of his *futa* and came out with a small metal canister covered with nicks and scratches of varying sizes. He popped open the top and plucked out a thick ball of khat. The man rolled the weed between two fingertips, using his fingers like pincers to prepare the drug. Then he pressed the khat into his mouth, slotting it on the inside of his right cheek. He sucked rhythmically at the ball, staring peacefully out at the plateau as he did so.

'Care to partake?' he said.

Slater shrugged. 'Why not?'

'I thought it might take your mind off the past.'

'I don't need your help,' Slater said, making his stance clear. 'I'm not riddled with trauma. I'm fine. I'm just curious to try it.'

Abu shrugged. 'Suit yourself.'

He passed across a large wad of khat, the green leaves bundled together to provide maximum ease of use, and

Slater slotted the substance against the wall of his own cheek. He chewed on the leaves, letting the residue build up in his mouth, noting the bitter taste of the bush. He took his time, not in a rush to be anywhere or do anything. When the build-up of residue became too much he spat a glob of the gunk into the empty tin that Abu rested between them and took a swig from the water bottle in his back pocket.

'Doesn't do much,' he admitted after a long pause.

'It's not supposed to,' Abu said. 'Do you notice that slight euphoria? That gentle pleasant feeling on the back of your neck?'

Slater nodded. 'It's nice.'

'That's why three-quarters of the population consumes this stuff. It's also why I'm employed.'

Slater cocked his head. 'You don't look like a farmer.'

'That's good. Because I'm not a farmer. I'm a programmer.'

'A programmer?' Slater said. 'Wasn't expecting to run into a tech guy out here.'

'Not many do,' Abu admitted, smiling. 'But the government relies on me. I keep the mechanical drills and pumps running across all the khat farms in the region. I fuel the entire country's addiction. My services are in high demand, as you can imagine.'

'The drills and pumps?' Slater said.

'They are important. Khat is responsible for a fifth of Yemen's water consumption, my friend. Without me, the plantations would die of thirst, and there would be a fair few unhappy residents.'

'So you float around this region?'

'Somewhat. Usually I am escorted. It's dangerous out here, you see.'

'Why the lack of protection this time?'

'Lack of available units,' Abu said, shrugging. 'It's fine. I can handle myself. I just keep my head down. But I don't like this area much anyway.'

Slater cocked his head. 'Why's that?'

Abu hesitated, as if he were about to touch on a subject he would much rather keep quiet about. He shook his head and broke eye contact, staring vacantly out at the valley. 'It's nothing.'

'Tell me. Maybe I can help.'

Abu smirked and shook his head. 'No, my friend. It is not like that. It it just a hunch.'

'What kind of hunch?'

'The tribes are not acting how they are supposed to.'

'The tribes?'

Abu jerked a thumb back towards the sweeping, barren mountains behind them. 'Up there. The northern highland tribes. They're fairly common in this region.'

'How are they supposed to act?'

'Like idiots,' Abu admitted. 'It's half the reason there's such turmoil in the region. They fight amongst themselves. They have no particular devotion to any one cause. Usually they just receive orders and instructions from the highest bidder. It creates chaos, you see. If there was infighting and quarrelling amongst them, you would have never made it into Qasam in one piece. They would have shook you down on the outskirts of the town. They would be extorting the locals.'

'So it's a good thing that they seem to have died down in their activity, then? I don't see the issue.'

'It's odd, that's all. I don't like when things are odd. I haven't been here in months, but things are almost too peaceful. Especially given the nature of the rest of Hadhramaut.'

'Sounds like you're all worked up about nothing.'

'Perhaps, my friend. Perhaps.'

'You're sharing an awful lot with a stranger you just met.'

'I like to think I am a good reader of people,' Abu said.

'And what did you read about me?'

'That I can tell you what is on my mind, and trust you with that information. As you can imagine, I don't get much of a chance to speak of these matters to many people. I am always on the move, you see. Always darting from place to place.'

Slater smiled wryly. 'Same here, Abu. Same here.'

'Where are you staying tonight?'

'I hadn't quite worked that out yet.'

'I have a room,' the man said, bowing his head again. 'It's only a temporary shelter, organised at the last minute. It's not much. But it's a roof over your head, if you need it.'

Slater waited a beat to let the offer settle over him. He regarded the man before him inquisitively, and came away satisfied with what he found in his initial assessment. 'I'd be grateful for that.'

'Of course.' Abu flashed a glance at the old-fashioned wristwatch above his left hand and pursed his lips accordingly. 'I'm afraid business calls. I'm due for a visit to one of the plantations in thirty minutes, to make sure their systems are running okay. It was great to meet you, Will. I'll be back in the evening. If you get tired before then, the home is just up the road from here. It's a blue wooden door — only one of its kind on the street. You can't miss it.'

Slater nodded his understanding. 'Thank you.'

'Enjoy the rest of your day.'

Abu left as quickly as he had arrived. The man packed up his bundles of khat and scurried away into the streets of Qasam, integrating with the bustling town life.

Slater stayed where he was, pausing to have a moment to himself.

It meant that — five minutes later — when he had soaked in as much of the view as he possibly could, he chose exactly the right time to leave the lookout.

It meant that he strode out into the laneway at the same exact second as the boy came running past.

It meant that the two bumped into each other.

And then everything changed.

7

The boy thudded into Slater's thigh and ricocheted off, sprawling into the dirt with a distinct '*oof*' of surprise. He had been sprinting full-pelt when he passed across the entrance to the laneway, meeting Slater just as he exited into the steep mountain street.

Slater's senses heightened all at once, sensing trouble. It had been ingrained into his subconscious over a decade ago to treat any unannounced situation with alertness and readiness. He was ready for a fight to the death by the time he realised the boy posed no significant threat.

The kid sat up, eyes scrunched shut as he laughed with glee. A mop of curly hair sat atop his head. He evidently spent much of his life outdoors — his skin was sun-drenched and deeply tanned. Slater couldn't help but share the kid's happiness. His smile was infectious.

The boy got his feet under him and sprung up, utilising his wiry athletic frame. He couldn't have been much older than eight.

'English?' Slater said softly.

The kid stared back at him blankly.

What were you expecting? he thought, scolding himself for his stupidity.

Slater clasped his palms together in front of his chest and bowed his head — an apologetic gesture. He didn't want the kid to think that he'd deliberately hurt him.

The kid smiled, shook his head, and pointed to himself.

My bad.

Slater smirked. He wiggled two fingers back and forth, signifying legs moving at a crazy speed.

You're fast.

The boy chuckled and pointed up the steep laneway, towards the top of Qasam and the towering rocky mountains beyond. He beckoned to Slater.

Come with me.

Slater looked left, and he looked right. There was no-one around, and it seemed that by now he had experienced everything the town had to offer, save chewing a truckload more khat. Perhaps it was the euphoric nature of the leaves he'd consumed back at the lookout, but he felt at peace in the presence of the kid.

He nodded, smiled and thrust a hand forward, palm facing outward.

Lead the way.

The boy set off at a cracking pace up the slope, tearing past groups of locals sitting outside small mud buildings and rundown shopfronts. Everyone was splayed out on frayed carpets and rusting car seats, each positioned so that the groups could face one another and shoot the shit while munching on khat in obscene quantities.

Wasting the afternoon away with small talk.

Slater could see the appeal in such a life.

But he was afraid he couldn't live it himself.

Before long the town centre faded away, replaced by a

barren track that weaved between two towering cliffs. He found himself dwarfed by his surroundings, broad rock formations spearing into the sky on either side. The two mountainous chunks of land shrouded the trail itself in shadow, protecting it from the dazzling glare of the Yemeni sunshine. The boy hurried away from Qasam's outer limits.

Slater paused at the foot of the trail.

He peered up at the dusty, sand-coated track, twisting into the hot mountains above them. The land out here seemed barren, just a few dozen feet from the outskirts of the town. Slater watched the boy hurry up the trail, beckoning him on with every step.

He stayed put.

Something about the trail tickled him the wrong way. He thought of Abu's stark observations regarding the highland tribes. He wondered if they were close enough to Qasam to pose any problems to locals. He didn't doubt his ability to protect himself should the opportunity be presented, but his limbs were acutely heavy after the altercation with the three security checkpoint guards earlier that day.

Besides, if he spent the rest of the day antagonising thuggish northern highlanders, he doubted it would bode well for getting a restful night's sleep. He didn't want anyone to come hunting for his head.

He'd experienced enough of that recently.

Halfway up the trail, the boy turned and froze on the spot, pouting at Slater's inactivity.

Slater shook his head solemnly, repeating the apologetic gesture.

'Not today, kid,' he called out. 'Just being cautious.'

The boy shrugged — likely unable to understand a word that Slater said — and continued his mad dash up the trail.

Probably off to a remote village tucked away in the mountains. Maybe he lived there. Maybe he had family there.

It wasn't Slater's business.

The encounter had been brief, but heart-warming.

It had been some time since he'd seen such innocent joy
in the eyes of another human being.

His life didn't often involve itself with people like that.

He remained milling on the spot until the sight of the
kid had vanished into a tiny blip on the mountainside,
forgotten in the span of seconds. Slater let the sweat flow
free from his pores, kicked back into perspiring by the short
walk up the hillside. In heat as intense as Hadhramaut's, it
didn't take much to kickstart the process.

Then he turned on his heel and made his way back
down into Qasam, taking care not to bother any of the clusters of locals he'd passed on the way up. They eyeballed him
just as viciously as they had when he'd encountered them
the first time. It seemed like he was welcome enough — the
men were not hostile in their mannerisms, and no-one
approached him to shepherd him out of the mountain town.

They simply studied him like he was a touring circus.

He didn't blame them.

He didn't think that many incidents appeared to disrupt
their routine very often.

Still slightly affected by the khat, he called it a day as the
sun fell quickly towards the opposite horizon. It was only
late afternoon, but the trek from Fughmah to Qasam had
been long and arduous, despite his best efforts to shut the
physical exertion out of his mind. The long day — coupled
with the act of subduing the three checkpoint guards — had
tired him considerably.

He decided to go looking for the blue wooden door that
Abu had spoken of earlier that afternoon.

It didn't take long to find it.

The man hadn't been lying when he'd told Slater that it couldn't be missed. Set deep into a niche in the wall of a rundown block of quaint Yemeni homes, the blue door was lit dimly by a paraffin lamp hanging off the wall at head-height. Slater strode up to the door with purpose, worried that if he approached it tentatively his actions would arouse suspicion.

The door was unlocked.

He pushed it open and went inside.

He found himself in a sparsely-furnished, low-ceilinged space that housed both a living area and a kitchen-dining quarters. There were no couches or chairs — instead, the shoddily-carpeted floor in the living room was dotted with broad cushions to sit on. All the seating was floor-level, a sight that created an air of homeliness and comfort in the space.

Several paraffin lamps identical to the light in the entranceway were dotted around the space, each glowing softly, gently illuminating the room. Slater peeled off the long-sleeved shirt he'd been wearing to protect his bare skin from the sun over the course of the day and dropped onto one of the cushions, welcoming the relief. The sheen of sweat across his bare skin only served to accentuate his musculature.

He rested his back against the wall and closed his eyes, sinking softly into a doze as he waited for Abu to return from his business venture.

'What are you doing?' he whispered to himself as he dropped off. 'Why are you here?'

Every now and again he questioned himself. He had enough money in anonymous offshore accounts to live out the rest of his days in unbridled luxury. Instead he was bare-chested, sweating his bodyweight away in a humid room atop a rocky promontory in war-torn Yemen.

But, time and time again, he came back to the same conclusion.

Discomfort made him feel alive.

He fell into unconsciousness.

8

The noise of the front door shifting gently open caused him to stir.

He heard the noise and shot upright off the cushion, beads of sweat flying uncontrollably off his forehead. Adrenalin flooded his senses, lending him an exhilarating burst of energy. He flew toward the entranceway with his fists balled and his teeth bared.

Abu stepped into the room, apprehension and surprise on his face.

Slater froze where he stood, grimacing at his instinctive reaction to being disturbed. He took a moment to ponder exactly how he'd acted. Then he shook his head in disappointment and dropped back down onto the cushion.

'Sorry, Abu,' he said. 'Don't know what came over me.'

Abu stared at him wordlessly, which did nothing but heighten the discomfort Slater was feeling.

'You told me at the lookout that you were fine,' the man said. 'But I think you were trying to tell yourself that instead.'

Slater began to craft a retort, but stopped himself halfway. There wasn't always the need for a counter-point. Abu had made his case clear, and Slater decided to let that sit in his mind for a while.

Maybe he really had been affected by his career.

He realised he'd been coasting for as long as he could remember on maximum output. He used to offset the mind-numbing thrills of combat with a healthy cocktail of high-stakes gambling and casual sex. He never slowed down. When the risk-taker's life had been stripped from him, and he'd been forced to dwell in his thoughts for longer than a few hours...

Maybe he really was damaged.

He shrugged the thought off and wiped a hand across his forehead. It came away saturated.

'How did the trip to the plantation go?' he said, attempting to steer the conversation onto more banal matters than the cracks in his psyche.

'About as well as it could have,' Abu said, crossing to the kitchen and powering up the stove. 'I'm about to cook dinner. Would you like some?'

'Please.'

'Chicken and rice tonight.'

'Fine by me.'

'You're not a fussy man?'

'Not at all.'

'And what did you get up to while I was gone?'

'I met a young boy. Briefly.'

Abu raised an eyebrow. 'Did you talk to him?'

'No. He didn't speak English.'

Slater shifted uneasily on the cushion. There was a wet patch underneath him where his sweat had dripped into the material while he dozed. 'Abu, tell me more about these tribes.'

Abu cocked his head, turning away from the ingredients simmering in the frypan on the stove. 'Why?'

'I have a weird hunch. Like you do.'

'About what?'

'Just tell me more about them.'

'There is not much to say,' Abu said.

'How close are they to Qasam?'

'The first major tribe lies just a few miles into the mountains. I hope you're not thinking of going looking for trouble up there. No matter how fearsome you think you are, you will not make it out alive.'

'Does anyone venture up there?'

Abu shrugged. 'A handful of people. There are a few remote villages amongst the rocky crags. They don't have electricity, and there's barely any running water. It's rather primitive up there.'

'The boy went into the mountains,' Slater said solemnly, staring at the opposite wall, deep in thought.

'Why would that bother you?' Abu said.

'Something about it felt off. Like he didn't really belong up there. Like he was just heading up in search of adventure.'

Abu shook his head. 'I believe I may have put too much fear into you, my friend. The tribes are uncivilised and reckless, but they are not monsters. Your young friend will be fine.'

Slater nodded. 'I don't know why I'm worrying anyway. I don't know enough about this place. The culture is complicated.'

'It sure is.'

'But you said you thought something was odd up there?'

Abu shrugged. 'As you said, just a hunch. I have no

evidence to prove anything. I simply feel they are with-drawing into their encampments, for good or bad.'

'Like they're guarding something?'

Abu smiled. 'You are full of conspiracy theories, Will.'

'Just speculating.'

'There's nothing wrong with a bit of healthy speculation every now and then,' Abu said. 'But in this case I believe it is foolish. I never should have brought it up. It's more than likely because of the civil war. They don't want to tread on the toes of an entity that might take offense to their rash behaviour. Or they might be getting paid to lie low while other organisations handle business elsewhere. Either way, it's none of my business and it's none of yours either. And it's a welcome reprieve for the townspeople.'

'I guess so.'

'It's in your blood to go searching for trouble, isn't it?' Abu said.

Slater paused. 'Yes, I think it is.'

'You hope there's something going on up there. You'd love nothing more than to dive into the thick of it. Am I right?'

'You're right.'

'Be a vigilante elsewhere, Will. This town doesn't need it.'

Slater nodded. 'I think I'm just looking for something to do.'

'Here's something to do,' Abu said, handing over a bowl full to the brim with stringy chicken and jasmine rice.

Slater tucked in, suddenly ravished after realising that he hadn't eaten anything since he'd set off from Fughmah earlier that morning. Abu had laced the meal with a mouth-watering combination of various herbs and spices. When

Slater cleared his bowl and was offered another serving, he graciously accepted.

The food satisfied him enough to shift his consciousness into a groggy stupor. He leant back against the cool mud brick wall and waited for Abu to finish his meal in turn.

They talked long into the evening, their low voices surrounded by the quiet hissing of the paraffin lamps and the distant rumblings of vehicles echoing in through the open window. They spoke of family, and occupation, and stories from their youths. Slater made a point to stay reservedly guarded about his career, opting to let bygones be bygones instead of revealing what he had done during his time in the United States Armed Forces.

It was close to midnight by the time Abu withdrew to his bedroom, leaving Slater to get comfortable on a cluster of floor-level cushions in the living quarters. He dropped his head to the plush material, suddenly intensely comfortable. The night had cooled, lending his pores a break from perspiring.

He drifted into a dreamless sleep, too exhausted to bother reminiscing on his past. He had never been plagued by the deeds he'd carried out in service of his country — not like many others. He was grateful for that. He wondered how long it would take for the nightmares to kick in, how separated he would have to be from his storied career before the whirlwind came back to haunt him.

Until then, he would enjoy life.

And carry on enjoying it for as long as he was physically and mentally able to.

He slept a long eight hours relatively undisturbed.

When the sun speared over the horizon the next morning, he was woken by anguished screams of despair.

9

The horrified wailing shot through him like a bolt of energy.

He reared his head, reacting harshly to the piercing noise, this time providing a justified reaction to being awoken by a strange sound. By the time he made it to his feet, Abu had materialised out of his room, dressed in a light blue *futa* and a new business shirt.

Ready for the day's proceedings.

The man had been similarly startled by the screaming. In a mountain town as calm and subdued as Qasam, the noise tore through the laneways like lightning. Slater met Abu's wide-eyed stare, and together the two made straight for the door.

They exited just as the morning prayers roared to life, blasting from the loudspeakers. Coupled with the yet-unidentified screaming, they melded together into a cacophony of jarring noise.

Slater searched for the source of the commotion.

He saw the woman running up the hill a second before he identified her as the source. She was dressed in a black burqa that covered every morsel of bare skin, apart from her eyes. The garment had been thrown on haphazardly, sheer grief overpowering the traditional customs. Slater noted the additional items she was wearing — black gloves, black socks, and a tall hat made of straw.

Then his gaze floated down below her hat, to the pair of eyes visible through the slit in the face mask.

They were racked with horror.

The woman ran with everything she had, eyes fixed on the top of the slope, ignoring all of her immediate surroundings apart from the path ahead. Her arms flapped wildly on either side of her thin frame, the burqa bouncing up and down in wild fashion. It must have been intensely hot underneath the garment.

Slater watched her approaching with a certain resignation. Despite knowing nothing about her circumstances, his gut told him that he knew exactly why she was behaving erratically. He connected the dots fast enough to grimace, wondering if it really could be what he was thinking.

Then Abu stepped out into the middle of the street and wrapped a wiry arm around the woman's waist as she flew past, stopping her in her tracks.

She reacted harshly, continuing to scream and slapping at Abu's chest with both gloved hands. He spoke fast into her ear, never raising his voice, only attempting to calm her down. It was effective enough to make her stop struggling and instead dissolve into giant sobs that wracked her whole body as she let out her unease and worry.

Slater stayed put, loitering on the side of the laneway, refusing to take the grimace off his face.

He knew why she was distraught.

It couldn't be anything else.

You should have trusted your gut, Will, you dumb fuck.

'Ask her what's wrong,' he said to Abu.

The man nodded and muttered calmly into the woman's ear, taking care not to heighten his tone and cause any more stress than absolutely necessary. She took a long while to respond, battling against the crippling sadness in her bones. Slater saw her physically cowering as she provided Abu with a string of panicked Arabic.

Her voice cracked as she spoke.

Abu froze where he stood. As he listened to what she was saying realisation spread across his face.

He looked up at Slater, eyes wide.

'Her boy is missing,' the man said in English, stretching out every word as if he didn't want to believe it himself. 'He said he was going into the mountains as an adventurer yesterday afternoon. She smiled and laughed. She didn't believe him. He still hasn't returned, and he's always home by six in the evening. He's twelve hours late now...'

Slater's legs turned weak as the blood drained out of his face.

You should have done something.

Anything.

He couldn't believe that a wild hunch had been accurate. Something about the boy's mannerisms had subconsciously told him that he didn't live in the mountains. He seemed too energised, too excited and invigorated by the prospect of adventure, to be returning home from a day in Qasam. Slater had suspected that the boy lived in the town, but had opted to bite his tongue, out of worry that he would come off as overly suspicious.

Should have done something, he repeated.

The woman spoke, staring hard at Slater.

Abu translated. 'She's asking if you saw her boy.'

Slater nodded.

She spoke again.

'She's asking if you saw him head into the mountains.'

Slater nodded again.

With her voice wavering, the woman spat a question.

Slater didn't need Abu to translate to know what she had asked, but the man did so anyway.

'She's asking why you didn't stop him.'

Slater shifted from foot to foot, scolding himself and running through a list of possible scenarios simultaneously. In all likelihood the boy was fine, having stumbled across a remote mountain outpost and been taken in by a couple of caring villagers.

Or Abu's hunch was right, and the boy had accidentally found something that the tribesmen didn't want anyone seeing. He could have been quietly eliminated and buried before anyone knew what had happened.

Something deep within him — perhaps past experience — told him that he would never see the boy again.

That brought about a fresh wave of emotions — disgust, sadness, fury. It all balled into a tight gut-punching sensation that wracked Slater's insides.

He realised that Abu and the woman were waiting for a response.

'I don't know,' he said. 'I'm sorry.'

He spent far too long watching the woman's eyes produce fresh tears as the realisation hit her that her young son had really taken off into the mountains. If he hadn't returned by now, Slater imagined he never would. He found himself encapsulated by her grief, and it began to fuel him in a way that he couldn't quite put his finger on.

But he couldn't deny his anger.

A steely aura fell over him. His mouth became a hard line. He wrapped up the emotions he was feeling into a tight package and balled it down, suppressing the tension for now. Determination seared through him.

He started to form a plan — to go and find the tribesmen responsible for what had happened. He tuned out his surroundings, drawing into the inner workings of his own mind.

To his own detriment.

He didn't hear the pick-up truck's engine until it was too late.

With his back to the slope, he had no clear view of oncoming traffic.

The roar of the approaching vehicle filled his eardrums at the last second.

He turned to peer down the steep road, expecting to see a vehicle screeching to a halt and predicting a verbal torrent of abuse from its occupants.

He saw neither of those two events.

Instead he saw the broad hood of a Toyota Land Cruiser filling his vision, only a foot away from impacting his torso.

The car had no intention of slowing down.

Slater leapt off his feet at the last second, which created enough momentum to topple him over the hood instead of being knocked underneath it when the Toyota slammed into his legs.

He sprawled across the hood, slammed against the windscreen, and dropped off the side of the pick-up truck onto the hot pavement below, landing in a pathetic heap on the ground.

10

It took a moment for the incident to register in his mind.

He'd reacted instinctively, saving himself from getting crushed underneath the Toyota's giant off-road wheels in the space of a half-second. It meant that he sprawled to the pavement with disorientation clouding his senses. It took him a beat to stare at the Toyota in an adrenalin-induced haze and recognise one of the occupants.

One of the checkpoint guards from the previous day.

The man sat in the passenger seat, sporting a grievous purple welt on the back of his neck from where Slater had struck him with the butt of the Kalashnikov.

Slater hadn't seen the driver before. The unknown man had both hands on the wheel, with his face twisted into a contorted scowl of concentration. He was applying the brakes after realising that he hadn't incapacitated Slater with the initial ram.

The checkpoint guard was in the process of twisting in his seat, trying to keep an eye on Slater while the driver slowed the Land Cruiser to a halt in the middle of the street.

The tyres squealed and thick grey smoke wafted into the air. When the Toyota finally ground to a stop, Slater saw Abu and the crying woman standing frozen only inches from the hood of the vehicle.

He saw red.

In the confusion, he wasn't sure whether the newcomers were armed. He realised that it would do him well to take advantage of the rapidly changing situation. The driver and passenger would have expected to hit him and incapacitate him with the first charge. They had failed to do so, and were clearly attempting to improvise.

Slater lived and breathed improvisation.

He scrambled to his feet and sprinted straight up to the driver's door. The guy still had both hands clasped on the wheel — the Land Cruiser hadn't fully come to a stop just yet, still in the process of squealing to a halt. Slater shot a hand through the open window and reached blindly into the space between the driver and the door.

If his hunch proved correct, the man would have stowed his weapon in the door's compartment while he concentrated on driving.

Slater wrapped his fingers around a smooth metal object and came out with an IWI Jericho 941 semi-automatic pistol, manufactured in Israel. He had the barrel jammed into the soft centre of the driver's exposed throat before the checkpoint guard in the passenger seat had a chance to react.

A Mexican standoff ensued.

Now that Slater had time to get his bearings, he acknowledged the fact that the checkpoint guard was armed. The man wielded the same Kalashnikov AK-47 that he'd held at the checkpoint, but in the cramped cabin of the Toyota it proved a cumbersome weapon to manoeuvre. It had taken the guy a couple of seconds too long to get an aim on Slater.

By the time he had the Kalashnikov aimed at Slater's temple, Slater had the driver at gunpoint.

Silence descended over the laneway.

It proved a strange sight — a Toyota Land Cruiser parked diagonally in the centre of the dusty street, smoke wafting off the tyres, two men frozen in the cabin and another man standing outside the vehicle with his arm holding a gun to the driver's throat.

Nobody said a word.

Slater noted the unstable grip the checkpoint guard had on the AK-47. His palms were slick with sweat, and his wrists shook with fear.

Out of the corner of his eye, Slater noticed Abu and the woman still standing in front of the vehicle. Neither of them had moved a muscle.

'Abu,' Slater said quietly. 'Come here.'

Abu skirted around the hood of the Toyota and drew to a halt alongside Slater. Both of them peered through the driver's window, across the driver, to the checkpoint guard in the passenger's seat.

'Am I correct in assuming that this man here,' Slater said, gesturing to the driver, 'is a mercenary?'

Abu stared at the driver, who had his gaze fixed straight ahead in horror. The guy squirmed uneasily under the pressure of Slater's gun barrel.

'Yes,' Abu said in a voice barely above a whisper. 'He's AQAP.'

'What?'

'Al-Qaeda in the Arabian Peninsula.'

'Does that mean my friend over there hired him to help do his dirty work?'

'Probably. How do you know that man?'

'Bit of trouble at a security checkpoint.'

Abu nodded understandingly.

'Tell my friend,' Slater said, 'that this won't end well for him either way. If he kills me, this pistol will go off and his al-Qaeda buddy will get his neck blown to shreds. Ask him if he understands how that particular organisation will react if they find out one of their own was killed helping police. Ask him to think long and hard about this.'

Slater had entered a different zone. There was a loaded gun barrel pointed at his face, and it had shifted him into a primal state, the kind of state where he thrived. He would do absolutely anything necessary to survive this encounter. Instincts had kicked in.

And all concept of mercy had fallen away.

He had done the guards a favour at the security checkpoint by keeping them alive. Now, he would not be so gracious. If the initial hit with the Land Cruiser had incapacitated him, he would have caught a bullet through his skull while lying helpless and injured on the hot ground.

Abu began to speak to the checkpoint guard, talking in a low tone just as he had done to the woman minutes previously. The man had broken out in an uncontrollable sweat, affected by the stress of the situation and the stifling humidity of the Land Cruiser's cabin.

Abu continued to talk.

The guard kept his eyes fixed firmly on Slater.

Slater kept his gaze fixed equally firmly on the guard.

The guard faltered first.

In the midst of Abu's speech, the man said something that attracted the attention of the guard for a brief few milliseconds. The guard's pupils flickered over to Abu for an instant, and the barrel of the Kalashnikov dipped a half-inch in the air.

He had broken concentration.

Slater pulled the trigger of the Jericho 941, sending an unsuppressed Parabellum round through the soft tissue of the al-Qaeda mercenary's throat. It killed the man instantly, but before the guy's brain had even registered the overwhelming roar of the gunshot, Slater had wrenched his aim around to face the guard in the passenger seat.

He pumped the trigger once more.

Two deafening blasts, loud enough to resonate throughout the entire town.

And two dead occupants.

The second bullet had sliced through the checkpoint guard's forehead, jerking his head back into the opposite window and spraying blood over the upholstery.

Slater saw none of it, because he had tackled Abu to the ground as soon as he unleashed his shots, hurling them both below the line of sight just in case the checkpoint guard spasmed against the Kalashnikov's trigger in his death throes.

Nothing happened.

Ears ringing, pulse pounding, Slater took a deep breath and composed himself.

Situation handled.

11

He didn't think there would be a single person in the mountain town who hadn't heard the altercation unfold. As he rose back to his feet and confirmed that the two men in the Toyota were dead, he exhaled softly, stilling his nerves.

He knew the dangers of letting the rush of cortisol get to his head.

He had to remain tactical.

For all he knew, the other two checkpoint guards were on their way.

'Are you okay?' he said as Abu clambered tentatively to his feet.

The man nodded, his cheeks pale, still in shock. 'I've only ever seen gunfights like that from a distance.'

'How common are they around here?'

'What do you mean?'

'I need to know if what just happened will cause an uproar.'

'Not an uproar,' Abu said, shaking his head. 'There are many fights around here. For the last couple of years death has become more and more common in these parts. But there has not been commotion in this town for quite some time, as far as I can tell. There'll be attention on you.'

'Might need to retreat away from here for a bit then.'

'I'd say so.'

Slater paused and stared at the vehicle with its two dead occupants. 'Lucky I have a ride, then, isn't it?'

Abu hesitated. 'I hope you're not about to do what I think you are.'

'And what would that be?'

'Something foolish.'

'That's all I ever do.'

He set about opening each of the Toyota's doors in turn and hauling both corpses out onto the pavement. He made sure to drag each body away from the main road to allow traffic to pass by. Death had long since lost its mystique, and he had no qualms with handling bodies.

Not after what he'd been through.

He propped each man up against one of the mud brick walls lining the laneway and crossed back to the Toyota. Thankfully, no arterial veins had been severed by the gunshots. They'd bled, but nothing Slater hadn't seen before. The cabin was relatively tidy, considering he'd killed two people in it moments earlier.

'What do I do with them?' Abu said, grimacing as his gaze drifted from the man with no throat to the man with no forehead.

'Whatever you want,' Slater said. 'Blame it all on me if you need to. I can take the heat.'

'And where are you going?' Abu said.

Slater paused by the driver's door, staring across the street at the woman in the burqa. Her eyes were still transfixed on the shocking scene of violence that had unfolded before her, but he could see the pain behind the stare.

He could see that if nothing was done, the unanswered questions would plague her for the rest of her life.

'I'm going to go find her son,' Slater said. 'She deserves that much. It's my fault I let him go up into the mountains.'

'It certainly isn't,' Abu said, suddenly furious. 'How on earth could you have known?'

'I did know,' Slater said. 'Subconsciously, I did. I just didn't do anything about it.'

'And what do you intend to do about it now?' Abu said. 'I fear it is too late.'

'It might be. I can still knock a few heads together.'

'I wouldn't lay a finger on the tribesmen up in those mountains,' Abu said. 'Please. I know we barely know each other, but it would be fatal, and I quite like you, Will. I consider you a friend. I don't want you to go getting yourself killed.'

Slater slotted wordlessly into the driver's seat and slammed the door. The rolled-down window gave him a hole through which he could communicate with Abu.

'I wouldn't worry about it,' he said. 'I can take care of myself.'

'I'm sure you can. But what about me? If it comes out that I've been seen with you, and you cause havoc up there ... how will I end up?'

'I'll make sure it doesn't come out,' Slater said.

'But...'

Slater seized the man's wrist and locked onto his gaze.

'Look at her,' he hissed. 'Look.'

Abu turned and glanced at the woman behind them, standing sheepishly on the sidewalk, covered in the shadow of a three-storey building.

'She needs to know what happened to her boy,' Slater said. 'I'm not walking out of here without knowing. Okay?'

'Okay,' Abu said.

He offered little in the way of resistance, obviously aware that Slater had made his mind up.

Slater pressed his foot down on the brake pedal and slotted the gearstick into drive. With a glance in the rear view mirror, he noted a cluster of civilians forming at the base of the street, further down the hill. It wouldn't take long for news of the firefight to spread through Qasam like wildfire. Most of the town would have heard the gunshots.

It would do him good to set off as soon as possible — both to let the recent violence fade away, and to possess the highest chance of retrieving the boy. The sooner the kid's mother knew his fate, the better.

He nodded once to Abu, wordlessly exchanging a farewell with the man who had shown him such hospitality when none was needed, and pressed the accelerator. The Toyota took a moment to lurch off the mark, as the revving of the engine shot through the tyres. The rubber eventually found purchase on the steep incline and Slater set off.

Toward the mountains.

Toward uncertainty.

12

The town fell away instantly, replaced by imposing cliff-faces on either side of the Land Cruiser. Slater tuned out the grim thoughts swirling through his head, opting to believe — for the time being, at least — that the boy was unharmed.

He had been intuitively trained to expect the worst in every possible situation.

But he wasn't employed anymore.

He was here by choice.

The thought rattled him, icing his veins, narrowing his vision. For years he had justified the violence and the rage and the devastation as the simple act of carrying out orders. Sure, the adversaries he'd faced over his career had all deserved it — at least, in his eyes — but he fully understood that the events he'd taken part in would have an undeniable toll on even the most hardened operative, unless a justifiable excuse was made as to why.

That thin veneer was beginning to fall away.

Now he was a free man, voluntarily heading for confrontation.

Looking for a fight, it appeared.

He told himself that was nonsense. Just as it had been justified to wage war against mercenaries, drug barons, bio-terrorists, and the scum of the earth in general, it was necessary that he retrieve an innocent boy from the hands of northern highlander tribesmen.

Who knew the things they might be doing to him...

Everything's fine, Slater told himself. *The boy's safe.*

He passed the first remote mountain village less than five minutes into the cross-country journey.

The twisting path guided the Toyota through the midst of a maze of crags in the mountainside. When the shadows across the truck fell away, replaced by an open view of the Hadhramaut Valley, Slater caught the first glimpse of human activity.

It didn't instil confidence within him.

The village was a ghost town, nothing more than a collection of mud brick huts, entirely abandoned and crumbling away under the intense glare of the Yemeni sun overhead. It had been erected in the centre of a smooth plateau, this one positioned far above Qasam. The wadis stretching out for hundreds of miles appeared small from this height. Slater touched his foot to the brake and slowed the Land Cruiser to a crawl as the track passed by the village.

He gulped back apprehension, at the same time quashing a dizzying sensation as he realised the altitude. It made him acutely aware of a potential fall, to the point where his breathing became more laboured. He sucked in air, wound down the window, and studied the village and the view beyond.

There was no sign of life whatsoever.

The majority of the huts sported roofs that had caved in weeks or months earlier. Coupled with wooden doors hanging off their hinges and stone bricks crumbling to pieces before his eyes, Slater imagined that no-one had lived at this site for at least a year.

The hairs on his forearms rose.

Out of instinct, he killed the engine, letting the desolation of the mountainside wash over him. The cabin turned to an oven in seconds, sweltering in the desert heat. He listened hard for anything notable — either the howl of a wild animal, or the squawk of a bird, or the cry of a child, or the clanging of pots and pans.

Nothing.

Just wind and heat.

Dejected by the uncertainty, Slater fired the Toyota back into life and continued on the path.

He stayed on edge, checking intermittently that the Jericho 941 in the centre console had its safety off and its trigger ready to fire. Over the course of his career he had come to learn that he preferred raging madness and total confusion to the pulse-pounding silence that signified an ambush.

The altitude steadily rose.

Over the next ten minutes, the thought began to creep into his mind that he had set off on a fool's errand.

What are you expecting to find?

Optimistically, he anticipated that any twist in the road would reveal a strongly-populated mountain village bristling with activity in the mid-morning heat. He would pull up to find the young boy from the day before beaming with glee, just as he had been fourteen hours previously. An elderly highlander couple would approach Slater's vehicle without fear, handing over the boy so that he could be returned to his mother without incident and the entire ordeal could be chalked up to a frightening but ultimately harmless misunderstanding.

Instead, moments after visualising a warm-hearted ending to the search, Slater swung the Land Cruiser around a steep bend in the road...

...to reveal one of the most horrifying sights he had ever laid eyes on.

13

Slater later stamped on the brakes.

The Toyota screeched to a halt in the middle of the uneven track.

Dust wafted off the fat off-road tyres. The engine rumbled idly as he clenched the steering wheel double-handed, knuckles white. Sweat began to leech off his forehead — but not because of the heat.

There was no doubts or qualms about what lay ahead. It couldn't be interpreted any other way. Slater considered turning back, pretending he had never seen anything, calmly informing the woman that he had found no sign of her son.

Anything would be better than the truth.

He forced himself into motion and trundled the big Land Cruiser over to the side of the road, steering it out of the way of any passing traffic. He stifled a curse at the foolishness of his own actions — there was as much chance a vehicle would pass by as there was of the boy making it back home for dinner.

Slater parked the Toyota, yanked the handbrake on, shut

the engine off, and stepped out of the cabin onto the potholed mountain track.

He grimaced, suppressed a wave of nausea...

...and crossed the road to scrutinise the boy's severed head.

Three distinct emotions rolled over him as he observed the scene of the haphazard execution.

First, regret.

He couldn't believe he hadn't stopped the boy in his tracks. At the very least he should have communicated through rudimentary sign language to ask if the boy's home rested in the mountains. Had he recognised that the kid didn't belong in the highlands, he never would have let him out of his sight.

Then, that passed, replaced quickly by confusion.

The hairs on the back of Slater's neck rose and he pondered exactly what the boy had done to deserve such a horrific fate. Like he had thought earlier, the kid couldn't have been older than eight. There was nothing that an eight-year-old could have done to antagonise anyone to this extent.

Slater studied the scene, even though he would have rather been anywhere else.

The kid's rigid body had been dumped in a shallow ditch by the side of the mountain trail, arms and legs awkwardly splayed in random directions. His neck consisted of nothing more than a bloody stump. The head — sporting a grotesque expression of abject terror — rested upright in the dust, covered in sand and barely recognisable.

That brought on the third emotion, a sensation that was accompanied by the blood rushing to Slater's face, the veins in his forearms and legs beginning to pump, his heart rate rapidly increasing.

Pure, unadulterated rage.

A particularly vicious gust of wind blew up the mountainside, whistling between the surrounding crags, kicking up particles of sand and dirt and dust. Slater let his gaze follow a soft cloud of dust that shot away from the boy's corpse.

That was when he saw it.

Someone had used the kid's arterial blood to paint a crude arrow atop the rocky ground just a few feet away from his corpse. Slater's attention had been so consumed by the sight of the decapitation that he hadn't noticed the symbol until now.

It pointed straight back down the mountain, delivering a clear message.

Back.

Slater lost track of the amount of time he spent staring at the arrow. He paid attention to every stroke that had been painted, every crimson speck. It had all come from the most innocent person he had met in months. A boy frolicking happily into the mountains. He spent so long looking at the symbol, enraptured by the brutality of it, that he didn't notice the voices until they were right on top of him.

By the time he broke out of his dazed stupor and heard coarse Arabic echoing off the rocky crags all around him, he knew he only had seconds to act.

The voices came from further up the trail, where the majority of the ascent was hidden behind a maze of natural rock formations. Slater's attention jerked directly to the sound.

Three men.

Maybe four.

He crouched low and slunk away from the track.

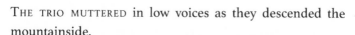

THE TRIO MUTTERED in low voices as they descended the mountainside.

After a beat of reasonably loud conversation, the leader hissed in a low tone at the other pair, instructing them to lower their voices.

Just in case any of the townspeople had dared to venture up in search of the child.

They had been speaking of protective measures, and the necessary actions that had come about as a result of staying loyal to their mission.

One of them had suggested they should check to see whether the signal had been received.

There was nothing else to do, so two of them snatched up their Kalashnikov AK-47s and the other fetched his traditional curved dagger — called a *jambiyah* in their native tongue.

As a pack, the trio set off for the place they had left the boy.

Striding purposefully to ensure they didn't turn an ankle on the loose, steep track, the three of them rounded the final bend to see the kid still resting where they had left him.

Untouched.

Unmoved.

Then one of them caught the glint of steel out of the corner of his eye.

He sucked in a sharp intake of breath and brought the AK-47 up to shoulder height in one swift motion, locking the barrel onto whatever he had found in his peripheral vision.

It was the rear tray of a pick-up truck.

Parked motionless on the other side of the track.

Most of the Toyota Land Cruiser's body was obscured by

a jagged rock formation the height of a two-storey building. The other two men had yet to notice the rear wheels poking out from behind the rudimentary cover.

The first man barked a coarse warning, seizing the attention of his comrades.

The trio noticed the vehicle.

Its occupants had to still be on the mountain.

There was no other way up here.

With both automatic rifles aimed tensely at the idle vehicle, and the third man clutching his curved dagger in a white-knuckled grip, the trio moved in on the truck.

Step by step.

Taking no risks.

Leaving nothing to chance.

Then the first man heard a footstep in the dirt, inches behind him.

His heart rate skyrocketed.

An arm wrapped around his throat and locked him in a grip so tight he thought his head might burst off his shoulders.

14

S later had a muscular forearm wrapped around the man's neck before the guy even sensed that anyone was in the vicinity.

With the other hand, he jammed the barrel of the IWI Jericho 941 into the side of the tribesman's head hard enough to cause him to audibly yelp in surprise.

The other two tribesmen spun, reeling, seized by panic.

'*Down!*' Slater roared at the top of his lungs. 'Down! Gun down!'

The guy he had taken as a human shield had a Kalashnikov AK-47 resting in his hands, but there was nothing he could do with it at close range that Slater wouldn't see coming well in advance.

The only other threat was the second armed tribesman.

The third had a traditional dagger, but it would prove useless from anything more than a couple of feet away.

Right now, he stood facing off with the other two tribesmen from a distance of at least five feet.

The sheer confusion that came along with the sudden high-stakes development caused the second tribesman to freeze in his tracks. He had his AK-47 aimed at the dust, and had missed the half-second of opportunity to bring it up before panic took over and he instinctively followed Slater's demands.

An uncomfortable, tense silence settled over the track.

Slater could have sent a Parabellum round through each of their foreheads from a safe distance away, concealed in a shadowy rocky formation that they had passed by seconds earlier, but he had to make sure that they were the cause of the boy's death.

As savage and primal as the highlander tribesmen might be, Slater wasn't about to shoot three of them dead on a hunch.

He instantly recognised that he had the upper hand. The pure aggression in his actions had stunned the trio into muted obedience. They were probably accustomed to getting their way, known around these parts as an unpre-dictable, dangerous group. When someone showed them zero respect and manhandled them around, they caved.

As most did.

Slater twisted the warm steel of the Jericho's barrel harder into the flesh above the tribesman's ear. The guy squirmed, and bucked, and finally let out a helpless cry of pain.

It was the nail in the coffin.

'Down!' Slater commanded, staring daggers across the track at the other two tribesmen. He let his eyes go wide, revealing the animalism in them.

The savagery.

The no-holds-barred willpower.

It intimidated the other two men into dropping their weapons into the dirt.

With the arm he had wrapped around the tribesman's throat, Slater beckoned with two fingers toward himself.

The pair of now-unarmed tribesmen got the message, and started walking over to Slater with their palms spread.

Stepping out of reach of their sand-coated weapons.

When he was satisfied that they were nowhere close enough to mount any kind of retaliation, he released his hold on the human shield and thrust the guy over to his comrades. The man went stumbling across the dusty track, thrown off-balance by the gradient.

His two friends' caught him and held him upright.

Slater levelled the barrel of the Jericho 941 at the trio, and they froze in place.

Right where he wanted them.

Effectively disarmed and rendered collectively useless in under a minute.

Standing in the middle of the trail, with no cover to dive behind or weapons to seize at.

Slater motioned with the barrel of his gun at the corpse of the boy, resting a few dozen feet down the track.

One of them turned and followed his gaze, noting the position of the kid.

The guy turned back to face Slater.

'You?' Slater said, thrusting the Jericho's barrel at the trio.

The guy who seemed to be in charge — dressed in faded rags and sporting a wretched expression of satisfaction — looked left, then looked right. As if checking to see if there was anyone else to blame the deed on.

Then he shrugged, nodded...

...and smiled.

Slater knew what he was supposed to do. Detain the three men, which would be a simple enough procedure.

Drive them back down to Qasam and funnel them into
Abu's residence. Get the man to translate for him, and find
out exactly why the trio had decided to enact such a savage
act of violence on an innocent child.

Then deliver them to whoever the proper authorities
were.

Suddenly, the rage came back to wash over him in waves
of furious red.

And he realised he had never done things that way.

Unable to resist his impulses, he locked on with his aim.

The reports of three separate gunshots tore through the
mountains, resonating off smooth cliff-faces and echoing
along deep chasms in the rock.

Slater admired his handiwork for less than a second.

Then he cursed his impulsiveness, gathered up the
tribesmen's Kalashnikov rifles, and hurled them into the
back of the Toyota just a few feet away.

15

S later considered the bloody arrow painted onto the rocks nothing but a challenge.

He peeled away from the corpses — now numbering four — and continued his ascent up the mountain. Anyone who stumbled upon the scene in the meantime would no doubt be awfully confused by what they found.

A dead child, and three bullet-riddled tribesmen.

Slater would be back to clean up the mess later.

Something about the arrow frustrated him to no end.

He had to defy it.

He knew he never would have forced answers out of any of the tribesmen. Even if he had somehow managed to breach the language barrier — with the help of Abu, perhaps — it would take little effort on the tribesmen's part to send him on a wild goose chase, crafting lie after lie about what their true intentions were.

Slater knew, as always, that the truth would be revealed in what lay further up the track.

The adrenalin ebbed steadily from his veins as he made

for the peak of this particular mountain. There wasn't far to go — every now and then he would catch a glimpse through the rock formations and find himself awestruck by how far he had risen above the desert floor.

Sand particles flicked against the dirty windscreen inter-mittently, kicked up by the fat off-road tyres and the wind howling through the stone on either side. Slater squinted against the bombardment, narrowing his vision on the road ahead. The Jericho rested by his side.

Just in case.

The trio of tribesmen could have dozens of comrades, for all he knew.

Suddenly, his vision narrowed to a pinpoint, condensing fast enough to make his head droop with vertigo. He rattled his skull from side-to-side and composed himself, battling to keep the Toyota on the track instead of careening through the rock formations to a hundred-foot-drop.

Nausea.

Dizziness.

Unease.

They all struck him at once. He couldn't figure out if it was the sight of the decapitated boy that had affected him so strongly, or whether the combination of constant perspira-tion and intermittent meals had made him sick.

Whatever the case, he pressed on.

There was no alternative.

Amidst the hazy smog of swirling dust ahead, he made out the rock formations on either side of the track falling away, opening out into some kind of flat ground. From his position in the Toyota's stifling cabin, Slater couldn't see anything more than that.

It told him enough.

He slowed down and tugged the handbrake into place,

grinding the fat wheels to a stop in the middle of the trail. Roaring into open ground and engaging in vehicular warfare with a yet-unknown number of hostiles could only result in disaster.

He wrapped the Jericho in one hand.

Glanced briefly at the Kalashnikov AK-47 on the passenger seat.

Shook his head and slipped out into the heat.

He had always preferred sidearms — especially in close-range situations such as this. They suited him better. He could whip the four-inch barrel from target to target at an unbelievable pace. He knew, because he'd done it before.

Hundreds of times.

They all dropped like bowling pins.

Kalashnikovs had their uses. They were reliable as all hell, and could pose an advantage when one needed to enact overwhelming force.

Spray-and-pray, in other words.

Slater considered himself a little more refined than that.

He palmed the Jericho and set off at a low jog up the mountainside, keeping as quiet as he could. It was almost entirely unnecessary — the wind resonated throughout the mountaintop like a howling wraith. Nevertheless, Slater had never experienced a situation where he didn't employ caution, so he stayed disciplined and focused.

He stepped out into the mouth of the plateau, sweeping the barrel of the Jericho from left to right, searching methodically for any sign of resistance.

Nothing.

He looked right, squinting against the glare of the sun to gaze out over the Hadhraumaut Valley. At the end of the flat expanse, the ground simply fell away into nothingness. It was a sheer cliff-face that dropped hundreds of feet to the desert below. The rest of the promontory twisted into the mountainside, the ground uneven and unstable. The flat stretch trailed past a line of shadowy caves, each of which speared into the rock itself. Their mouths hung empty and foreboding.

Slater stared at the open ground in front of the caves.

It took him a moment to spot the encampment.

Visually, the collection of mud brick huts were near-identical to the deserted village Slater had passed earlier. But there was something indescribable in the air, a palpable tension that cast a sinister gloom over the entire area. The hairs on his forearms stood on end and a cold chill worked its way down his spine.

He didn't belong here.

Keeping the Jericho raised, Slater moved tentatively across the open ground. He couldn't shake the feeling that he was awfully exposed. At any moment he expected a gunshot to ring off the walls of the surrounding slopes.

If the first shot hit home, he wouldn't be around to hear the report.

Slowly but surely, it set in that there was no-one home. The tension that he initially mistook for an ambush petered out, replaced by isolated silence. He stepped into the midst of the encampment.

His stomach twisted at what he saw.

Altogether, it combined to form a confusing picture — none of it bode well for Slater's nerves. His gaze passed from food scraps to steel canisters full to the brim with water, to a collection of weaponry large enough to outfit an entire militia, to grenades and traditional curved daggers and spartan tribal garments.

None of the individual objects inherently bothered him.

What set him on edge was the way everything had been

thrown around the camp, completely disorganised, almost abandoned. It seemed as if the entire mountain had been ditched in a hurry. There were enough general supplies and weaponry and clothing in the village to house more than a dozen tribesmen.

Slater couldn't imagine that the trio he'd encountered were the only people on the mountain.

Where are the others?

He spent a second pondering that question before something else seized his attention, right on the edge of the encampment.

The corner of a tarpaulin sheet flapping in the wind.

Slater quashed a brief stab of reluctance and crossed over to the sheet. The tarpaulin was draped over a section of the dusty rock behind one of the mud brick huts, hammered into the ground with inch-thick steel posts. There was no intention of keeping whatever it was covering secure — each of the edges flapped mercilessly as they were bombarded by the mountain gale.

He crouched by the corner of the blue sheet and lifted up the edge with his free hand, peering into the murky recess underneath.

The breath caught in his throat.

A lump formed in his chest.

He stared at a collection of gas masks and oxygen tanks sprawled at random across the ground.

16

Slater had no misconceptions as to what the presence of the objects meant.

He had been involved in the realm of bioweapons for years — a popular pastime amongst the scum of the earth. The dangers of chemical and biological warfare posed a trickier and more significant threat than any kind of conventional weaponry. Of course, the gas masks littered across the ground underneath the tarpaulin didn't inherently mean that foul play was afoot.

It certainly didn't instil confidence in Slater, though.

He stood up, reeling. From his brief assessment, it appeared that the breathing apparatus' had been used. Mouthpieces were detached from their holsters, the back harnesses supporting the oxygen tanks had been tightened to varying degrees, and there were flecks of dried saliva stained into the insides of some of the gas masks.

They weren't there as a precautionary measure.

Something had unfolded that had required their use.

Suddenly, the tension that Slater had felt as he stepped out onto the promontory crept back in.

All was not as it seemed.

He squatted in the centre of the deserted encampment and tried his best to gather his thoughts. There were a million worming around inside his brain. He recalled the times he had encountered weapons of a chemical nature — each time they seemed to carry with them more heightened stakes than the last. Technology advanced, terrorists got smarter, and weapons gained lethality.

The thought of a bioweapon out here sent shivers down his spine.

Despite the Yemeni sun scorching the promontory, heating the back of his neck until it grew uncomfortable...

... inside, an icy chill worked its way through him.

Then — sudden alertness.

His heart rate spiked as he heard the noise. It came from deep within one of the caves, barely audible over the gale-force winds. But it pinpricked at the edge of Slater's hearing just enough to send the barrel of his Jericho lurching in the direction of the cave.

Some kind of clattering.

A man-made sound.

He lined the sights of the Jericho directly into the mouth of the cave, his eyes searching the shadows for any sign of movement. Nothing stood out to him. He stayed frozen, still as a statue, for a long half-minute. There was a pause in the wind buffeting up through the edge of the promontory, and all sound died out briefly, replaced by an eerie silence.

Hearing nothing out of the ordinary, Slater advanced steadily toward the cave.

Its mouth was shrouded in shadow, blocked from the sun by an overhanging rock formation. He wiped sweat off his forehead with the sleeve of his shirt, preventing drops of perspiration from running through his eyebrows and affecting his vision.

He stepped into the darkness.

It took a moment for his eyes to adjust. He didn't dare look down at his feet, even though the view was near pitch-black. The daylight leeching in through the mouth of the cave quickly fell away, only a dozen feet into the lair.

He kept his breathing muted and his footsteps silent.

No-one would hear him coming.

He had worked tirelessly his entire life to disappear when it was deemed necessary.

He would do the same now.

The path inside the mountain curved slightly, twisting almost imperceptibly to the left. Slater followed it round, now nearly entirely swamped in darkness.

His eyes began to adjust to the low light.

He paused in the gloom as he made out the outlines of man-made objects.

More guns. A collection of old-fashioned video cameras with flip screens, their battery lights softly blinking in the darkness. Scraps of food, upended plastic bottles.

More gas masks.

Slater's heart began to pound and his hands turned clammy. The space between his palm and the Jericho's grip quickly became soaked with sweat. The warm air seeped through the cave, stifling in its intensity, but that wasn't what was causing him to overheat.

He hadn't been anticipating anything like this.

At worst, he had expected a ragtag collection of infuriated tribesmen looking to unleash their bloodlust on whomever wandered into their encampment. He would have dealt with them accordingly, exacting revenge in the name of the young boy he'd barely known.

Instead, he'd stumbled upon something far worse.

Slater crouched by the collection of belongings and snatched up one of the video cameras. A green light blinked intermittently on its side. He flipped open the screen — still locked into place against the side of the device — and the camera automatically fired to life.

There was nothing on the memory card.

He hadn't been expecting much — certainly not incriminating evidence that would reveal the exact reason for all the breathing apparatus'.

It still crippled his morale, though.

He was nowhere close to the truth. He had nothing to go off besides the remnants of something horrific. Every voice that could reveal anything about the situation had either fled, or been killed.

He never would have forced anything out of the trio of tribesmen down the trail anyway.

Dejected, he thumbed a button on the side of the video camera and the flashlight on the front of the device flickered into life.

For no good reason, he pointed the white beam down the length of the cave, peering further into the mountain.

The light glinted off a set of beady eyes watching him in the darkness.

17

He had the Jericho trained on the face in the blink of an eye.

There was no fear — nothing but intense focus and concentration. He tuned out everything else in his surroundings and narrowed his vision onto the eyes sparkling in the darkness. He dropped the video camera in one swift motion. The device clattered to the cave floor and came to rest on its side, flashlight still aimed directly down the length of the tunnel.

The tension amplified.

No-one made a move.

No-one made a sound.

Then the eyes began to move...

...and Slater froze.

He assumed the man had been crouching down, hovering a foot off the ground for tactical purposes. But when the head floated slowly forward, drawing closer to the mouth of the cave, he realised that it was no man at all.

It was an animal.

The creature slunk toward him, deadly silent, shackles

raised. Slater scrutinised the outline for a long moment, until finally the beast came close enough and the camera light illuminated it.

A red desert wolf.

Eyes glowing menacingly in the dark.

Slater hesitated, unsure whether to gun the animal down where it stood. He knew little about the beasts, other than the fact that a handful of them roamed the desert. He didn't imagine they would be unnecessarily confrontational, but to reassure himself he kept the Jericho fixed on the wolf's snout.

Then it drew closer still, and he took a back step, recoiling in horror at what he saw.

In all his years as an operative, through all the mind-boggling situations he'd been involved in and the horrific sights he'd been witness to...

... never had he seen anything quite like this.

The animal limped pathetically into view, barely able to hold itself upright due to its condition. As it stumbled and lurched into clear view, its features illuminated by the harsh white light still emanating out of the video camera, Slater found himself completely stunned by what he was witnessing.

The wolf was coated from head-to-toe in crimson blood. The liquid seemed to leak out of every orifice, dripping gruesomely from its mouth and both its nostrils. The beast's eyes — usually piercing and calm — were wracked with pain, bloodshot and rabid. As Slater's muscles temporarily locked up in confusion, the wolf bowed its head and retched, hacking up a glob of blood onto the cave floor. It looked up at Slater, locking eyes with him.

For a moment, everything else fell away.

He stared into the gaze of the helpless creature. The wolf

could barely stand, only able to drag itself out of the position it had been resting in to respond to the new arrival. When it made it into the glare of the camera light, it snarled once — feebly, with nothing behind the gesture — then collapsed in a pool of its own blood, its breath coming in rattling gasps.

Slater lowered the Jericho, shocked.

The first idea that came to mind was that the tribesmen were more sadistic than he had ever thought possible. Perhaps they had captured this red desert wolf when it wandered curiously into their encampment, and used it as a prisoner to take out their frustrations at the world. It was a grim idea, but Slater had been dealing with the unimaginable for as long as he could remember.

Nowadays, nothing surprised him.

But that didn't make any sense. The wolf didn't appear to be trapped in this cave.

It didn't explain the gas masks, or the breathing apparatus', or the fact that half the mountainside had been hastily deserted.

Then a second thought came roaring into his head, along with the blood rush of adrenalin flooding his senses.

Perhaps this was the reason for the masks. Perhaps this was a weapon like nothing he had ever seen before, a sinister infection that caused symptoms straight out of a horror film.

Perhaps the wolf had been a test subject.

As soon as the thought entered his mind, he turned on his heel and broke into a full-pelt sprint for the mouth of the cave. A terrifying wave of nausea washed over him, bringing with it the notion that he might already be infected. He knew enough about bioweapons to recognise the dangers of a test subject out in the open.

Probably why the mountain's abandoned, he thought.

He didn't understand how the tribesmen could have been so foolish.

He never would have imagined that a test would have been carried out anywhere other than a laboratory, expertly sealed to prevent any unexpected consequences.

Then again, that didn't exactly align with the intellect of highlander tribesmen.

Still in disbelief, he broke out into open ground, legs pumping with maximum exertion.

Where on earth did they get a bioweapon?

What the hell is it exactly?

How virulent are the particles?

What are they going to do with it?

Question after question bombarded him relentlessly, to the point where he shut everything out and focused solely on the breath pounding in his lungs and his feet pounding against the smooth rock.

He made it to the encampment — halfway across the promontory, several dozen feet from the cave — and snatched up a gas mask from underneath the tarpaulin sheet on his way through. He never eased off the pace. The mask would likely achieve nothing, but if remnants of the virus hung ominously in the air all around the plateau, he wanted to use every available opportunity to avoid inhaling a particle.

Maybe it didn't matter.

Maybe he was already doomed to the grisliest death imaginable.

With his heartbeat pounding in his ears and the foggy breathing mask pressed awkwardly to his face, Slater found his senses clouded. He could barely see where he was going, let alone concentrate on his surroundings.

It meant that — as he tore across the encampment and burst out between a pair of mud brick huts on the opposite side — he didn't hear the pick-up truck barrelling in his direction.

He didn't even know anyone else was in the area.

So when the hood of the vehicle crunched into his abdomen — a head-on, albeit slow-moving collision — and flung him off to the side, he couldn't believe what was happening until it was too late.

Again?

He thudded into the rock, rolled once, twice. Lost the gas mask in a frantic scramble. It tumbled away.

Sizing up the situation in an instant, he made out the shape of another Land Cruiser — this one jet black — towering over him, having screeched to a halt alongside him. It had been on its way into the encampment when it hit Slater hard enough to cause serious injury.

He spotted automatic weapons in the hands of the men piling out of the cabin. They were panicked, scrambled, unfocused. They hadn't spotted the location he'd come to rest at just yet.

Fuck, he thought.

Instinct took over, and he jammed the Jericho desperately into the back of his waistband, hiding it from sight.

He had a zero percent chance in a head-on gunfight against three heavily-armed hostiles.

It was time to play the role of an innocent, hopelessly-lost tourist.

Long shot — but the only chance he had.

He prayed that he wouldn't end the day in a bodybag.

18

'H*ey!*' he screamed, contorting his features into twisted terror. 'Help!'

There were three weapons in his face before he had the chance to say anything else. He stared up at the steel and the faces beyond, wondering if this would be it, if a decade of defying the odds and making it out of situation after situation with his life would come to an abrupt end on a scorching Yemeni mountainside.

It would only take a single twitch of a trigger finger to send him into the great beyond.

With nothing else to do but feign naivety and hope for the best, he studied the features of the three men holding the weapons.

They were vastly different to the initial trio he'd encountered. These men must have come from Qasam, unless there was another way up to the promontory.

Two of them wore neatly pressed, official-looking military uniform. Slater noted the plush black caps on their heads and the shiny combat boots on their feet. The breast pocket of each outfit sported some kind of official military insignia, but Slater had no idea who or what it symbolised.

The pair looked to be in their early twenties, youthful yet determined. There was no hesitation in their eyes. They were ready to kill on this mountain, if it was required.

The other man hung back, wielding a similarly fearsome rifle — another Kalashnikov — but dressed differently to the two soldiers. He wore the traditional dress of the other tribesmen, albeit with a little more flair. He was older and angrier, with sharp lines creased into his forehead. Slater put his age at somewhere near sixty. Despite his cracked skin and sun-scorched features, he looked agile, sporting a wiry frame mostly covered by traditional cloth.

'Help me,' Slater said, pointing to himself, making eye contact with each of the soldiers in turn.

The older man might see straight through his lies, but Slater was banking on the inexperience of the soldiers to save his life. There could be little doubt as to how he had ended up here. But there was always the chance that...

'You are American?' one of the soldiers said, scowling.

Slater paused. He hadn't been expecting that. 'Yes. You speak English?'

All three barrels remained trained directly on his face.

The soldier nodded. 'Little bit. Just me. These two — no.'

'Who are you?' Slater said. 'Please help. I don't mean any trouble — I just want to get the hell out of here, man.'

'What are you doing?'

'Lost. Very lost.'

The soldier scowled, staring around at the plateau. 'No. Not lost. Up here for something.'

Slater widened his eyes, charging his expression with fear, shaking his head from side to side and stammering for relief. 'Definitely not. Very lost. Took a wrong turn. Someone was shooting at me. He killed three people down there.'

It caused the soldier to hesitate. That was all the reprieve Slater needed. Immediately, the life-or-death tension injected into the confrontation melted away, enough to convince Slater that he would make it through the next minute without catching a bullet. He'd slid enough intrigue and mystery into his vague statements to make the soldiers want to know more.

'Shooting?' the soldier said. 'Explain.'

'Can I get up?'

The soldier looked across at his comrades. The other soldier shook his head vigorously. The elderly tribesman paused for a long moment, regarding Slater with an intense stare. Then he nodded once, barely noticeable.

'Yes,' the first soldier said. 'Up. Now.'

Slater clambered slowly to his feet, keeping his arms spread to indicate that he meant no harm. He stood up, and a searing hot flash of pain gripped his mid-section. He winced, but avoided doubling over in agony. The Land Cruiser hadn't been travelling fast, but even a ten mile-per-hour impact with a truck hurt like all hell.

He wondered if he had torn a muscle.

Goddamn hope not.

'W-who are you?' Slater stammered, hunching over to accentuate defeat and submission. He didn't want them thinking he might put up a fight at any moment.

The two soldiers shifted in their body language, dropping their guards ever so slightly.

The elderly tribesman was too experienced for that.

He remained deathly still, unwavering with the grip of his Kalashnikov.

The first guard jabbed a finger in the direction of the old man. 'This is Sayyid. He leads this camp. What are you doing on his premises?'

'Like I said,' Slater muttered. 'I'm completely lost.'

'This is a long way to get lost,' the man said, raising an eyebrow. 'Long way up the mountain.'

He stepped a little closer and re-aligned his aim. Slater shifted uncomfortably from foot to foot. He wasn't going anywhere fast.

They were still highly suspicious.

And they had every reason to be.

Behind the pair of soldiers, Sayyid cast a dark look around the encampment. His beady eyes flicked across the contents of the site. He grumbled under his breath, and his gaze wandered across to where the gas mask lay wedged between two sheets of rock, half of it buried in the crevasse. It had skittered away when Slater had been hit by the vehicle.

The man's eyes widened at the sight of it.

Slater recognised a shift in the atmosphere. Suspicion turned to outright disbelief. He watched Sayyid freeze as he noticed the gas mask. The elderly man raised a finger and pointed it accusingly at the mask. His eyes locked onto Slater, full of questions and anger.

The first soldier got the drift of Sayyid's discontent. 'What were you doing with that?'

Slater shrugged, feigning innocence. 'It looked strange. I picked it up. Please, I don't know what's going on.'

Sayyid scowled and shook his head. The man strode away, heading for the cave on the opposite side of the encampment.

The cave containing the infected desert wolf.

Slater hesitated. There were a thousand thoughts racing through his brain — and he couldn't let any of them show.

Was the elderly man involved with this?

Was he oblivious?

There was too much happening to process. The terror of a potential infection had been temporarily subdued by the arrival of the new party, but now that an uncomfortable silence had settled over the encampment Slater had all the time in the world to worry.

He watched Sayyid continue his strides and disappear into the mouth of the cave.

Ten seconds later, a yell emanated from the darkness.

Slater froze.

The outburst wasn't typical of someone who had encountered a shocking sight. It sounded more like frustration.

Sayyid was involved.

And he knew that Slater hadn't been here for no reason.

The contents of the cave had clearly been tampered with.

The elderly man came hurrying out of the mouth of the cave, back into the sunshine, pointing another accusing finger at Slater from across the promontory.

He began to bark a command to the pair of soldiers holding Slater at gunpoint.

Both men turned their heads ever so slightly to listen to the tribesman's orders.

Slater had no doubts as to what Sayyid was demanding.

Kill him.

He reached out, wrapped a hand around the thin barrel of the nearest Kalashnikov, yanked the gun away from his own face, and broke the guy's leg with a single vicious side kick.

19

The first soldier — the man who spoke rudimentary English — had been standing far too close for comfort. It played to Slater's strengths. He thrived in close quarters combat.

Incredibly foolish from a tactical standpoint, but the guy had likely been trying to intimidate.

Slater didn't imagine that the Yemen military were at the forefront of combat strategy.

In fact, he doubted they had any experience against highly-trained combatants.

It would be disastrous for them.

The first soldier slackened the grip on the Kalashnikov as his right leg gave out completely. Slater heard the audible *snap* of bone as he slammed his shin into the side of the guy's knee, but by the time the man hit the ground Slater already had the weapon trained on the second guy.

He didn't quite have the urge to kill the soldiers.

Not just yet.

He had no idea if they were truly involved in this or not.

So — before the man could even register how the situation had changed — Slater lowered the barrel of the AK-47 and sent two rounds through the guy's kneecap, blisteringly loud.

He ducked for cover behind the rear tray of the Land Cruiser as Sayyid let loose with a volley of shots from across the plateau.

There was nothing like the pulse-pounding jolt of energy that came from the emergence of combat to eliminate the fear of infection. Slater forgot all about the presence of the mystery virus as he flattened himself against one of the Land Cruiser's panels.

Heavy gunfire cracked all around him.

Sayyid was a good shot.

There was no noise from the two downed soldiers on the other side of the Toyota. Slater imagined they were tending to their injuries. The man who had been shot would be scrambling to stop the blood flow, fully aware of the consequences if he let himself bleed out. The man with the broken leg was less of a threat, seeing that Slater was clutching the guy's weapon.

The torrent of bullets ceased temporarily. Whether Sayyid was out of bullets or had simply chosen to hold his fire, Slater kept himself pressed against the Toyota regardless.

After a beat of hesitation, he leant around the rear tray, taking a peek through the middle of the encampment.

There was no sign of Sayyid.

The mouth of the cave lay empty.

Then, movement.

Slater silently raised the barrel of his Kalashnikov.

An animal limped slowly into the light, emerging from within the cave.

The red desert wolf.

Still bleeding horrendously.

The rabid animal had heart — that much was clear. It hadn't accepted its death yet. Slater stared into its broken eyes and paused.

Sayyid had yet to appear.

'Fuck this,' he muttered to himself.

There were too many uncontrollable variables. The two soldiers on one side of the Land Cruiser could recover at any moment. One of them was still armed. Sayyid could be anywhere — this was his encampment, after all. There were a dozen different ways he could manoeuvre himself into a better position without Slater being any the wiser.

And — most importantly — right now Slater could be choking down loose viral particles of God-knows-what. The longer he spent on the mountainside, the less confidence he had in his ability to survive unscathed.

Swearing under his breath, he ducked his head and threw caution to the wind.

He skirted around the side of the Toyota, using the vehicle as a barricade to separate him from the two soldiers. He didn't know how lucid they would be.

The driver's door was unlocked. Slater threw it open and ducked into the cabin.

The windshield detonated under the impact of a bullet, glass shards cascading inside the vehicle. Slater brushed a smattering of the fragments off the steering wheel and slammed the Land Cruiser into gear.

He twisted the wheel, keeping his head low, clueless as to Sayyid's location. He heard panicked yelling outside, coming from everywhere at once.

To hold them at bay, he reached up with the Kalashnikov and fired a blind three-round burst out the gaping hole in the front of the cabin where the windshield had once rested.

The shouts died off.

Hopefully Sayyid had ducked for cover.

Slater completed a hundred-and-eighty degree rotation in the Land Cruiser and stamped on the accelerator. The truck surged across the uneven ground, its suspension jolting and bouncing as the vehicle lurched from rock to rock.

When he felt it was safe to lift his head, he shot upright and spotted the same trail leading back down the mountain, boxed in by towering rock formations.

He yanked the wheel to the left, correcting course.

Twin streams of automatic gunfire riddled the back of the Land Cruiser, ricocheting off the rear tray and sinking into the back wall of the cabin. Slater grimaced and ducked again, opting to avoid catching a bullet for his troubles.

When the Toyota roared onto the dusty track and the entire cabin shuddered under the stress of handling the off-road terrain, he righted himself again.

He let out a long exhale, trying to calm down.

To no avail.

The trail was frighteningly steep — too much pressure on the accelerator and Slater would enter into an uncontrollable skid. Despite every fibre of his being screaming at him to get away from the plateau as fast as humanly possible, he kept a measured pace.

When he came across the portion of the trail where he had gunned down the first three tribesmen, he slammed on the brakes and skidded to a halt alongside the identical truck he'd initially ascended the mountain in.

The truck belonging to the Al-Qaeda mercenary.

Veins pumping with determination, he abandoned

Sayyid's vehicle. The trio of corpses rested where they had been shot. Out of the corner of his eye, Slater noticed that one of the bodies had been turned over.

Sayyid and the two soldiers must have passed this point on their way up.

They would have suspected Slater from the get-go.

He had bought himself just enough time with the talk of getting shot at to make them hesitate, wondering if there was another assailant somewhere on the mountain.

It was the reason he was still breathing now.

He kept his eyes away from the headless kid on the side of the road, aware that if he spent too long scrutinising the body he would head back up the trail in a blind rage.

He had to keep his anger reined in.

For now.

He ducked back into the first Toyota, firing it up and setting off down the path. Sayyid's Land Cruiser rested abandoned, doors open, in the middle of the trail. Hopefully it would confuse them long enough for Slater to put distance between himself and the mountainside.

Things were moving too fast.

He needed time to stop.

Time to think.

He fixed his gaze on the track ahead and kept his mouth shut, kicking up dust on either side of the vehicle.

Racing toward Qasam.

20

He roared back into Qasam's limits at mid-morning, causing enough of a scene to attract the attention of any townspeople he passed by. They looked up from their seated positions on doorsteps and modified car seats, taking a break from picking leaves off khat plants to watch the pick-up truck fly past at breakneck speed.

Slater screeched to a halt in front of Abu's residence, praying that the man was home.

As soon as he stepped out onto the potholed laneway, the familiar blue door flew open. Abu hurried out onto the street, worry creasing his features.

There was no sign of the boy's mother.

Good, Slater thought. *I'm in no state to explain anything to her.*

He still needed to process exactly what had transpired.

'You're not working today?' Slater said, crossing the street to pull up alongside the man.

The small talk felt ridiculous in the wake of what had unfolded in the highlands.

Abu shook his head. 'Not after what happened. I delayed my visit to another plantation. I needed to see whether you'd make it back.'

'Here I am.'

'What did you find?'

Slater grimaced. 'Let's go inside.'

Abu ushered him back into the same spacious living quarters. He gestured to the same cushion that Slater had slept on the night before.

Slater dropped gratefully to the floor.

For the first time since the day had begun, he could let the tension out of his limbs.

Ever so slightly.

No-one would shoot at him in here.

Abu sat on one of the cushions opposite. 'You look like you've seen a ghost.'

Slater exhaled softly and dabbed his forehead with the corner of his shirt. It came away soaked in sweat. He hoped more than anything that the constant perspiring was a result of the intense heat, and not a more ... deadly condition.

'I have no idea what the hell is going on,' he muttered under his breath, shaking his head slowly from side to side.

Still in disbelief.

'What is it?' Abu said. 'What happened?'

'The boy is dead,' Slater said.

He felt the need to get that out of the way first. Abu's face fell, and Slater could tell that the man felt genuine distress at the announcement.

Unfortunately, the kid was now the least of Slater's worries.

In fact, as much as he was ashamed to admit it, the head-less body had passed from his mind entirely.

His thoughts were choked with images of the dying wolf.

Something sinister was at play here.

He was sure of it.

'I can inform his mother,' Abu said. 'She might take the news better if it comes from a fellow Yemeni. I think if a total stranger told her that, she might not be able to stomach it.'

'She won't be able to stomach it regardless,' Slater said.

He had seen grieving parents before.

Too many times to be comfortable with.

'May I ask how he died?' Abu said.

'You may,' Slater said. 'But it's not an answer you want.'

'What do I tell the mother?'

'He passed away. That's it. It was quick and painless.'

'Was it?'

Slater said nothing.

Abu hesitated before changing the subject, furrowing his brow as the realisation set in that the boy's death had been anything but brief. He bowed his head, composed himself, and resumed conversation.

'I don't think that is what's bothering you,' he said. 'You seem rattled, Will.'

'I am rattled.'

'Would you care to explain?'

Slater shook his head again. 'I can't put it into words.'

'There is blood on you.'

'What?'

Abu gestured to Slater's forearms — he looked down to see tiny crimson spatters lacing his skin.

'Ran into a problem or two,' he muttered.

Abu leant forward, uncomfortably close.

'Tell me,' he demanded. 'Maybe I can help.'

Slater told him. He started with the discovery of the

boy's corpse, leaving out the more gruesome details about the decapitation, then moved onto the encounter with the three tribesmen. He explained pressing up into the encampment, discovering remnants of some kind of bioweapon. He described the wolf as best he could, bleeding from every orifice, barely able to keep itself upright, hacking up blood and stumbling around. Then he finished on running into the soldiers, and the mysterious tribal leader known as Sayyid.

He imagined Abu would believe none of what he had just explained.

Surprisingly, the man's face turned deathly pale.

'The soldiers,' he said. 'What were they wearing?'

'Pressed uniforms,' Slater said, cocking his head at the strangeness of what Abu had decided to focus on. Out of all the odd components of his tale, he hadn't imagined he would be quizzed on the military outfits. 'They were dark navy. Almost black.'

'Were there any insignia on them?' Abu said, his tone abrupt.

He needed answers.

Fast.

Growing increasingly worried, Slater shrugged. 'There was something on their breast pockets. I couldn't quite tell.'

'Give me any details.'

He narrowed his gaze, sinking back into his memory, trying his best to remember accurately. 'I think it was a gun and a sword, crossed together. With some kind of arrow in between. I wasn't paying much attention to it.'

Abu froze, paling even harder. Slater became worried he might faint.

'What?'

'I don't understand...'

'What's not to understand? I mean — besides most of what I told you.'

'I'm fairly certain they are the private guards to the Brigadier-General. Not military. Private soldiers.'

'Same thing, right? They were contracted, I assume.'

'No,' Abu said sternly. 'This doesn't make any sense. I know of the Sayyid man you speak of. He has lived in the highlands his entire life. He does not associate with the Armed Forces in any capacity. I cannot imagine this would occur. The Brigadier-General hates the tribesmen with a passion.'

'People change.'

Abu shook his head. 'Not these kind of people. Are you sure they didn't have Sayyid in custody?'

Slater paused for a moment. 'No. Definitely not. If anything, they were working for him.'

'That doesn't make any sense.'

'None of it does. I don't see why you're so fixated on the soldiers. Who cares what they were doing there?'

'Because if the Brigadier-General is involved,' Abu said. 'Then there is reason to worry. I don't think the tribesmen pose much of a threat on their own.'

'They hacked a young kid to death,' Slater hissed. 'Of course they pose a threat.'

'If what you said is true, then I was right.'

'About...?'

But Slater knew. He almost didn't want to admit that this was happening. He pressed a pair of fingers into his eyelids in frustration as Abu began to speak.

'I told you they were hiding something,' the man said. 'It's always been a hunch. What you saw seems to confirm it.'

'I still don't know what I saw.'

Slater trailed off, thinking hard.

'You're hesitant,' Abu observed. 'What's the matter?'

'I just can't believe something like this is happening again,' Slater said. 'I'll admit it — when my old occupation petered out, I went looking for trouble. I came to this country looking for confrontation, in any way, shape or form. I guess it's an addiction. It's how I'm wired. But ... this?'

'We don't know anything yet.'

'I know,' Slater said. 'I know this is worse than anything I could have been anticipating.'

'It's not your responsibility, though.'

'Yes it is. Like I said, it's how I'm wired.'

'So what are you suggesting we do?'

Slater stared out the window as the sun speared above the opposite building and filtered in through the frame. He stayed quiet, deep in thought.

'Will?' Abu said.

Slater looked up.

'I think we pay the Brigadier-General a visit.'

21

'This is a terrible idea,' Abu said, squirming restlessly in the passenger seat of the Toyota.

Despite relentless protests, and a full half-hour of warning Slater about the consequences of sinking too deep into the political mess, Abu had been herded into the vehicle and they had set off down the mountainside. Now they sped along one of the countless dusty tracks weaving and winding through the flat Hadhramaut Valley, heading for parts unknown.

At least, unknown to Slater.

'Who is he?' Slater said as he peered at the far horizon, a thin yellow line from this far across the wadi.

'The Brigadier-General?'

'Yes.'

'Abdel al-Mansur,' Abu said.

'How much do you know about him?'

'Enough.'

'I need details.'

'What kind of details?'

'Everything. How long's the drive?'

Abu peered out the windshield. 'Just over an hour.'

'Then we have all the time in the world.'

'Not if we run into a checkpoint,' Abu warned. 'Trust me when I say they'll be looking for you.'

'Who?'

'If you keep up this pace — everyone. You're already public enemy number one.'

'Then it's beneficial to us that there's a civil war going on,' Slater said. 'Keeps the attention off us.'

'Not the kind of attention you're attracting.'

Slater paused, focusing on the shuddering suspension under his rear, weighing up what Abu had said. 'You don't have to be here, you know…'

Abu glanced across. 'What on earth are you talking about?'

'No-one's forcing you to come along.'

'And what are you going to do without me?' Abu said. 'Drive around Yemen in circles until you stumble across what you're looking for? Learn Arabic in the space of an hour? I don't think so.'

Slater shrugged. 'I didn't say I don't need you. I need you more than anything. But I don't want to ruin your life. Been doing that a lot lately.'

Abu sighed. 'You already have, my friend.'

'Abdel al-Mansur,' Slater repeated, bringing the conversation back to its initial subject. 'You said he wouldn't be seen dead with the tribes?'

Abu shrugged. 'From what I've been led to believe, he despises them. I've seen him in the media a handful of times and every time he refers to them as primitive and despicable. You never know, though…'

'How long's he been in his position?'

'A few years now. He was a controversial figure even before the war broke out. Now he's untouchable.'

'Untouchable?'

'He controls a substantial fortune, you see. Did so even before stepping foot in office. Many think that's how he got to the rank of Brigadier-General in the first place. Bought his way in. Now that he's in an advantageous position, he uses his wealth to employ a small army of private security. Precisely why I was telling you not to try anything. Yet here we are...'

'How'd he make his money?'

'Property, oil, construction. The same way anyone does out here.'

'Is it rare to be that wealthy?'

'It's rare to hit it big and then choose to stay in Yemen by choice. Especially the Hadhramaut Valley. It's why I was so surprised to see you here. No-one comes voluntarily. Maybe that's why he's met little resistance. It's seen favourably that he's stayed true to his roots.'

'Where does he live?'

'On the outskirts of Seiyun,' Abu said. 'That's where we're headed.'

'I assume he has a nice place.'

'Very nice. It's a mansion.'

Slater didn't respond. He was assessing, analysing, weighing things up.

'What exactly do you propose to do?' Abu said, his tone bitter. 'What do you intend to achieve? I'm curious.'

'I just want to talk to him,' Slater said. 'You heard me the first time.'

'You won't be allowed to set foot anywhere near him. His guards will shoot you down the second you open your mouth. They're trigger happy, given the current state of Yemen.'

'Then we'll have a problem,' Slater said.

Abu reached across, seized the wheel, and wrenched it toward him, deliberately veering the Toyota off the road.

Slater clenched his teeth in frustration and battled for control, stamping on the brakes. The rear of the Land Cruiser fish-tailed wildly, barely keeping traction on the loose sand.

When they ground to a halt, Slater reached across impulsively and slammed Abu back into his seat.

'What the fuck are you doing?' he hissed. 'You could have got us killed.'

'Oh, really?' Abu said. 'It looks like that's what you're trying to do anyway.'

Slater let out the breath that had caught in his throat and leant back against the headrest, eyes closed, calming himself. When he opened them, he began to speak.

'You think I'm a reckless idiot looking for a fight,' Slater said. 'And you don't think I can grasp what's waiting at al-Mansur's mansion. You think I'll storm in on my high horse and get myself arrested, beaten, or killed. Maybe all three.'

Abu nodded. 'Exactly.'

'There's nothing I can say to change your mind,' Slater said. 'I have a past. It's taught me a lot. I'm not going into detail about it, because I came here to get away from it all. I came here to do my own thing. But I'm not swimming in deep waters — I can handle almost anything. I don't expect you to believe that, but it's why I offered you the opportunity to get the hell out while you still have the chance. Good things don't happen to people around me. Seems I'm just that type of person, and there's nothing I can do about it.'

Abu spent a long time contemplating what Slater had said. He drummed his fingers incessantly against his thigh.

Then he spoke.

'How many people did you kill in the highlands?' he said.

'Three.'

'What did you used to do?'

'Black operations. For my country.'

'You were good at them?'

'I'm sitting here in front of you, aren't I?'

'How long was your career?'

'Close to ten years.'

'Non-stop?'

'Barely got a chance to catch my breath.'

'How close have you come to dying?'

'The closest it's possible to get.'

'How'd you survive?'

'I don't have an answer for that. I just do my thing.'

Abu sighed. 'Okay. Let's go.'

'Just like that?'

'I don't know who or what you are, Will. I haven't met anyone like you. I guess that makes me trust you.'

Slater shrugged. 'It's your call.'

'Do you really think there's something sinister going on?'

Slater thought back to the sight of the red desert wolf, succumbing to a world of symptoms the likes of which he didn't imagine were possible. He thought of the sheer devastation a weapon like that could cause.

'Never been more sure,' he said.

'Then I will do what it takes to help you.'

'Why?'

'I am scared. You seem determined to sort this out. I have

more faith in you than anyone else in Qasam. If I can provide any assistance, I feel like that's my duty.'

Slater nodded, re-applied his foot to the pedal, and coasted back onto the endless highway.

'Thank you, Abu,' he said. 'But don't touch the fucking wheel again.'

The man nodded silently and settled back into his seat.

22

B y the time they crossed a significant portion of the Hadhramaut Valley, Slater had devised a barebones plan to breach the heavily-fortified perimeter of the Brigadier-General's mansion.

Abu shifted back and forth in the passenger seat, clearly uncomfortable. Slater didn't blame him. The man had been taken from his relatively uneventful life as a computer technician and thrust into a world he knew nothing about, always under the threat of attack from any number of parties that wanted Slater out of the picture.

Sometimes, Slater had to remind himself that his life wasn't ordinary.

Sometimes, the madness blurred together and he lost sight of what ordinary looked like.

'You really think there's a chance this could be something huge?' Slater said as they approached the town of Seiyun from afar.

'Times are unpredictable,' Abu said. 'Yemen is a melting pot right now. I would not say anything is out of the question. You are dealing with desperate men here.'

'Men who are likely to work together, though?'

'Sayyid is intelligent. Al-Mansur is intelligent. I wouldn't put it past them to exploit the jihadists for a common cause.'

'Is that a risk?'

'It is now. Times are changing. The war is tearing us apart, which means young men who can't find work and need to eat turn to more desperate measures. Our population is growing too fast to sustain anything. Half the country is unemployed. I've been incredibly lucky — my services are in demand almost everywhere. Probably because everyone turns to khat to calm their nerves while Yemen tears itself apart all around them. It keeps the plantations pumping out the stuff.'

'You think it leaves room for something like a bioweapon?'

Abu shrugged. 'Here would be the place to create one. Where everyone's so busy focusing on staying alive that they don't pay attention to what's being crafted next door.'

'Here we are,' Slater muttered, staring at the grand mansion resting in the middle of a bare rocky plain. Further ahead, the city of Seiyun rested in the shadow of a gargantuan mountain range.

The property was surrounded on all sides by towering brick walls, topped with barbed wire and patrolled by perimeter guards who appeared as nothing but specks from this distance. Slater scrutinised the compound as they approached, running through what he intended to do over and over again in his mind.

'This could get me killed,' Abu said. 'This could get my wife and child killed.'

'You have to decide whether that risk outweighs what might happen if we do nothing.'

Abu paused. 'You certainly have a way with words, my friend.'

'What do you say?'

'What *can* I say? I already had a hunch before you stumbled across the wolf. I can't let this go. These are my people.'

'You think Qasam is the target?'

'I can't see why it would be. There's nothing going on there.'

'There's no other concentration of civilians anywhere near those mountains,' Slater said, deep in thought.

'What if the mountain was just a testing ground?'

Slater stared at the upper levels of the foreboding mansion. Everything else was blocked off by the perimeter wall. 'We'll find out.'

He turned onto the twisting gravel path that led up to a set of giant steel gates set into the front of the property. Clusters of dead undergrowth dotted the surrounding plains at random. The sheer isolation of the compound resonated with Slater.

'Why *does* he live here?' he said.

Abu shrugged. 'Beats me.'

'You remember what to say?'

The man nodded. 'It'll work. Trust me.'

'You sure?'

'If there's one thing that never goes out of fashion in this country,' Abu said, 'it's corruption.'

They pulled up at a snail's pace to the gate. Slater made sure not to make any sudden movements. There was good reason for the compound's guards to be wary — namely, they had never seen either he or Abu before in their lives.

He forced down a pit of nervousness, shoving it away for the time being. He had to employ full concentration for what came next. If it went wrong, they would be caught in no man's land.

He gulped back apprehension and watched as a pair of soldiers loitering by the gate strode slowly up to the stalling Toyota, weapons clutched firmly in their hands.

More Kalashnikovs.

Slater grew queasy at the knowledge that he had his own firearms resting in plain view on the back seat. Abu had assured him that it didn't matter — everyone was armed out here — but he couldn't shake the thought that al-Mansur's guards would take it as a sign of hostility.

Abu wound down the grimy passenger window and stuck his head out into the stifling desert air, greeting the approaching guards with a warm smile.

One man skirted to each side of the vehicle. The barrel of an AK-47 tapped three times against Slater's window, and he rolled it down without protest.

The guy stared at Slater with wide eyes, sneering through yellow teeth.

As per usual, a ball of khat rested inside one of his cheeks.

Abu fell into hushed conversation with the guard on the passenger side, gesticulating with both hands to get his point across. Slater had no idea what the two were saying, but the conversation quickly entered mutually agreeable territory. After less than a minute of quiet back-and-forth, the guard on the passenger side of the vehicle ushered them through without a second thought.

'Told you,' Abu whispered in English as Slater took his foot off the brake and they slunk through into the compound.

23

It had been a simple enough procedure.

Abu had informed him en route to the Brigadier-General's mansion that, in Yemen, one thing held more weight than any other form of persuasion — bribery.

Slater had suggested offering al-Mansur's perimeter guards a wad of cash in exchange for a meeting with the General, but Abu had quickly shaken his head.

'No. I will approach with knowledge of something I know he has his fingers in.'

Abu had the credentials to prove that he was a technician for the khat plantations, which inherently meant that he held close connections to many of the men who ran and operated the farms. Apparently, khat was a lucrative industry — Abu told Slater that three-quarters of the Yemeni population actively consumed the plant.

Obviously, al-Mansur and other wealthy political figures were able to skim profits off the top of each plantation through what effectively amounted to extortion.

It was impossible for all the Brigadier-General's security to stay up to date on the man's dealings — in fact, most of the details surrounding corruption were obviously kept private.

It meant that when Abu quietly informed the guards that he was carrying a bag of dirty profits from the khat plantations across the Hadhramaut Valley, they had been at no discretion to stop him in his tracks.

They knew how much importance al-Mansur placed on maintaining a steady cash flow.

When Abu produced the documents and identification proving his position, they waved him through without a word of protest.

As Slater entered the compound, he sized up what he could see, paying close attention to the level of security.

There was little manpower within the walls themselves.

It seemed that even a man of al-Mansur's power had his restrictions. He could station five or six men around the outskirts of his property, but riddling the grounds themselves with a similar number of guards must not have fit his budget. Slater counted two men in the security detail within the compound — one patrolled the sweeping balcony running the length of the mansion's top floor, and the other waited patiently in the courtyard to welcome visitors.

'What will happen when the truth comes out?' Slater muttered.

'They do not know me,' Abu said. 'They do not know where my family live. I will have time to go collect them. As long as you hold up your end of the bargain.'

'You bet,' Slater said.

He felt the weight of responsibility on his shoulders — one slip-up on his part, and it wouldn't be just his own life on the chopping block. If he wasn't there to protect Abu, the man would be detained and his family would be tracked down to pay for his treachery.

The very thought quickened Slater's pulse.

He slowed the Toyota to a crawl, and the guard out the front of the mansion approached. With both windows rolled up, he wouldn't be able to hear the conversation within the cabin.

It was their last chance to talk freely.

A bolt of nervous energy ran through Slater. 'What if they recognise the car?'

Abu cocked his head. 'Whose car is this, again?'

'The al-Qaeda guy I killed in Qasam. The gun-for-hire.'

Abu smiled wryly and shook his head. 'All these guards are here to protect al-Mansur from AQAP. You can be sure that he has never seen this vehicle before. Besides, how many Toyota Land Cruisers have you seen during your time in Yemen?'

Slater nodded his understanding. 'Does the government have an official contract or something? They're literally the only car I've seen.'

Abu shook his head. 'No-one pays much attention to the government anymore.'

The guard pulled up to the driver's door and tapped on it once, more courteous than the two men manning the gate.

Maybe it had been relayed to the guards within the complex that the guests had come bearing cash.

Money created all kinds of conveniences.

The notion of it would get them in the front door, at least.

That was all Slater needed.

He felt the acute presence of the language barrier as he stepped out of the driver's seat and the guard barked a question in his direction, staring at him with a raised eyebrow. Slater cocked his head, as if deep in thought, and turned to

Abu. The man was on the way around the hood of the vehicle.

He would be there in seconds.

The guard fired the same question off again.

Slater chuckled, shook his head, and waited patiently for Abu to arrive. Inwardly, his heart pounded in his chest. He knew that if it became obvious that he couldn't speak Arabic, the suspicion would heighten significantly.

They might be blocked from entering the mansion.

Abu pulled to a stop between them and smiled warmly at the guard, responding with a long string of Arabic. His tone was reassuring and his mannerisms calm. Instantly the guard relaxed, nodded, and gestured for them to make their way up to the marble porch running along the front of the building.

Slater nodded back, eyeing the sidearm holster attached to the belt of the man's uniform. Inside rested another Jericho 941, a weapon clearly popular in these parts. The most notable factor was the leather strap designed to loop over the back of the gun, securing it in the holster.

The guard had left the strap undone.

Likely to be able to respond to any sudden confrontation in the blink of an eye.

Luckily for Slater, he didn't know how fast his adversary was.

Slater kept that in mind as he stepped up onto the terrace, feeling the smooth marble under his shoes. A towering set of double doors rested half a foot back into the face of the mansion, made of oak. They had been recently polished.

The guard muttered something.

Alongside Slater, Abu whispered, 'He's asking you to knock.'

'You're the one with the money,' Slater muttered back.

'Good point.'

Abu stepped forward and rapped twice on the enormous doors, then folded his arms behind his back to wait patiently for a response. It created a line of people trailing away from the door — first Abu, then Slater, then the guard.

The door opened.

Abdel al-Mansur stood in the vast lobby, shrouded by the relative darkness of the mansion's interior. It seemed that the man opted to keep minimal natural light from filtering into the building, maybe to seal the heat out.

Al-Mansur was relatively young for his position — Slater guessed he was in his early thirties. He had thick black hair slicked back with greasy product, and a sharply defined face with prominent cheekbones and a strong jawline. The man wore a plain long-sleeved shirt and a traditional *futa,* with matching flip-flops. He stood a few inches taller than Slater, somewhere close to six-foot-three.

Same height as Jason King, Slater thought.

For a beat, he wondered where his old comrade was now.

Probably not infiltrating a government compound in war-torn Yemen.

Lucky bastard.

Al-Mansur smiled and stepped aside to let Abu through to the compound. He must have been informed by a phone call from one of the perimeter guards, explaining the reason for Abu's sudden arrival.

Slater instantly noticed the man's burning desire for money. He'd lost count of the number of times he'd witnessed the mannerisms of a man enraptured by financial gain. He had encountered hundreds of the scum over the course of his career.

The type of people who would do anything for a quick buck.

The idea of an extra package of compensation must have excited al-Mansur, for he barely looked at the arriving party before welcoming them into his home.

Abu passed through the grand entranceway, and Slater followed suit.

He waited for the guard to follow them inside and the door to close behind them before he wrapped two burly arms around Abu's mid-section, locked his fingers together behind the man's back, and hurled the computer technician like a rag doll into al-Mansur.

24

A bu and al-Mansur sprawled to the marble floor of the lobby in a wild tangle of limbs. Both were unarmed, and little threat. Together they slapped against the ground loud enough to startle the guard behind Slater into a moment of hesitation.

Slater whipped around and snatched at the Jericho in the guy's holster, prodding with two fingers like pincers. He succeeded on the first attempt, and yanked the weapon free from the guard's grasp.

But the man was fast.

Before Slater could slot his finger into the trigger guard and reverse his grip on the sizeable pistol, the guard charged into range, dropping his shoulder low in an attempt to tackle Slater around the mid-section.

There was no stopping the manoeuvre.

The guy was too close.

Slater had to accept that he would be taken off his feet, and adapt accordingly.

The guard effectively speared Slater in the stomach,

driving a shoulder up into his torso like a defensive end taking a quarterback off his feet.

However, it left an untrained opponent open for all kinds of choke holds.

Slater locked in a guillotine choke with his free hand, looping an arm around the guy's neck as he tackled Slater to the floor. When the two sprawled onto the ground awkwardly, Slater kept his vice-like grip around the man's throat, applying a mountain of pressure with his forearm.

The guillotine choke was one of the more painful submissions in jiu-jitsu. By trapping the guard's head underneath his armpit, face pointed at the floor, Slater was able to apply downward pressure on the back of the man's skull, forcing his head into a horrifyingly uncomfortable position.

The man bucked and squirmed and writhed, and his face turned the colour of a beetroot.

Slater kept the choke tight.

If he wanted to, he could have shot the man through the top of his head with his free hand — but he felt like he'd killed enough people for one day. This man wasn't objectively guilty of anything — not just yet.

Until Slater knew more, he opted for temporary rather than permanent incapacitation.

The guy's limbs went limp in less than twenty seconds, as the blood flow to his brain was shut off by Slater's meaty forearm. Slater dropped him to the marble floor face-first, where he lay still.

Unconscious.

Unarmed.

Useless.

He rolled onto his side to see Abu and al-Mansur locked in a wild brawl across the lobby. Both scrambled around on the slippery floor like drunken thugs, swinging their sagging limbs, neither doing much damage at all to each other.

This wasn't their world.

Slater got to his feet and strode across the lobby. Al-Mansur saw him coming and recoiled away, noticing the unconscious soldier lying motionless on the floor behind Slater.

The man realised what he'd gotten himself into.

Slater reached down and snatched al-Mansur to his feet as if he were scolding a child. He simply lifted the Brigadier-General off the ground, letting his legs dangle uselessly, kicking in protest.

Slater slammed him into the far wall hard enough to knock the breath out of the scrawny man's lungs.

Al-Mansur dropped pathetically to the floor, whimpering, rendered useless by the barrage of force applied to his body.

Alongside Slater, Abu picked himself up off the marble floor, wiping a drop of blood away from his lip.

'Did you really have to do that?' he muttered, angry at being treated like a discarded plaything.

'Had to use my surroundings,' Slater said. 'Sorry.'

'It's fine.'

Slater gestured to the Brigadier-General at his feet. 'I'm going to ask him a few questions. You're going to translate. Got it?'

Abu didn't respond. A look of sheer shock had settled over his features. His gaze flicked from the unconscious guard — only now starting to twitch as his motor functions kicked in and he began to return to the realm of consciousness — to al-Mansur, beaten into submission with overwhelming force.

'I don't think I fully grasped what it is you do until I saw it up close.'

Slater nodded. 'Uh-huh. Can we deal with that later, though? There's about six men around the perimeter and one upstairs who'll shoot us dead if they see this.'

'Of course.'

Slater handed the Jericho to Abu.

'If he moves,' he said, pointing to al-Mansur. 'Pull the trigger. Don't hesitate.'

Abu said nothing. Slater doubted the man would do it — there was a world of difference between maintaining drills on khat plantations and shooting unarmed members of political office dead — but al-Mansur didn't know that. The more terrified the Brigadier-General was, the less chance he would attempt anything brash.

Slater hurried back across the lobby and forced the security guard back down to the floor. The man offered little resistance, dropping onto his stomach and lying still. He was still neurologically rattled by the quick trip into darkness. Slater knew the intricacies of shutting down the human body — it would be almost an hour before the man's brain returned to normal.

For reassurances sake, he ripped the man's shirt off, tearing through the cheap buttons, and used it to fasten his hands securely behind his back. The man didn't utter a word of protest.

He lay with his forehead pressed to the cool floor and accepted his fate.

When the shirt had been yanked around the man's wrists, almost tight enough to cut off the circulation in his hands, Slater nodded satisfactorily and turned his attention back to al-Mansur.

He could see it in the General's beady eyes. Al-Mansur

knew he was in deep shit. Slater had stormed the houses of innocent men before, and he knew the subtle cues that signified someone wasn't involved in foul play.

Innocent men showed more fear. Their eyes brimmed with terror, as they truly had no idea what was happening to them — or why.

Al-Mansur knew. His expression was one of resigned acceptance, like he had just been caught red-handed. The man could barely hide his defeat. He seemed dejected, dismayed, as if the rug had been swept out from underneath his feet.

Then the Brigadier-General composed himself, and his face turned to stone.

Slater noted the shift in demeanour.

Perhaps it would be hard to wrestle the truth out of the man after all.

'Abu,' he said. 'You might not like what I have to do here.'

Abu stared at Slater. 'We don't know if he's involved. We don't know what is going on. I don't feel comfortable with hurting him just yet.'

'He's involved,' Slater said. 'I don't know what capacity, but something's going on. Something involving a chemical weapon. I can't hesitate here. I've shown restraint with his men — even the pair I found on the mountain. I left them alive. I won't show restraint with him.'

'He might not talk,' Abu said.

'I'll make him.'

'Do I have to be here?'

'I need you to translate,' Slater said. 'I'm sorry, my friend. There's no other option.'

Abu said nothing.

'Think of what might happen if we don't feel like doing

the dirty work. Imagine an entire town in Yemen under attack, the infection spreading from host to host. Blood in the streets....'

He shivered at the thought, remembering what had happened to the wolf.

Rivers of blood, he thought.

'Do you think he knows what we're discussing?' Abu said.

Slater stared at the Brigadier-General, refusing to take his eyes off the man. Al-Mansur had adopted a look of oblivious confusion, but it was a poor performance on his part. Slater had seen the man's morale break initially, before he masked it.

That was all he needed to be sure of.

'He knows what we're here for.'

'What reason would he have to do that to a city?'

'I'm about to find out. Go find me a chair.'

Abu bowed his head, clearly uncomfortable, and shuffled through to the next room — some kind of office on the ground floor. As he disappeared from sight, Slater covered the distance between himself and al-Mansur and squatted down next to the man.

He seized the Brigadier-General by the throat.

'I know you don't speak English,' he hissed in a low tone. 'Look into my eyes.' He jabbed two fingers at his own face. 'I'll get it out of you. Whatever it takes. Don't delay it any longer than necessary.'

He knew he was onto something. It didn't take confirmation from al-Mansur to recognise that there was foul play afoot.

But what came next chilled him to the bone.

'Will...' Abu called from the office.

Slater stiffened at the man's tone. He had never heard

such fear in Abu's voice, such uncertainty and confusion and worry all at once.

He grimaced even before he hurried through into the room, dragging al-Mansur along with him.

'What is it?' he said.

He noticed the expression on Abu's face before his eyes turned to the setup in front of the man. Never had he seen such apprehension in a man's eyes. Slater looked past Abu, who had frozen in place in the middle of the room, to peer at a strange computer setup splayed across a sweeping oak desk.

The central CPU looked like something out of a bad Hollywood film, a towering brick of a device packed with an unimaginable amount of processing power. On either side of the CPU, eight screens were arranged in twin grids, each displaying a different grainy image.

The feeds flicked across to new angles on self-timers, providing an unparalleled view of a metropolitan area.

CCTV feeds.

People bustled to and fro, choking the sidewalks with congestion, rugged up in winter clothing and thick scarves. Slater could almost make out the details in their expressions — the camera feeds switched between the overhead views of hundreds of pedestrians with each passing second.

'Oh, Jesus,' he whispered.

'This is something else,' Abu muttered, visibly horrified. 'He shouldn't have access to this.'

It didn't take long for Slater to recognise the location. He had been there several times — sometimes for work, sometimes on vacation. He spotted several distinct landmarks, each time wishing that his mind was deceiving itself.

Clearly, there had been some kind of mistake.

Then one of the video feeds cut to an unmistakeable

view of the River Thames, like a scene straight off a post-card. He spotted Big Ben, and beyond it the London Eye, both landmarks staggering in scale.

'This is government software,' Abu said, leaning in to study one of the closest monitors. 'I don't know how he set this up, but he must have needed help.'

'You think it has something to do with the bioweapon tests?' Slater said, almost wishing he had been kept in the dark.

But now he did know.

And he needed to do something about it.

'Why else would he need this?' Abu said.

'I thought his target was somewhere in Yemen...'

'So did I. I just assumed. There was never any reason to believe otherwise.'

Slater turned to face al-Mansur, who had slumped against a wall on the far side of the room with his hands resting squarely in his lap. Clear unease spread across the man's face — almost anyone would react the same way if their private dealings were stumbled upon — but underneath the veneer was something else, a quiet smugness of sorts.

Slater knew the look.

It was confidence — the knowledge that no matter what anyone did to try and stop him, enough failsafes had already been put into place to ensure that the deed would go ahead regardless.

Standing in the humid, high-ceilinged office of the Brigadier General's mansion, surrounded on all sides by armed perimeter guards unaware of what was going on inside, battling to comprehend what al-Mansur had to do with the deserted tribal encampment and a blood-soaked, disease-ridden desert wolf, Slater took a deep breath and let the gravity of the situation settle over him.

He sensed that — underneath all the mystery — there lay something he wasn't fully prepared for.

Something that could cause more devastation than he ever thought possible.

PART TWO

25

London
England

Hussein had been told to collect the package at precisely two in the afternoon.

Not a minute before.

Not a minute after.

He would never dare to displease those who gave the instructions.

He had been promised a world of luxury and fulfilment if he followed them to a tee.

The grimy one-bedroom flat in Kingston had been his home for close to three months now. Even though there were no records that his journey had originated in Yemen — his superiors had been painstaking in that regard, forcing him through an intricate web of complicated air and boat travel until finally he was granted permission to fly to Heathrow — he had spent much of the initial cooling-down period in constant fear.

Not of arrest.

Not even of death.

But of letting his leaders down.

Men who had selected him to carry out an act that had taken years of preparation. He was the individual who had been entrusted to pull the trigger, and the responsibility was certainly not lost on him.

He would not let them down.

He paced back and forth across the freezing apartment, restless as the first major hurdle approached. It hadn't been within the budget of the operation to secure him a flat with heating.

Or maybe it had, but his superiors had decided that Hussein would be better off integrating with the poorest residents of London.

Nobody cared about the poor, after all.

The three months had passed without incident. Now the day was upon him, and Hussein had never been more prepared for anything in his life. It had taken some time to acclimatise to London — upon arriving, almost everything had rattled him. He could now ignore his surroundings, though. He had come to expect anything.

The first world was a strange place for a Yemeni native.

An alarm he'd set on his smartphone three months ago kicked in, blaring across the room. Hussein crossed to the dresser and tapped the snooze button, staring at the screen for far too long.

Now that the moment was upon him, the pressure had him rattled.

All he had to do was go downstairs and sign for the package.

He slipped out of the flat, quashing his nerves — at least outwardly. Inside his guts churned and his heart pounded, but he didn't let it show. There was no-one around, but he knew the importance of caution.

The little girl he always seemed to pass was nowhere to be seen.

At two in the afternoon, the residents of the Kingston apartment complex were either at work or so high on drugs that they had no intention of leaving their flats. Hussein imagined even the time of day at which he was supposed to collect the package had been assessed and determined based on minimising the amount of witnesses.

Nothing had been left to chance.

He knew that more than anyone.

His time in London had been lonely — nothing he wasn't used to, though. Given where he had come from, he considered his living conditions luxurious.

Not that it mattered, in any case.

He wouldn't be here much longer.

He made it to the end of the corridor and entered a dilapidated stairwell descending into gloom. During the three months he'd spent cooped up in his tiny flat, no-one had bothered to fix the flickering stairwell lights. After weeks of disrepair, most of them had eventually petered out entirely.

Once again, it didn't bother him.

He reached the lobby — the most dangerous part of this entire ordeal. The receptionist was a kind-looking Western woman who had only ever been accommodating to Hussein. He held no ill will towards her. But if she ended up accidentally witnessing any part of the exchange, he would have no choice but to remove her from the equation entirely.

He exited cautiously into the open space and froze when he saw the scene before him.

The little girl from a neighbouring flat had her head pressed into the receptionist's bosom. She was sobbing incessantly. It made Hussein falter — he hadn't borne witness to emotion like that in this foreign land. Everyone here seemed detached, disinterested in sharing their emotions with the world. They were like robots to Hussein.

Not this time.

The receptionist looked up and noticed him standing there in the shadow of the stairwell. She gave a sad smile and shrugged, as if to attempt to wordlessly explain the interaction.

Hussein smiled back, nodded his understanding, and carried on across the lobby.

He had a deadline to meet.

The strange situation heightened when the little girl lifted her head off the receptionist's chest and turned to face the new arrival. Hussein met her innocent eyes, brimming with tears, and noticed the swollen red welt under her left eyelid.

He hid a grimace.

He smiled warmly to her, trying to reassure her that everything would be okay.

Then he carried on.

The afternoon air had a biting chill to it. Hussein stepped out onto the bustling sidewalk at one minute to two, shooting daggers up and down the street in search of the vehicle that was expected to meet him out the front of the building.

Briefly, he wondered if circumstances had changed.

An indistinct grey van with a logo Hussein couldn't read screeched to a halt directly in front of him. The driver shot out of the cabin with a practiced urgency — fast enough to hurry the encounter along but slow enough not to attract attention. He threw open the rear doors and lifted a heavy cardboard box off the van's floor, one of only a few packages in the vehicle. Hussein imagined the others were simple decoys.

The box carried the same logo as the van, and the man wore a uniform sporting the insignia too.

Hussein knew it was imitating a popular postal company in the area.

He had no idea which one, or what it was called.

That didn't concern him.

The driver played his part well. He dumped the box down on the sidewalk like it had no importance whatsoever, letting out an almighty huff of exertion. Playing up his discontent, just in case any cameras were watching intently.

Hussein didn't imagine they would be.

In fact, he saw no flaws in the plan at all.

The sequence of events had been painstakingly prepared and practiced.

The driver turned to Hussein and babbled something in English.

A question.

Hussein nodded, playing his own part, going through the motions.

The driver handed across a clipboard and a pen, gesturing to the lower half of a piece of paper that had been attached. Hussein had been told what to do. He scrawled a signature and returned the clipboard.

The driver got back into the cabin and peeled away from the sidewalk just as fast as he had arrived.

Hussein had been fed scraps of information about the effort it had taken for this box to reach his Kingston flat. There were rumours in the pipeline, rumours that what he had been deemed responsible for would change the shape of the world itself.

Truth was, he knew little detail about what exactly would transpire after he was done.

All he knew was that a button needed to be pressed.

At the right place.

At the right time.

Nothing else mattered.

He hauled the box into both arms and put into action a specific chain of commands that had been drilled into him for weeks on end. He had practiced the actions many times. The confident smile, the spring in his step, the straight shoulders.

He wasn't hiding anything.

At least, that's what anyone watching would think.

He doubted there was anyone watching, but it was better to be safe than sorry.

He sauntered jovially back into the lobby, outwardly displaying his happiness. Not in a rush to hide anything, not pent up with nerves. Just a happy Kingston resident receiving a package they'd been waiting on for some time.

Nothing to see here.

The receptionist and the little girl were sitting side-by-side when he strode back into view. From the brief glance he threw in their direction, he noticed the receptionist attempting to distract the young girl from her troubles, pretending that she was a co-worker and handing her one document after another in a playful manner. The girl giggled, barely paying attention to her surroundings.

Relief trickled through Hussein. He wanted nothing more than to avoid suspicion, not just for his sake and the sake of his superiors, but for the little girl's.

If it had been deemed necessary, he would have stabbed the young girl and the receptionist in a back-alley.

If it meant the operation had been compromised.

But the pair didn't even look at him as he made the quick journey back across the lobby to the stairwell.

They would live to see another day.

Quietly pleased with that outcome, he took the stairs three at a time, hurrying now that he was out of sight. He made it back to his flat in record time, passing no-one else along the way.

When he closed the front door behind him and set the cardboard box down on the thin mattress across the room, he breathed a long exhale, diffusing the tension that had locked up his muscles ever since he'd picked up the package.

Everything had gone off without a hitch.

Just as he'd suspected.

Barely able to contain his excitement, he ripped the packaging tape off the top of the box and folded its four sides outward, staring at the contents within.

All the smaller parcels had been labelled with the same Arabic scrawl.

Apis mellifera yemenitica.

It had been a crucial part of the process. To successfully smuggle the true contents in-country, a believable cover story had to be crafted. It didn't matter how many plants they had in the British postal service, or how heavily they had researched the chain of delivery.

At the end of the day, the contents had to be embedded deep within boxes of Yemen's luxury honey.

Hussein had lived in the Hadhramaut Valley all his life, yet despite that he had never tasted the top-shelf products that the region was renowned for. He had been privy to all the usual details — Hadhramaut exported over thirty tons a year of the honey, famous worldwide for its rumoured medicinal advantages.

After he had been recruited to carry out an unprecedented task for his superiors, he had also been told other details — like how the luxury honey was often ignored by customs officials due to the unavoidable mess it created in searching its contents.

Maybe that was how they had done it.

Or maybe it was the string of devout agents they had embedded through the chain of delivery.

It didn't matter.

The box was on his bed.

Now nothing would get in the way.

Hussein tore open one of the tins, full with the shiny golden syrup, and dug his bare hand straight into the goop. His fingers touched a small parcel inserted deep into the centre of the tin. He shook his head in disbelief as he extracted the sealed device.

A steel bomblet, packed tight with a lethal virus.

It had been that easy...

There were three of them in total.

He had a traditional set-up tucked into the back of his wardrobe. It hadn't been hard to secure the plastic explosives — he'd done so two months ago. They were fairly common on the black market. There wasn't much damage that could be done with traditional explosives, especially the minuscule amount he had ordered. Any larger quantity of C-4 would attract unwanted attention.

However, if you used the plastic explosives as a trigger for something more devastating...

Hussein extracted each of the bomblets from the tins of

luxury honey and lay them out on the bed, ignoring the golden stains on his mattress.

He couldn't believe the gravity of the devices that lay before him.

He closed his eyes, whispered a silent prayer, and asked that the rest of the journey would unfold as seamlessly as the first portion.

There wasn't long left now...

26

D iana could still feel the sting on her cheek from where Steve had struck her.

She didn't know what she had done to deserve it. In fact, she hadn't said anything all day. The arguing had reached a climax earlier that morning, so vicious and unrelenting that Diana had broken down in tears and run straight to her room.

She must have slammed the door too hard.

Steve had burst in with venom in his eyes. She hadn't been able to see him charging across the room, because her face had been buried between two pillows — the usual routine.

Steve hadn't liked that.

He'd ripped the top pillow away and hurled it across the room.

'Slam the door, bitch?!' he'd yelled. 'Not in my house.'

Diana remembered her mother screaming from the living room, but that hadn't changed a thing. Words didn't stop strikes.

The backhand had caught her in the side of the face

hard enough to turn her whole cheek numb. By then, the tears had already been flowing.

Somehow, she'd managed to stumble past Steve and out the front door. He'd let her through, perhaps a little shocked by the force he'd put into the blow. By the time he came running after her, she had made it to the stairs.

He hadn't opted to follow.

Beryl had visibly stiffened at the sight of her face when Diana had burst out onto the ground floor, looking to go anywhere but home. The elderly receptionist had applied an ice pack underneath her eyelid for most of the morning, but it seemed that the skin would inevitably turn a dark shade of purple within a couple of days.

Now they sat silently in the empty lobby.

Diana could tell that Beryl was unsure of what to say.

'Darling,' the woman finally said. 'I need to take you to the police.'

Diana shook her head. 'That'll make Steve more mad.'

'That's exactly why I need to, my dear.'

Diana didn't know much, but she knew that the police would be a bad idea. Her mother might never talk to her again. 'He didn't mean it.'

'I doubt that.'

The facade melted away. Diana let out a nerve-wracking sob, unable to hold it in any longer. That triggered a wave of emotions, none of them pleasant. She bowed her head and let the tears flow.

It didn't take long for Beryl to reach over, whispering reassurances in a soothing voice, and press Diana's head to her chest.

Diana let the warmth seep into her. It calmed her at the darkest point of her life, letting her know that everything was going to be okay.

A footstep scuffed against the floor from across the lobby.

She lifted her head to meet the gaze of the nice Middle-Eastern man. The one who always smiled at her. She watched him cross the lobby in front of them. He seemed startled, or rattled, but she thought nothing of it.

There were tears rolling down her cheeks and one side of her face had become a swollen mess.

No wonder he froze in his tracks.

Then the man smiled briefly at her, and it sent a wave of calm through Diana's tiny body. Beryl was always there for her, after all, but a complete stranger displaying such an outward sign of reassurance warmed her insides. She smiled back, returning the gesture. The man carried on his way, but even after he stepped outside Diana found the nerve and the courage to compose herself.

There were people out there who cared.

She might not know them ... but not everyone was like Steve.

That gave her hope.

Beryl set into a routine of handing Diana documents and instructing her to answer the phone in an official voice. Diana smiled and laughed and played along, momentarily distracted by the charade, but she couldn't take her mind off the Middle-Eastern man.

Maybe he could be her friend.

Then a strange thought entered her mind.

Maybe he could stick up for her. She pictured the man striding into their cramped flat and yelling at Steve for laying his hands on her. It brought a smile to her face. When the man re-entered the lobby a couple of minutes later carrying a large cardboard box in both hands, looking jovial, Diana pretended she didn't notice him.

But out of the corner of her eye, she watched his every move.

He had seemed like a pleasant fellow in all the encounters they'd had. She couldn't imagine him posing a threat. Her mother always said not to talk to strangers, though...

Diana shrugged it off. She had little confidence in her mother anymore.

As he disappeared into the stairwell, walking noticeably quicker than before, she made a mental note to talk to the man the next time she saw him.

She returned to Beryl's game, comforted by the thought.

It didn't matter that her mother would yell at her when she got back. It didn't matter that Steve might hit her again.

She found herself clutching onto the thought of the Middle-Eastern man being some kind of vigilante hero.

He would help her.

She was sure of it.

27

S later used a stretch of rope he found in a long-unused cupboard to fasten al-Mansur to one of the swivelling office chairs.

He tied the thick, frayed ends together, uncomfortably tight across the Brigadier-General's chest. The man squirmed and bucked with little success. When he had been effectively secured, and Slater grew confident that the man was going nowhere, he pulled up one of his own chairs and sat facing al-Mansur from across the wide space.

'I'm sorry you have to be here,' he said to Abu.

The man shrugged, standing at the ready between the two parties. 'I trust you. I can stomach this if it means getting to the truth.'

Slater hesitated before diving into the questions. He recalled the lone security guard patrolling the balcony on the third floor of the mansion. He considered that the only significant, immediate threat. The men stationed at the outer perimeter wouldn't dare venture inside while al-Mansur was conducting his private dealings.

Especially when it involved information they had no

business overhearing, like skimming dirty money off the khat plantations' profits.

He let the silence turn uncomfortable, listening intently for any shred of noise from upstairs.

Nothing.

Satisfied that the man had been ordered to remain on the balcony, he skittered a little closer to al-Mansur, dragging the wheels over the shiny office floor. They squeaked harshly, echoing off the walls.

He opted to start fast.

'I know everything,' he said, allowing a pause after each sentence for Abu to translate his statements into Arabic. 'I know about the tests in the mountains above Qasam. I know your targets. But you don't know who I am, or who I work for. Correct?'

Al-Mansur listened to the spiel with a wry smile plastered across his features. As the time had passed since the initial brawl, the man had settled into a cocky, confident mood. His initial shock and fear had come to pass. Slater didn't want to let it show, but the behaviour didn't exactly instil confidence in him.

Al-Mansur began to speak for the first time.

Slater found himself shocked by the man's tone.

He talked with a gravelly, high-pitched rasp. Slater couldn't fathom a reason for such an affected tone, but it made him sound ludicrous. The man talked fast, and Abu struggled to keep up with the translation.

'You're coming to me,' Abu said in English, 'with your hands shaking and your face trying desperately to hide the fact that you know nothing. I won't bother saying a word to you. No matter what you do. You're naive enough to think you can get details out of me with physical pain. Do you know where I've come from? Do you know what my life was like before I was rich? I'm bulletproof. You should leave. Save yourself the embarrassment. You're too late, anyway.'

Slater listened to the spiel with clenched teeth. When al-Mansur's wild ramblings finally petered out, he slid his chair forward and seized the man by the throat. He applied pressure to the carotid artery with a practiced squeeze, cutting off the blood supply to the man's brain.

Al-Mansur turned the colour of beetroot, writhing pathetically against the restraints.

He was going nowhere.

After enough time had elapsed to bring the man close to the pull of unconsciousness, Slater released the hold and sat back.

'I can do this all day,' he said. 'I'm not happy about it, but I don't have a choice.'

Abu translated.

Al-Mansur smiled with glee and spat a retort.

'He asks how long you can keep this up before the perimeter guards come storming in?' Abu said.

'I'll deal with them too.'

Al-Mansur said something else.

'You sure?' Abu said, mimicking the man's confident tone.

Slater paused.

Something seized his attention, barely perceptible amidst the hollow quietness of the mansion. His reflexes tingled and he spun in his chair, staring out through the wide passageway into the marble lobby.

There was a man on the staircase.

Within a half-second, Slater identified the shadowy figure as the guard from upstairs. The man who he'd spotted patrolling the third floor balcony minutes earlier. The guard must have had the footsteps of a ghost, for he had materialised seemingly out of nowhere. It had been the faintest echo that had attracted Slater's attention, and now he found himself panicked.

His heart rate skyrocketed and he snatched for the IWI Jericho 941 by his side.

The man — in his mid-thirties, with a bulky physique and fat fingers — began to raise a hefty Kalashnikov assault rifle as he spotted al-Mansur fastened to the chair against his will.

Slater fired once, sending an unsuppressed round through the top of the man's skull. An arterial spray of blood painted the staircase like a grotesque piece of artwork, and the guard collapsed in a motionless heap across the steps. The Kalashnikov thudded uselessly by his side.

The noise of the gunshot speared through the silent mansion like a nuclear bomb. Abu and al-Mansur simultaneously recoiled, ducking away from the horrific sound. It rattled off the walls, tearing through the empty high-ceilinged rooms, blisteringly noticeable.

Slater swore under his breath.

The noise was unmistakeable. Jerichos were heavy, powerful sidearms, and the sound of their reports couldn't be passed off as anything else. It would attract the attention of every soul in the compound.

Recent memories tore through his mind. He thought of every perimeter guard he had spotted patrolling the exterior of the complex, as well as the man who had greeted them within the walls.

At least six men.

Men who were devoted to protecting their employer.

He imagined the Brigadier-General was held in high regard by his underlings. They likely received a pretty penny for their services.

Slater's stomach twisted at the situation.

He looked across to see al-Mansur staring at the Jericho pistol in Slater's hand with unrestrained glee. The man knew what the gunshot meant. He knew his forces would be inside the mansion in seconds.

Slater picked up distant shouting outside, growing rapidly closer.

Abu went pale.

Slater shot off the chair and thundered a boot into al-Mansur's chest, toppling the General's chair over with sheer kinetic force. The chair and its occupant thudded onto the hard floor, facing straight up. Still pinned into place by the rope, al-Mansur was in no position to move. His gaze was fixed toward the ceiling.

He couldn't see what Slater was about to do.

Thinking fast, he snatched hold of Abu's forearm with a vice-like grip, seizing the man's attention.

'You're going to stay here,' he said.

'What?!' Abu shrieked, shooting a glance at al-Mansur's placid form across the room.

'He can't speak English,' Slater said. 'He won't know. I need you to hide out in here. You'll get killed if you step outside.'

'Where are you going?'

'I'm the centre of attention. I'll draw them away. You get me?' Slater heard the whir of an electronic gate crawling open. 'There's not much time. I need an answer.'

Abu flapped his lips like a dying fish, trying to comprehend the gravity of what Slater was asking him to do. 'They saw me come in with you.'

'I'm going to kick up a storm,' Slater said. 'They'll assume you slipped away if you stay hidden in the madness.'

'What if there's cameras in here?'

'If there were cameras, they would have been onto us the second I fought that guard.'

Abu said nothing. Slater could see the terror on his face.

'If we both leave, we won't get back in,' Slater said. He jabbed a finger toward the state-of-the-art computer setup. 'I think that's the key to all of this. We can't lose what little progress we've made.'

'What do you want me to do about it?'

'You're a computer technician...?'

'Yes, but...'

'Abu, some serious shit is happening here. Isn't it obvious?'

'I know, Will.'

Something crashed into the front doors, out in the lobby. It sounded like a battering ram, rattling them on their hinges. Slater remembered he had locked the doors from the inside. He raised the Jericho and fired a single round. The bullet hammered through the wood, shredding a fist-sized hole in the left-hand door.

The incessant thudding ceased momentarily.

They were probably ducking for cover.

He'd bought himself a few seconds.

'You have a phone on you?' he said to Abu.

Abu nodded.

'Give me the number. Right now.'

Abu rattled off almost a dozen digits, speaking fast, his voice laced with nervousness. Slater listened hard, pulse pounding as he considered the ramifications of forgetting the number.

If he couldn't communicate with Abu, the man would be effectively trapped within the compound's walls.

'Got it,' he said, committing the string of digits to memory as best he could.

Abu furrowed his brow, already sweating. 'Will, this is madness.'

'You got another option? Get upstairs. Find a wardrobe or something. Wait for my call.'

Abu froze in place, paralysed by fear. Slater ground both rows of his teeth together to prevent a furious outburst, painfully aware of how little time they had. He grabbed two handfuls of Abu's business shirt and hurled the man toward the grand staircase in the lobby.

'Go!' he hissed.

Abu stumbled out into the lobby, just as another vicious impact smashed against the other side of the lobby's front doors.

Hinges snapped.

The doors flew open.

28

S later watched Abu dive for cover, slamming into the first few steps and ducking behind the exquisite banister running the length of the staircase.

Gunshots cracked from the front porch, passing through the open doorway and taking chunks out of the wall above Abu's head.

Dangerously close.

Slater cursed and squeezed off two shots with the Jericho, both tearing through the gap in the doorway and whizzing outside to destinations unknown.

He wasn't sure if he'd hit anyone.

He doubted it.

But it bought another couple of seconds for Abu to sprint up the stairs, racing past the dead guard. The man took the steps three at a time, reaching the second floor of the mansion at an unbelievable speed. Slater could recognise the effects of adrenalin when he saw them.

Abu was scared for his life.

The computer technician disappeared from sight, hurrying into the depths of the mansion. In such an enormous building, Slater prayed that the man would find a suitable hiding place to burrow down until the attention faded.

The most dangerous game of hide-and-seek in history, he thought.

Only if Slater could make it out of the complex alive.

Just as Abu vanished across the second-floor landing, a trio of fully-armed perimeter guards poured into the lobby. Slater ducked back into the office, electing to avoid remaining out in the open. He spotted al-Mansur still facing the ceiling, rendered immobile by the chair's restraints.

Kill him, a voice in his head hissed.

It would be simple enough. A single round through the man's skull would eliminate him from the equation, but Slater knew it would achieve nothing. If he wanted to get to the bottom of the infected wolf and the CCTV feeds across London, he would need al-Mansur alive.

His gut told him that al-Mansur was at the heart of something gravely sinister.

So he snatched the Brigadier-General and his chair off the floor, wheeling them into position and crouching behind the man instead of turning him into a corpse.

Instead, he used al-Mansur as a human shield.

It carried the risk of losing his most valuable asset, but Slater had no other choice. He watched as — almost in slow-motion — the trio of hired security hurried into the office, guns raised, sweeping methodically across the room for any sign of hostiles.

They were doing all the right things.

But, one by one, they saw al-Mansur tied helplessly to his seat in the centre of the room. They hesitated, unwilling to kill their boss in the crossfire.

It cost them their lives.

Slater blasted each man's head apart with a trio of well-placed shots, his aim barely wavering as he worked the Jericho from man to man. He killed them all in the space of a couple of seconds, opting to end it quickly so that none of the trio would ever know what had hit them.

They would have seen their boss tied to a chair, then the silent figure crouching behind him.

Then nothing at all.

Slater had thrown rationality away at the sight of the CCTV cameras dotted across London. He wasn't willing to pull punches anymore. He remembered leaving the Brigadier-General's men alive on the mountainside above Qasam with nothing but superficial bullet wounds.

Mercy.

There was no mercy left here.

He knew what he would have to do to prevent a greater evil from unfolding.

He knew the ramifications, and accepted them.

He had for years.

This was nothing new.

There were fifteen rounds in Jericho magazines, so he knew he had more than enough ammunition to deal with the last three perimeter guards. So far there was no sign of the others, obviously opting not to follow their comrades inside the mansion.

For a moment, Slater considered the fact that the other three might have employed caution. They might have hung back, waiting in the dark corners of the compound for Slater to slink away and send a bullet through his back when he tried.

Then he remembered the phrase that had been drilled into him for over a decade.

Combat is hell.

It took a near-impossible level of self-control to remain

level-headed and clinical in the midst of chaos. Lead and blood created hysteria, a panic which sent hardened men fleeing in the face of adversity. Slater had seen it many times before. Soldiers on the battlefield were fully prepared for combat, able to psyche themselves up before war.

But in the face of the unexpected, few could control themselves.

And this was the definition of an ambush.

Keeping low, Slater slunk out into the lobby, stepping around the three corpses now bleeding profusely across the marble floor. He kept his hearing acute. Any kind of advantage he could seize — whether that came from the soft noise of a distant footstep or the racking of a rifle's slide — he would take.

Nothing.

He couldn't hear a peep.

He pressed his back to the right-hand front door, still firmly shut. The left hung open, revealing the same sun-baked courtyard he had seen on the way in. Slater leant across and flashed a glance out into the open, revealing himself for less than a second.

Then he ducked back, anticipating a barrage of gunshots to head his way.

But nothing happened.

Tinnitus piped up in his eardrums, an incessant whining after such an unrestrained volley of unsuppressed gunshots indoors. Above that, Slater couldn't hear a thing. There was no panicked shouting, no sound of running footsteps, no gunshots or panic to speak of.

It was like the entire compound had been deserted in the blink of an eye.

He opted to take one more look, leaning into view of any hostiles, placing himself in mortal danger. With his pulse booming in his ears, thudding underneath the high-pitched whine of tinnitus, he leant around the doorway and took in what he could see.

One of the military vehicles, packed with the other three men, hurtling desperately for the front gate.

Fleeing in the face of chaos.

Just as he expected.

Then he noticed something else. Out of the corner of his eye. A strange blur in his peripheral vision.

He turned his attention to the sight...

...and the blood drained from his face.

From his elevated position on the mansion's front deck he could see over the top of the perimeter fence, able to view the sweeping wadis of the Hadhramaut Valley for dozens of miles into the distance. The trail he and Abu had come from — crossing the wadi from Qasam — was now packed with a convoy of pick-up trucks, each jammed with a handful of occupants. Even from such a distance, Slater spotted the sun glinting off automatic weapons.

A small army — headed straight for the compound.

The three perimeter guards weren't fleeing because they were scared. They were fleeing because a mercenary force of tribesmen were on the way.

Slater put two and two together in an instant. If he hesitated another second, he wouldn't make it out of the compound in time — and he would find himself trapped against at least fifty juiced-up, barbarian tribesmen.

All armed to the teeth.

With his heart rate skyrocketing, he leapt off the porch and sprinted across the courtyard for the Land Cruiser they'd arrived in.

29

I t was the definition of a race against the clock.

Slater screamed toward the Land Cruiser he and Abu had exited minutes earlier, the same vehicle taken off the al-Qaeda mercenary who had stormed into Qasam in search of his head. He heard the drone of approaching engines resonating over the walls of the compound. Now that he had stepped down onto the hot, dusty earth, his view was blocked. He couldn't see a thing, operating off his hearing alone — a dangerous notion, given how the conflict inside the mansion had impaired it.

The sweat began to flow freely from his pores.

Underneath the baking desert sun, he dove into the cabin, wrenching open the driver's door and slotting into the seat. It was stifling within the Land Cruiser, its interior having been fully exposed to the sun while Slater and Abu were inside.

Abu.

A bolt of fear rang through Slater. An overwhelming number of tribesmen were heading for the compound, and if they searched the mansion all at once they were destined to stumble across the man at some point.

Slater needed to cause a scene.

One that would make everyone forget about searching for the computer technician.

He also needed to make it through the front gate before it was blocked off by the motorcade.

He watched the military vehicle containing the three perimeter guards barrel out of the compound, twisting radically on the hot earth and screaming out of sight.

At the same time, the din of the approaching convoy grew louder.

He slammed the truck into gear and stamped on the accelerator — as he did so, the front gates began to trickle closed, accompanied by an electronic whir.

'Oh, fuck,' Slater muttered.

The tyres spun on the loose sand, kicking up geysers of the stuff as he battled for control of the Land Cruiser. He slammed back into his seat as they found purchase and the truck rocketed off the mark, spearing toward the gate.

It inched steadily closed.

A couple of seconds into the mad dash, he realised he would make it through the gates in time. He breathed a momentary sigh of relief, ignoring the sweat drenching his forehead.

Then the convoy roared into view all at once. Three pick-up trucks led the pack, racing into the narrow mouth of the compound's entrance. The two vehicles on the far side had a little more ground to cover — they were aiming to form a tight semi-circle, blocking off the entrance to anyone attempting escape.

And they were about to succeed.

A head-on collision was imminent. Slater passed

through the closing gates with inches to spare and aimed for the far side of the fast-moving blockade. The third truck moved to block him off.

He pressed down harder on the accelerator.

It was all or nothing.

In the blink of an eye, the cabin of his vehicle passed out onto open ground. The truck packed with tribesmen speared nose-first into his Land Cruiser's rear tray, accompanied by a horrific metal screeching. Sparks flew, and automatic rifle fire crackled in the air.

Slater realised the men in the enemy truck were firing on him, even as the collision took place.

The driver's window shattered, spraying glass across both his arms. He ducked instinctively and wrestled with the wheel as the enemy truck lodged into the side of his rear tray.

But he'd picked up enough momentum.

The Land Cruiser separated from where it was pinned between the compound wall and the enemy pick-up truck. Its rear wheels fish-tailed in the sand and Slater's heart skipped a beat as the vehicle lurched up on one side.

For a moment, he thought the truck would roll.

Then there would be nothing he could do to prevent a grisly demise, surrounded on all sides by vehicles loaded with heavily-armed occupants.

But the big pick-up truck slammed back down onto flat ground and shot away from the compound, its rear tray crippled.

Another half-second of hesitation, and enough of the vehicle would have been log-jammed to freeze him in place.

He wouldn't have lasted ten seconds if his course had been halted.

You're not out of the woods yet, he thought.

Bullets flew from seemingly everywhere at once. He had roared out onto open ground in full view of the arriving convoy, and every tribesman with a weapon had decided to unload their ammunition to prevent him from leaving.

He fired several shots from the Jericho, aiming out the open window, hoping to send men scattering for cover.

Out of the corner of his eye, he saw one of the gunmen jerk unnaturally and cascade off the back of his truck.

He'd killed one.

Slater's eyes widened at the sight and he threw himself below the line of cover. Each impact from the following barrage of Kalashnikov rounds thudded against the Toyota's chassis, resonating through the cabin, horrendously loud in the confined space.

He felt the vehicle mount the trail outside the compound — the trail that led to Seiyun.

He twisted the wheel and gave the engine everything it had, redlining the tachometer. The engine screamed, the bullets poured, the tyres spun...

They found purchase and Slater rocketed away down the road.

He considered it safe enough to raise his head back into view. Any more time he spent driving blind ran the risk of ending up in a ditch, helpless to prevent the convoy from tracking him down.

He kept the Land Cruiser running at close to eighty miles an hour and wrapped both sweaty palms around the wheel.

In the distance, Seiyun beckoned.

Distant, intermittent shots pinged off the back of the rear tray, but Slater barely flinched. He glanced in the rear view mirror and spotted the congestion around the front of the compound. The convoy had been so desperate to cut off the entrance that they had manoeuvred themselves into a logjam. Most of the vehicles had rumbled off the trail in an attempt to cut to the gates, and now they were in the desperate act of backing up and recovering their position.

None of the stragglers on the outskirts of the convoy felt the urge to pursue Slater.

Aside from a handful of potshots still spearing in his direction, he had made it out of harm's way.

With inches to spare.

As the occasional incoming bullet faded away into sheer quiet — at least, compared to the roar of a close-quarters gun battle — Slater checked himself for any wounds. With his vision wavering and his head throbbing from the overwhelming dose of adrenalin, he knew the risks of failing to recognise that he was hit.

It had happened before.

Thankfully, he was clear. He patted himself down, searching for blood or a sharp jab of pain in a specific area. Coming away with nothing, he settled into a measured pace along the track to Seiyun, making sure not to overheat the Land Cruiser's engine. A breakdown at this point would spell certain death.

Every few seconds he checked to see whether the convoy of tribesmen had elected to give pursuit. Each time showed the cluster of vehicles growing further and further into the distance. He squinted in the glare, analysing their movements.

The group seemed frozen around the compound's entrance, like deer in headlights.

They hadn't anticipated that he would make it out alive. Their entire game plan had been predicated on the element of surprise, opting to throw everything into sealing him into the compound.

Despite everything, the rapidity of the encounter brought a smile to his face. If he had been sucked into a drawn-out skirmish with automatic weapons and a horde of corpses, attention would have almost certainly been drawn to the mansion in the event of his escape.

But everything had happened so fast.

None of the tribesmen had managed anything more than a fleeting glimpse inside the vehicle.

Slater imagined they would assume Abu had come with him.

He hoped that they did.

Otherwise the computer technician would meet a grisly demise...

...and there would be hell to pay.

As Seiyun grew closer and closer on the horizon, the reality of the situation began to set in. He'd been forced to flee from the one man who knew anything about the complex riddle he'd stumbled across. He had next to nothing to work with, apart from a man he'd forcibly trapped inside an enemy compound and a strange bioterror incident on a dusty Yemeni mountainside.

'You're clutching at straws,' he muttered under his breath.

The steering wheel rattled in his hands as the Land Cruiser bounced and jerked over a series of increasingly jarring potholes. Ahead the road turned smoother, freshly paved and leading toward a strange formation of bright-green trees surrounding the outskirts of Seiyun.

An oasis amidst the wasteland.

With his morale crippled, Slater considered turning back and waging war with the convoy.

He had always preferred combat. As far as he was concerned, it provided the solution to a swathe of problems.

He knew that it would be a suicide mission, and it would simply act as a defence mechanism so that he didn't have to confront the gravity of the situation at hand — but right now, the concept seemed appealing.

So far, he had dismally failed to achieve anything significant.

Senses reeling, he prepared to slam on the brakes and spin the wheel in a tight arc.

Heading back.

Going down in a blaze of glory.

His pulse quickened.

Then he noticed the passenger seat — or rather, the glove box hanging wide open. It had been unlocked by the blunt trauma applied to the Land Cruiser during its escape. Now it hung loose, its contents spilled across the footwell.

Slater took one hand off the wheel and leant over to rummage through the pile of tidbits that had come loose from their container. Most were indecipherable — sheets of faded scrap paper with half-complete sentences scrawled across them in Arabic. Save for finding another rare soul in the Hadhramaut Valley who happened to speak perfect English, he wouldn't be able to translate their contents.

But the device in the centre of the footwell, surrounded by the documents, seized his attention.

A portable GPS.

These were the possessions of the al-Qaeda mercenary who had stormed into Qasam earlier that morning. Slater had guessed the man had been recruited for a quick errand by the security checkpoint guard, paid a handsome sum to eliminate a common enemy.

Out of sheer curiosity, he reached down and plucked the GPS out of the footwell.

He checked through the dust-coated windscreen to see if

there was any oncoming traffic, but he might as well have been searching for aliens.

Seiyun lay a few miles away still.

Outside of that, there was no sign of civilisation.

Bouncing and jolting along the uneven sandy track, Slater braced himself against the rattling cabin as he flicked the GPS on by slamming its cord into the lighter socket, powering it up. The screen flared to life, stained with dirty fingerprints, displaying a pop-up message in Arabic, accompanied with an arrow looping back on itself.

Slater cocked his head.

Return to last available destination, he thought.

He hit enter.

A topographic map of the surrounding area materialised on the screen, complete with a small green circle to symbolise Slater's position in Hadhramaut. Directions ran across the top of the screen, instructing him to continue along the same track for just over two miles.

They led into Seiyun.

Slater raised an eyebrow.

'What the hell were you doing in Seiyun?' he muttered softly.

His voice fell on deaf ears. The only man who could answer that question had his throat obliterated by a bullet from Slater's handgun earlier that day.

Unashamedly curious, with no place to be and nothing to do until the attention on the compound died down and he could try and communicate with Abu, Slater decided to follow the trail.

Al-Qaeda never spelled anything but trouble, and he had no place to be.

He was in operational mode.

Always hunting for an objective.

Dissatisfied with anything other than forward momentum.

He dropped the GPS onto the passenger seat, applied more pressure to the accelerator, and went searching for the last place the al-Qaeda mercenary had felt the need to visit.

It's not a coincidence you took this car, a voice told him.

Somehow, someway, all the shady dealings taking place in the Yemeni desert were linked.

He was sure of it.

Corruption and mercenary work and illegal activities were secretly bonded more often than not. Experience had taught him that.

He quickened the vehicle's pace and pressed into Seiyun.

I t turned out to be the largest city Slater had come across in quite some time. He had grown accustomed to desolate mountain towns and long winding tracks twisting through the wadis, all devoid of human commotion.

He had considered Qasam a busy town.

That was nothing compared to Seiyun.

It unnerved him crossing from the isolation of the desert to the bustle of ordinary civilian life. The city sprawled across a sizeable portion of the desert, surrounded by a gleaming sea of green palm trees. A pair of towering mountain ranges much similar to the ridges he'd ascended earlier that day acted as a backdrop to the city. As he grew closer to the streets themselves, distancing himself from the desert, he passed swathes of oncoming traffic heading out into the Hadhramaut Valley, either on delivery runs or simply tending to business elsewhere.

It set him on edge to witness people going about their daily lives after the barbaric confrontation that had just unfolded several miles behind him.

The GPS guided him through streets and roads and avenues similar in design to Qasam's, albeit without the steepness of a mountain town. Seiyun had been erected on uneven ground, but in comparison to the vertigo-inducing rises of Qasam's laneways, Slater felt like he was floating on a cloud.

He caught the occasional odd look from a passerby, but fewer than he had the day before. Newcomers were more common here, he concluded. It was a little less secluded, as open and welcoming as a city in war-torn Yemen could be.

He pressed deeper into the city, acutely aware that the Land Cruiser was dotted with bullet holes. Strangely enough, that didn't seem to bother any of the locals. They barely glanced at him as the pick-up truck trundled past, concerned with their own business.

Slater guessed they had learned to ignore anything that didn't involve them.

Safest way to stay alive, after all.

The GPS instructions grew more complicated, devolving into a constant string of twists and turns down narrow back-streets. Foot traffic disappeared as residential buildings were replaced by low mud-brick business premises. Slater kept his eyes peeled for anything unusual, but he didn't know what to look for.

Out here, everything was unusual.

He sensed the entire city had become wrapped up in a constant state of wariness and distress. The effects of the civil war weren't clearly apparent, but he could almost taste the unrest in the air. It seemed like everyone was ready for a firefight at any moment.

He wondered if there was anything on the Toyota to signify it as an al-Qaeda vehicle. Maybe that was why no-one dared to look at it for longer than a few seconds.

He had only been pondering that for a moment when the GPS reached its last-entered destination — a long, low building set in the middle of a dusty stretch of land. The entire complex was fenced off with a chain-link perimeter, topped with grisly barbed wire and sporting multiple signs warning trespassers to keep out.

At least, he guessed that's what they were saying.

Before he could study the complex in any further detail — in fact, before his vehicle had even rolled to a stop in the middle of the quiet side street — a stern-looking mercenary came storming out of the front gate, fully automatic Kalashnikov assault rifle in hand.

Slater's heart skipped a beat.

The man looked young — early twenties, even — but there was iron-clad determination in his features. He obviously recognised the car Slater was driving, and had already seen that the man behind the wheel was not the original owner.

Slater wondered if this man had been friends with the al-Qaeda mercenary he'd killed.

It didn't matter.

What mattered was the speed with which he was approaching the vehicle.

Slater knew that if he snatched for the Jericho by his side, or his own rifle on the passenger seat, he would lose a battle of reflexes. The man had taken no chances, pointing the barrel of the Kalashnikov through the open window frame in the blink of an eye.

He would have to try something else.

Slater forced himself to hyperventilate, spreading panic across his features as the man strode up to him.

The guy jabbed the barrel of the Kalashnikov through the window frame, pressing it into the ball of Slater's throat.

A wave of heat infiltrated the cabin, heightening the discomfort.

Slater squirmed. 'Guessing you don't speak English.'

The man barked something.

Hostile.

'Thought not,' Slater said.

He began a complicated series of hand signals, attempting to portray a tale without making any sudden movements. It would only take a single knee-jerk reaction to blow the inside of his throat across the Toyota's interior.

First he placed both hands on the wheel and moved them from side to side.

The driver.

The al-Qaeda mercenary watched him like a hawk, enraptured by what was unfolding. Next Slater tapped the screen of the GPS and jerked a thumb back in the direction from which he'd came.

Which could mean anything.

The mercenary squinted in confusion and leant forward a little, trying to understand.

Slater smashed the barrel of the gun away with an open palm, moving like his life depended on it.

Which it did.

The sheer force behind the blow sent the rifle clattering onto the dashboard, pinning it awkwardly out of reach of both men. With his spare hand, Slater yanked the door handle downward, releasing the closing mechanism. He crashed a boot into the centre of the door, thrusting it outward hard enough to cause serious damage to anyone within range.

Namely, the driver.

The man took the majority of the blow to his torso, knocking the breath out of his lungs. Before he had any time to react to the chaos, Slater sprung out of the driver's seat and bundled the guy into the side of the vehicle. He left absolutely no room to spare, making the conflict awkward and ungainly.

Just what he wanted.

He threw an elbow with reckless abandon, putting his own weight into the strike. If he missed, it would put him at a horrendous disadvantage, thrown off-balance by his own momentum.

He connected.

The sharp point of his elbow shattered the guy's jaw, crumpling him into the side of the Toyota. His limbs went limp and he slumped into a strange state of semi-consciousness in the dust, overwhelmed by pain and confusion.

Slater spun in a tight arc, snatching the Jericho out of the empty cabin — the driver's door still hung wide open. If he had simply been searching for a fight with jihadists, he would have recognised the pointlessness of the exercise and high-tailed it out of this district of Seiyun before attention grew.

But there was no chance of that anymore.

In fact, a heavy sense of foreboding hung over him.

He'd seen something before the guard had approached his vehicle.

Amongst the Arabic-clad warning signs instructing civilians to keep out of private property, his attention had been momentarily seized by something that sent a bolt of unease through him like a raging fireball.

He had only studied it for half a second before the al-Qaeda thug had approached.

Now, he had time to confirm his worst suspicions.

A small, rust-coated circular sign hung low on the fence,

adorned with a sole symbol that translated across all languages.

A cartoonish gas mask inside a triangle, faded by the scorching Yemeni sun over the years.

Unmistakeable.

This was a chemical weapons site.

It explained nothing concrete, but it told Slater that everything was intrinsically connected.

The deserted camp on the mountainside.

The red desert wolf, bleeding from every orifice.

An isolated compound belonging to an established political figure with CCTV feeds of inner-city London.

And now, a mysterious complex in the middle of a desert city, guarded by al-Qaeda mercenaries looking for an honest payday.

Somehow, it all added up.

He resolved that he wouldn't leave Yemen until he had answers.

Deep down, he knew he didn't have a choice.

Under the watchful eye of perimeter security cameras, he stepped through the front gate and into the compound.

31

He had never felt tension like this before.

Slater recalled all the black operations he'd carried out over his time in the military, ranging from the stifling jungles of Ecuador to the congested streets of Chicago. He'd foiled dozens of terror plots over his life — each as grave and horrifying as the last.

But none of them had carried quite the weight of this situation.

He wasn't sure what it was. Ever since he'd ventured into the mountains above Qasam, every waking moment had been spent pondering what might occur. He felt sick to his stomach as he jogged steadily across the overgrown front lawn of the complex, making for the giant steel building in the centre of the lot. Weeds choked everything, as if the entire place had been left uncared for to disguise its true purpose.

It could be nothing, he thought.

What were the chances that the al-Qaeda thug who had been sent to kill him in Qasam would also be involved in the bioweapon plot he'd stumbled across in the highlands?

Don't overlook anything.

The one thing he'd learnt over a violent and unbeliev-able career as a Special Forces operative was that thugs and mercenaries had one thing in common, one thing they were drawn to time and time again — whether that meant guarding a compound from curious trespassers or elimi-nating a tourist who'd troubled a dirty law enforcement officer.

Dollar signs.

They swayed everyone.

It wasn't that unbelievable that in the Hadhramaut Valley, where the lines were blurred between honest work and earning a Yemeni *rial* by any means necessary, the busi-ness of the undesirables would overlap.

He kept that in the back of his mind as he hurried for one of the doors along the front of the compound.

The silence was overwhelming. As he moved, staying low, weapon raised, he found himself dumbfounded by the lack of resistance. There should have been a dozen men manning the front of the property if its contents were of the importance that Slater thought they were.

Another thought speared through him, but he ignored it.

He didn't want to think of the ramifications if it was true.

He remembered what al-Mansur had said earlier.

You're too late, anyway.

He sensed that the foundations had already been laid. The critical work had already been completed.

He realised he would more than likely be storming into a compound that had already served its purpose.

It had manufactured something sinister, and then been hastily abandoned as the project moved to its final stages.

Gulping back uncertainty, he finished covering the stretch of land in front of the main building and drew to a halt beside a single locked door. A keypad rested on the exterior of the building, near the handle.

An electronic locking system.

He paused apprehensively, trying to figure out how to proceed. Experience and common sense had taught him that firing a bullet into a lock never achieved anything worthwhile. Most of the time, it jammed in the steel and made matters worse.

Out of instinct, Slater reached for the handle and twisted it.

The door sprung open.

Despite the ease at which he'd penetrated the perimeter, the knot in Slater's stomach grew tighter. He'd been uncertain as to whether the compound truly had been deserted during his trek to the building. It might have simply been chalked up to a matter of inexperience.

Maybe he'd caught them at a bad time.

The door opening without resistance had shattered what little hope he'd had left.

Something was seriously awry.

With the Jericho aimed squarely at the empty space in front of him, he stepped into the building, feeling the physical relief on his skin as the intense sunshine was replaced by cooler artificial light. The building seemed hollow, like its contents had been gutted at a rapid pace. Slater tried his best to quieten his footsteps, but against the metal floor of the corridor even the slightest scuff of heel against surface echoed painfully off the walls.

He decided to freeze in the middle of the hallway and wait for someone to come running to his position.

If there was anyone here at all.

The unlocked door spelled a tactical disaster for Slater. It had thrown him off completely. It was such a gross display of incompetence that even the most senile fool on the planet wouldn't dare to make such a mistake.

They were baiting him into a trap.

He was sure of it.

Yet he placed enough faith in his skill set to know he would come out on top regardless.

His thirst for answers overwhelmed his natural instincts.

He pressed on.

The corridor banked sharply at the end, leading to a steel door set into the wall, also closed. Slater eyed a similar keypad resting at chest height, but this time he had a preconceived notion that he would get a similar result. He reached out, tugged the handle, and the door swung ominously open.

He led with the barrel of the Jericho raised high, now fully on edge. There was no mistaking what was happening. Someone had deliberately left the compound open, inviting trespassers inside.

But why?

They couldn't have known Slater was coming. Unless al-Mansur had warned the compound in advance, but there was no reason for him to think that Slater would target the facility. As far as he was concerned, Slater didn't know it existed.

In truth, he hadn't — until five minutes ago.

In fact, he still didn't know whether it was connected to whatever al-Mansur was doing.

Then Slater rounded the next corner and stepped into a ransacked viewing room, with one wall replaced by a one-way sheet of glass looking into an empty laboratory.

A testing facility.

Equipment had been gutted from both the viewing room and the lab itself, just as Slater had suspected. It had been done crudely, with a focus on speed over care. Wires dangled uselessly off steel countertops, some of them torn in half. The handful of screens that had been left in the facility displayed static, disconnected from whatever juicy electronics had needed to be removed.

More importantly though, there was a man sitting in one of the swivel chairs in front of Slater. He had scooted all the way up to the desk in front of the viewing window, staring vacantly into the lab. He had both hands resting on the steel surface in front of him, palms down.

Unarmed.

Slater realised he posed no threat, and stepped forward.

The man twisted in his chair, and Slater realised the source of his heavy, laboured motions.

The three-quarters-empty bottle of unlabelled whiskey resting on the floor next to the chair.

The man finished turning in a tight semi-circle and stared up at Slater with weeping, bloodshot eyes. He looked to be in his early fifties, with a tuft of wispy hair atop his head that stuck out at all kinds of angles. He hadn't bothered to do anything with it. He was Middle-Eastern, but Slater couldn't tell whether he was a Yemeni native or not.

He was still dressed in a white lab coat, but had rolled the sleeves up to prevent it from absorbing alcohol stains. His fingertips were grimy and his forehead was slick with sweat. His pupils were dilated, to the extent where Slater imagined hard drugs had contributed to his condition. Flecks of saliva riddled the sides of his mouth and he gave off the vibe that he hadn't slept in days.

He looked like absolute shit, all things considered.

Then he opened his mouth and did something Slater didn't anticipate.

He spoke English.

32

'I was expecting this,' the man said, eyeing the Jericho in Slater's palm. 'But who the fuck are you?'

'A curious stranger.'

The man managed a pathetic smile, exposing stained teeth and chapped lips, and shook his head pitifully. 'Leave. Nothing for you to see here.'

'I think there is.'

'You don't want to get involved in this.'

'I already am.'

The man lifted an eyebrow in curiosity. It seemed like the only gesture he could manage in his current state. 'Ah. Came here deliberately?'

Slater nodded.

'Fucking fool,' the man said.

'Who are you?'

'I run this place. Or, at least, I did.'

'And what do you do now?'

He lifted the bottle off the floor, his arm swaying as he presented it to Slater. His head drooped forward involuntarily. 'I drink. And I sit here waiting for someone like you to walk through that door. And I hope for the end.'

'Why?'

'I made a mistake.'

'What kind of mistake?'

'You are American?'

'Yes.'

'You are here for your government?'

'No.'

'Why are you here?'

'I told you.'

'Tell me again.'

'I'm a curious stranger.'

The man sighed and settled back into his chair. 'So you have no procedure to follow?'

'None.'

'No superiors to answer to?'

'No.'

'If I tell you what I have done, will you use that gun in your hand on me?'

'It depends. Probably not.'

'I'm asking you to.'

Slater let the silence hang in the air, opting not to respond. He weighed up the gravity of what the man was saying.

He had done something horrendous.

And it had evidently torn him up inside.

'Whatever it was,' Slater said, 'why did you do it? If it made you this?'

The man shrugged. 'That question will carry on as long as we live on this planet.' Then he scoffed. 'Which might not be long, after all.'

'I know the Brigadier-General is working with northern

highlander tribesmen to manufacture some kind of bioweapon,' Slater said. 'That much I've got. Is that what you were doing here?'

The man nodded. 'And that's all I know.'

'What does London have to do with it?'

The man spat a glob of saliva onto the viewing room floor. 'London...'

He pondered that statement for what felt like an eternity.

Slater realised the man hadn't known.

'They kept you in the dark?'

He smiled wryly and shrugged. 'Need to know basis. I wasn't told what would become of what I created. But they told me to check the news. Every day. They told me I'd know then.'

'Who told you?'

'Al-Mansur,' the man said. 'And his men. You already know that.'

'So tell me about what you created.'

Clear fluid ran out both the man's nostrils at once — either a result of the alcohol leeching through his system, or the drugs that had gone up his nose earlier that day, or the lack of sleep. Whatever the case, he spat again and composed himself.

'Have you heard of the Marburg virus?'

Slater paused, contemplating the words. None of them inspired confidence in him. 'Can't say I have.'

'Ebola's slimy cousin,' the man said, laughing pathetically at his own words. 'Three particles hanging around in the air are enough to cause the most painful death imaginable.'

Slater thought of the red desert wolf in the cave, horrendously damaged, separated from death by a thin sheet of agony. 'I saw an infected animal. Back in Qasam.'

'With your own eyes?'

'Yes.'

'Then you're one of the luckiest men alive to be standing here before me. You should be haemorrhaging by now. Your skin should be bruising as your capillaries burst. You should be vomiting blood and shitting uncontrollably. Consider it a blessing that you're doing none of those things.'

'What do you know about the tests they conducted on the mountainside?'

The man smiled again. 'Nothing. As I said — it's their business what they do with it. I was paid to manufacture it. Weaponise it. Seal it in bomblets and pass it along.'

'Why didn't you do anything to stop them?' Slater said, suddenly thinking the man might be faking his demeanour. 'Why the sudden change of heart?'

'Fear? Intimidation? Uncertainty? Why does anyone do anything?'

'Money,' Slater said.

'They paid me,' the man said. 'They paid me very well. Look how much I appreciate it.'

He waved an arm over himself, highlighting the state he'd devolved to. He took another swig from the bottle, letting the whiskey drain its way down his insides. Slater watched the man let out a sickening belch and slump further back into his chair, head drooping back.

Slater didn't move.

He wanted more.

'You said you weaponised it,' he said. 'Give me details.'

The man coughed. 'What use would it do you? It's too late to do anything about it. You're fucked. I'm fucked. The world's fucked.'

'How many bomblets did you manufacture?'

'Three.'

'How much damage could that do?'

The man didn't respond. It was difficult to tell in the lowlight, but Slater thought he saw the blood drain from the man's face.

Either fear had caused the reaction, or the alcohol.

But Slater knew.

He knew the signs of overwhelming guilt.

This man was going through a world of pain.

'I ... don't want to think about it,' the guy said. 'But it spreads fast. Really fucking fast. Especially after what I did with it.'

'Just you?'

'I had two assistants.'

'Where are they?'

The man touched two fingers to the side of his temple, pointing his thumb skyward, forming the distinct shape of a gun. He mimed the barrel recoiling as the weapon fired.

'You did it?'

The man shook his head. 'Couple of tribesmen. Came and picked them up a few days ago when the final batch was handed over. Never heard from them again.'

'You were okay with that?'

'I didn't have a choice in any of this.'

'So you say.'

'Guilt trip me all you want,' the man said. 'I can't feel any worse.'

'I should kill you.'

'Please do.'

'Back to what I said earlier,' Slater said. 'You weaponised the Marburg virus. How?'

'We passed it through a live incubator.'

Slater paled. 'You mean...?'

'Now you see why I am like this,' the man said. 'What I've done...'

'Who was he? Or she?'

'A homeless beggar we dragged in off the street. No-one bothered to wonder where he went. Anyone who knew him must have thought he succumbed to his life on the streets.'

'You're a piece of shit.'

'Tell me something I don't know.'

'How did he die?'

'About as horrifically as you could possibly imagine. It took a few days for the infection to set in. He went from headaches and queasiness to complete shutdown of his motor skills. The haemorrhaging began on the fifth day, and by that point everything went south fast. His body turned blue — almost black — and his skin began to break apart. He bled from everywhere at once. He constantly defecated — it was uncontrollable.'

Slater stood immobile, in a state of shock. 'What causes that kind of reaction?'

The man shrugged. 'Nobody's certain. We know it stops the body's ability to clot blood. Through shutting down platelets and the like. And it's highly contagious. The samples we took from his broken body were weaponised beyond measure. I was in shock when I handed them off. I couldn't believe what I'd done.'

'*I* can't believe what you've done,' Slater whispered.

'You're a tough guy?' the man said, his eyes moving from Slater's stern expression to the Jericho in his hand.

'I like to think so.'

'You need to stop this,' the man said. 'I was too weak, too pathetic, too much of a failure at everything. I don't think I need to stress what will happen if you let this unfold.'

'London,' Slater repeated, mulling in his thoughts. 'But why? Why is any of this shit happening? What reason does al-Mansur have?'

'You'll have to ask him that yourself.'

'I will.'

'And you'd better do it quickly...'

'Oh?'

'It's been four days since I sent the bomblets off to al-Mansur. He said he had systems in place to deliver them straight away. He told me that much, at least. Whatever he did — they should be in position soon.'

'What makes you think it'll be today?'

'It could be any day,' the man said, taking another swig from the whiskey bottle. Its contents were almost entirely depleted. 'But I told him to do it at sundown. Wherever he wanted to set it off, he needed to do it then.'

'Why?'

'It'll cause maximum infection that way,' the man said. 'Sunset creates an inversion in the weather. The cooler air in the sky covers the warmer air on the ground. Think of it as a giant bubble, sealing all the particles in.'

'You didn't have to tell him that,' Slater said. 'That was your own information that you offered him on a platter?'

The man nodded. 'I'm afraid so.'

'You weren't really doing this out of fear, were you?' Slater said. 'You were caught up in the moment. You did whatever he asked, blinded by the money. Only now you're realising the gravity of what you've done. That's what this pity party is.'

The man smiled, drained the last of the whiskey, and pointed the empty bottle at Slater. 'Bingo.'

Slater blasted his forehead to bloody shreds with a single shot from the Jericho. He had the sidearm trained on the man and the trigger depressed before the guy even knew what hit him.

The man deserved a whole lot worse than that.

Slater left the man to bleed out all over the swivel chair and moved past him to where a landline phone rested on its cradle. He snatched the receiver up, pressed it to his ear, and dialled the number he'd memorised back in the mansion.

Abu picked up on the second ring.

'You're alive?' Slater said.

'Obviously.'

'Good. We don't have much time.'

33

Yemen was two hours ahead of England, which meant Slater had just over five hours before dusk arrived in London. When he'd strode into the bioweapon complex the sun had been drooping toward the opposite horizon, but he imagined it wouldn't grow dark here for a few hours.

They had enough time to stop and think.

Barely.

'Any close calls?' Slater said.

'You've been gone an hour,' Abu said. His voice was muffled, its tone deliberately lowered to prevent detection. 'Not exactly a world of time to get discovered.'

'You're doing okay though?'

'No-one's been inside. Whatever you did out the front has their attention. They're not searching the place, that's for sure.'

'You think you'll be okay for now?'

'Al-Mansur uses ten percent of the house,' Abu said. 'I'll be fine. I heard them untying him before.'

'Pick up on anything they said?'

'They were scarce on the details,' Abu said. 'But...'

He hesitated.

'But what?' Slater said.

'I don't know,' Abu said. 'It's strange. He seems ... almost scared.'

'I don't blame him. We almost crashed his party. We still have the chance to.'

'No,' Abu said. Slater could almost hear the man shaking his head. 'Not like that. A different kind of scared. Like he was worried for himself.'

'What are you basing this off?'

A pause. 'Nothing. Just a hunch.'

'Keep an ear out for anything strange,' Slater said.

'What did you find?'

'The truck I stole from the mercenary that tried to kill me in Qasam. It led to a bioweapon facility here in Seiyun. The guy had been contracted to guard the place. Al-Mansur's been using it to manufacture a virus.'

'What kind of virus?'

'Something called Marburg. It's bad. Horrifically bad.'

'What do you want me to do?'

'Tell me everything about the security situation at the compound,' Slater said. 'I can't see any other way around this. I need to get back in. I thought you might be useful if you could get into the office without being detected, but there's no time anymore. I need al-Mansur to talk. It's the only option.'

'We tried that already,' Abu muttered.

'There's a weapon in London capable of decimating an entire city. We need to try again.'

'There's a dozen tribesmen spread around the

compound,' Abu said. 'They're not searching for me — they don't know I'm inside. But security is damn tight. Al-Mansur might be expecting you to come back.'

Slater sighed and bowed his head. Although he didn't vocalise it, memories he'd rather have left in the past came roaring back. Sieges on enemy strongholds.

One man against a small army.

He'd done it before.

He would have preferred to leave those kinds of risks in the past, but it seemed he had no other option.

'What kind of damage could you cause from the inside?' Slater said. 'I'll need all the help I can get.'

He heard Abu audibly gulp. 'I don't know...'

The man couldn't have been less versed in combat. Slater recognised that, and adjusted his approach accordingly. 'You know what — don't worry. I don't want you doing anything stupid. Buckle down. Wait for me to come storming in. Okay?'

'Okay,' Abu said, a little hesitantly. 'What are you planning to do?'

'What I do best.'

Slater ended the call and slammed the landline receiver back down onto its cradle. He left the scientist's corpse spinning slowly in its seat, bleeding profusely, resting awkwardly against the chair back. The guy deserved nothing less. Slater had spent years dealing with the incompetence of men who simply did as they were instructed.

This man was as much of a scumbag as the rest of them.

Even despite his late-notice change of heart.

It didn't alter what he'd done.

Slater took a moment to compose himself. So far, he had been lucky to absorb little damage. Amidst the madness of the past day there had been glancing blows and brutal impacts, but nothing significant enough to cause serious injury. He had made it through everything in one piece — and, all things considered, he was in acceptable shape to storm a hostile compound.

He had fared far worse in the past.

Drawing on that, he burst into motion, charged with energy. He pictured the scenario that the scientist had described in all its gruesome detail — the shocking effects of the Marburg virus on a human incubator.

He imagined all of London succumbing to the bioweapon.

It sent a shiver down his spine, simultaneously icing his veins with determination.

He didn't know why this was happening, or what reason al-Mansur had for inflicting such a terrible curse upon society.

But he had the tools to stop it.

He left the viewing room as quickly as he'd entered it, ghosting out into the deserted corridors of the complex. It didn't take long to stumble across a holding room designed for the use of the mercenaries employed to guard the compound.

The important work was done, and the rooms had been abandoned in haste as soon as the final product had shipped out.

Luckily, they'd left behind entire racks full of weapons and ammunition.

Slater eyed identical rifles and sidearms, all of which he felt like he'd seen a thousand times over during his time in Yemen. Kalashnikov assault rifles — AK-47s, AK-12s, AK-15s, AK-74s — littered the racks, all loaded with magazines and ready for use. There were a handful of sidearms — Beretta M9s and more IWI Jerichos — scattered across the countertops, but he ignored those. Loading up with every weapon under the sun simply proved cumbersome. Slater snatched up an AK-15 with an attached suppressor, bundled a handful of magazines into the pockets of his jacket, and turned on his heel.

He had never spent much time weighing up the tactical advantages of different approaches.

He simply picked a gun, got his mind right, and swung for the fences.

He was still here today — so his approach obviously held some merit.

He wondered if that could be chalked up to his blindingly fast reaction speed.

Shrugging it off, he left most of the weaponry where it lay and retraced his path through the complex. It had quickly become apparent that the lead scientist was the last man left in the building — leaving the doors open had been his form of committing suicide. Too scared to go through with the act himself, he must have figured that his ineptitude would have caused al-Mansur to send a few thugs in to deal with him.

He sure hadn't been expecting Slater.

Slater thought about many things as he made the trek back to his vehicle. He thought of a small package of bomblets somewhere in inner-city London, soon to be unleashed in an event that would no doubt be remembered for centuries to come. He thought of a computer technician with an uneventful life, currently trapped in a psychotic general's mansion in the centre of a desert valley all because he'd run into Slater earlier the previous day.

Above all else, he thought of the eyes of a red desert

wolf, wracked with unimaginable pain as its skin fell apart and it succumbed to a virus beyond comprehension.

He thought of hundreds of thousands of people suffering the same fate.

He shivered involuntarily.

34

The Toyota Land Cruiser shot out of Seiyun's city limits at close to eighty miles an hour, kicking up a barrage of dust and sand behind it as it screamed through the otherwise ambient streets. At mid-afternoon, there was little commotion amongst the locals — in fact, it was near-peaceful as the working day ticked by and locals floated for their homes.

It meant that when Slater rocketed out of the city at breakneck speed, it attracted a world of attention.

He had the faded, peeling steering wheel in one hand and a military-grade satellite phone in the other, plucked off the unconscious perimeter guard who he'd knocked out upon entering the compound. After a few seconds of deliberation, he had elected to leave the man in his current, pathetic state by the side of the road.

There were too many variables to bother killing him for no reason.

He didn't know if the guy was aware of what he had been protecting. For all Slater knew, the complex's security had simply been instructed to guard an unknown payload. In all likelihood the guy knew exactly what he was doing, but Slater didn't have time to weigh up the moral justifications of shooting him dead where he lay.

He simply ignored him and set off for al-Mansur's compound.

This time, the visit to al-Mansur had a clear, unwavering objective. Slater had wandered into the compound the first time with a world of questions. Everything had happened so fast that he'd barely had time to stop and think.

He still had limited details on what exactly was going on, but throughout his strange and muddled journey through central Yemen, al-Mansur provided the clearest link to the bioweapon yet. He was a key part of the process.

Exactly what that process was, Slater didn't know.

But he had concluded that al-Mansur was perhaps the only individual capable of calling the operation off.

With that understanding embedded in his psyche, he jammed Abu's number into the satellite phone and waited impatiently for the man to answer. As the phone rang once, twice, three times, Slater passed from the towering buildings of Seiyun into the arid desert of the Hadhramaut Valley. Civilisation fell away all at once, and he resumed the familiar bumpy journey into the heart of the plains.

Just when he feared that everything had fallen apart, Abu answered.

'When are you coming?' he said, sheer terror lacing his tone.

'Just wait,' Slater said. 'I'm on my way.'

'If you get killed, then what? I keep cowering in this office until someone finds me and kills me?'

'You'll find a way.'

'I have a family, Will. They need me back.'

Slater noted the words, but didn't respond to them. He

didn't want to scare the man any more than he already had been. 'Has anything changed out front?'

There was a momentary pause as Abu shuffled out of his position. Slater imagined the man staying low, peeking out one of the many windows at the front of the mansion.

'No,' Abu said. 'The same. There's about half the number of tribesmen that first showed up here. The rest headed back shortly after you fled.'

'Back to Qasam?'

'I'd say so.'

Slater drooped his head onto the top of the steering wheel out of frustration. He clenched his teeth and composed himself silently.

Despite that, Abu sensed his agitation. 'What is it?'

'None of this makes sense,' Slater said. 'Why would he test it in the mountains above Qasam? Why would he involve the tribes? He would know the risks that involved. They're effectively guns-for-hire, from what I understand.'

'You're right,' Abu said. 'They have a proven track record of serving the highest bidder. Al-Mansur could have used his own soldiers for any kind of manpower he needed. He's in charge of half the north-western military sector...'

'We can work it out later. I'm fifteen minutes out.'

'There's six men at the entrance. A few in the courtyard itself. None of them seem to know what they're here for. They all seem confused. You can take advantage of that.'

'They're all armed?'

'Yes.'

'Great.'

'There are men downstairs, too. With al-Mansur. I can hear them.'

'Can you hear what they're saying?'

'No. I just know they're there.'

'How many?'

'Three, maybe. There's around twelve total. I don't think you can do this. You should leave me. I can sort things out myself. It was my decision to stay, in the end.'

'Even if I did that — which I never would — everything comes down to that mansion. The cameras, the Brigadier-General. It's all a puzzle, Abu, and I can't solve it. But I can try to do it through sheer force.'

'Has it worked for you before?'

'Yes.'

'Then try your best, my friend.'

Slater nodded silently to himself in the empty cabin. Even if the answers lay elsewhere, he never would have left Abu stranded in the mansion. The man had been selfless in his actions, opting to trust a total stranger with his life.

Slater owed the man everything.

'Tell me exactly how things are set up out the front of the compound,' he said.

'Three men on each side of the gate,' Abu said. 'You seem to have broken it when you fled — it's jammed open. But they've parked their pick-up trucks in a barricade across the entrance. There's no getting through.'

'Are they alert? Are they paying attention to their surroundings?'

'They're all munching khat,' Abu said. 'Looking around every now and then. If I had to guess, I'd say their orders have been muddied. I don't think they know what's going on. I can sense confusion.'

'I hope you're right,' Slater muttered. 'It's my only shot.'

'I've seen you in action,' Abu said. 'I have faith.'

'We'll see.'

The compound appeared on the horizon like an ominous beacon, symbolising imminent carnage. Slater gulped back a sudden ball of tension as he made out faint features of the complex — the enormous building in the centre, the thick perimeter wall.

And the congestion out the front of the complex.

'Two minutes, Abu,' he said. 'Be ready. Just in case shit hits the fan.'

'I don't think there's any other option, my friend. It's going to hit it regardless.'

'I know.'

He ended the call and discarded the satellite phone into the opposite footwell. Sweat dotted his brow, leeching through his pores as the stress of the approaching combat played tricks with his nerves. He much preferred to be sprung unknowingly into a skirmish, rather than deliberating and weighing up the risks in advance.

He squashed the pedal into the floor and narrowed his gaze on the compound.

The details became clearer as the desert haze melted away. Slater's vehicle roared into proximity, attracting the attention of every tribesman stationed out the front of the compound. There was no chance of approaching with stealth — his Land Cruiser was akin to a screaming klaxon amidst a thousand square miles of unchanging flat rock and sand.

He would be visible to every man in the compound.

Immediately, the bullets started to fly. A muzzle flare exploded in front of the gate, and the next moment Slater's side mirror detonated in a shower of sparks. He ducked instinctively, returning fire with the AK-15. The three-round burst ricocheted harmlessly off the ground around the compound's entrance.

He was still a few hundred feet from the front gate.

Sizing up the distance in a heartbeat, Slater burst into

motion. He reached back and wrenched the seatbelt free, taking care not to pull too hard at risk of the locking mechanism kicking in. With the distant din of automatic gunfire echoing along the track, he looped the buckle through the bottom of the steering wheel and tied it tight.

The angle would have to line up perfectly.

Ignoring the chaos unfolding all around him, Slater concentrated hard on the trajectory of the Land Cruiser. He adjusted the seatbelt accordingly, tweaking its hold on the wheel an inch at a time to make sure it was headed on the right course.

When the wheel was locked into place — aiming slightly to the left in an arc that Slater hoped would impact at its intended destination — he reached across the seat, fetched the GPS device, and jammed it vertically into the driver's footwell, against the accelerator.

It kept the pedal mashed to the floor.

Then he twisted in his seat, opened the door, and simply fell out of the vehicle.

35

S till clutching the fully loaded AK-15 in his hands, Slater made sure to come down across the chain of muscles across his upper back. He rolled with the impact, tasting sand and hitting the earth hard enough to knock all the breath out of his lungs. The sensory overload as wind and sand and the sharp report of bullets buffeted him threatened to overwhelm him, but experience had taught him to keep a level head in times like these.

He flailed his limbs in an attempt to slow down, plowing into a soft portion of the side of the track and grinding awkwardly to a halt on the desert floor. He spat out a mouthful of the granules and found his bearings, looking up to witness the resulting destruction.

That was, if he managed to get the course right.

The Toyota carried on at full speed, roaring away in a cloud of dust as the GPS device ensured it maintained its acceleration. Manipulated by the slight pull of the seatbelt's restraint, it drifted to the left in a wide arc, veering off the trail at just the right moment.

Slater breathed a sigh of relief.

So far, everything had unfolded according to plan.

He was up and running by the time the Toyota finished its turn and demolished a portion of the tribesmen's barricade. The vehicle was travelling at close to eighty miles an hour when it speared into two of the stationary pick-up trucks, detonating with an audible *bang* of flying car parts. The rear tray lifted off the ground and the entire vehicle catapulted over the barricade, sending cars twisting away and tribesmen diving for cover.

Slater came to a halt in an advantageous position — right in the middle of the sandy track — and picked off two men on the outer limits of the barricade with a precise volley of shots. The AK-15 jerked in his hands, but he rolled with the recoil, predicting it in advance and adjusting accordingly.

Three of the men died in the space of a couple of seconds, thudding against the side of their pick-up trucks, leaving streaks of blood on the rusting metal.

Just as he anticipated, pandemonium struck.

These men — all together — acted as an intimidation tactic by whoever utilised their services. That much was clear. It was a similar situation to the first time Slater had an altercation at the Brigadier-General's mansion — soldiers and mercenaries in these parts were thoroughly unprepared for a trained professional.

Especially one with Slater's capabilities.

Those who had witnessed their comrades fall scrambled behind their vehicles, putting a solid object between themselves and the marksman who was picking off their friends. Slater hurried across the track, making straight for the front of the compound. As he grew closer, he was able to make out the twisted expressions on the tribesmen's faces.

Fear.

Good, he thought.

He crossed the most dangerous stretch of no-man's-land, a wide open expanse of uneven sand in front of the gate. Here he was totally exposed — thankfully, the three tribesmen still breathing outside the compound were preoccupied with ducking for cover.

One of them stuck their head out from behind one of the trucks, trying to get a better view of where Slater was.

Slater put a couple of rounds through the man's forehead.

He had sunk deep into operational mode. A nuclear bomb could have detonated on the far horizon and he wouldn't have noticed — every fibre of his being was tunnelled into the path ahead. There were two men still alive amidst the barricade, and he wouldn't stop until they were dead.

He sensed movement behind the pick-up truck directly in front of him — the furthest vehicle in the long line that made up the barricade. Acting on instinct, he sprinted for the truck and vaulted over its rear tray in one practiced motion, leaping over the corrugated metal and using the momentum to catapult him into the sand on the other side.

He came down hard, in ungainly fashion, but the element of surprise was on his side.

He landed directly alongside one of the two remaining tribesmen.

The man had a grizzled, pockmarked face, beaten down by years of tension. Slater imagined the toughness of life in the highlands, simply battling for survival by offering mercenary-style services to the highest bidder.

It was about to get a whole lot tougher.

Slater sent a scything side kick into the side of the man's rifle, battering it awkwardly against the truck. An audible *crack* ripped through the air as the man's finger was caught inside the trigger guard, squashed against the vehicle's rear tray. Instinctively, he released his hold on the weapon.

Slater caught it, tossed it behind him, and thrust a shoulder into the man's throat at close range. It crunched into delicate tissue and vital organs, turning him into a spluttering mess.

Slater didn't hesitate.

He raised his own AK-15, jammed it into the nape of the man's neck, and pulled the trigger.

A suppressed round sliced through the guy's throat, dropping him like a rag doll where he stood. As he fell, Slater continued bringing the gun up in a tight, controlled arc, searching for the last remaining tribesman in the swirling desert heat.

There.

A stationary figure at the other end of the barricade, tucked around a cluster of vehicles, somewhat protected behind cover.

Slater hesitated for the briefest of moments.

A round sliced through the top of his shoulder.

White hot fire needled his skin, spreading from above his collarbone, travelling sideways through his neck and thrumming against his skull with bolts of agony. He shut out the sensation and returned fire, used to remaining calm when everything was falling apart around him.

He made better use of his own shot.

The last tribesman's head snapped back amidst a spray of brain matter. He twisted on the spot — already dead — and disappeared out of sight.

Slater touched a hand to his trapezius muscle. It came away coated in blood. He grimaced as the pain began to roll over him. It only seemed to present itself when he received a visual signal of the wound — he had been struck by a bullet in the heat of combat before and hadn't noticed it until close to an hour after.

Now, he probed the injury with his fingers, ignoring the stabbing pain that came along with it. He breathed a momentary sigh of relief when he realised the bullet had sliced through the skin and passed straight through, leaving a tiny valley atop his muscle. There was nothing lodged inside him.

He would have full range of motion.

The wound was merely superficial.

He adjusted his mentality accordingly, ignoring the blood pooling down one side of his torso. He adjusted his grip on the AK-15, shrunk low, and headed straight into the compound.

There was no time to spare.

36

Hussein waited impatiently for the call.

He stared at the satellite phone on the bed with breath rattling in his throat. He couldn't help himself. Nerves were inevitable at this stage. He would mask them out in the open, but within the confines of the Kingston flat, he let all the symptoms show.

Maybe they would dissipate before the big moment.

He doubted it.

He knew they would only intensify.

Everything had been prepared in painstaking detail. The set-up that his superiors had run through over and over again was now complete, with all the necessities packed into an ordinary workman's backpack indistinguishable from the thousands of others that Londoners carried to their offices every day. Out on the street, he would appear as just another commuter on their way home from a dreary day in their cubicle.

No one would know.

No one would expect a thing.

It would make the resulting anarchy all the more confusing.

The room was cold, but Hussein hadn't stopped sweating since he'd woken that morning. His armpits were drenched, and his forehead never seemed to dry for a moment. He had changed his shirt three times now, stressing silently over whether the perspiration would give him away.

He had given up on trying to mask it by now. His state was uncontrollable — nothing could prepare him for what was about to occur. He knew he wouldn't be able to remain calm. He decided to change his shirt a final time before heading out, and simply hope for the best. He had been trained to disguise his fear — his superiors had known that the gravity of the day would affect him severely.

He would hide it.

Inwardly, he would be eating himself alive.

But the payoff will be extraordinary, he thought.

Growing increasingly restless, he settled into the usual rhythm of pacing back and forth across the tiny apartment. He couldn't take his eyes off the phone for more than a few seconds at a time. At any moment, he expected it to ring. He had been told that the call would come at dusk. It was now late afternoon in London, and the bleak day would soon turn to evening.

He knew, in all likelihood, the call would not come for another few hours.

He had been told not to act early under any circumstances.

'Why not?' he whispered to himself, alone in the freezing flat.

The line set something off in his head — an uncontrol-lable urge to *go*. It made no difference whether he went now, or when the call came through. His better judgment told him that, but the instructions that had been drilled into him subconsciously made him hesitate.

He ignored them, hefted the backpack off the bed, and made for the door.

No! a voice screamed in his head. *Don't abandon the plan.*

He ignored that too.

Still sweating, he realised he hadn't changed his shirt. He told himself it didn't matter — none of this mattered. Sweaty armpit stains would reveal nothing. There were a million reasons for a Londoner to be stressed.

The largest of which rested in the backpack slung over his shoulder.

He wasn't sure why he had decided to throw caution to the wind in the final hour. He *knew* he was being irrational, but couldn't do anything to stop it. He wanted nothing more than for the months of stress and tension and unease to come to their conclusion.

It doesn't matter if you do it now, he told himself.

It will unfold all the same.

Using a palm slick with sweat, he eased the front door of the flat open a crack and checked the corridor outside for any prying eyes.

Empty.

He stepped out into the hallway and shut the door behind him, breathing hard, taking in these last moments of solitude before he slipped out into the bustle of London foot traffic.

There was a slight creak in the damp floorboards further along the corridor. It resonated through the space, barely perceptible but akin to a bomb going off in Hussein's heightened state of awareness.

He jolted involuntary and turned to look down the length of the corridor.

Not quite empty.

The little girl from one of the neighbouring flats looked up at him, almost twenty feet away, entirely innocuous but strangely observant all the same. She was positioned in front of the door that Hussein often saw her emerge from as she headed off to school each weekday, sitting with her back against the flaking plaster wall and her tiny boots resting on the shoddy rug running the length of the corridor.

She had been crying.

Her eyes were red and puffy. Hussein couldn't understand how one person could elicit such emotion. It seemed like every time he saw her she was ailed by a new burden. Through the thick blanket of suppression that he'd drowned his emotions in over the years, a sliver of empathy squeezed through.

He destroyed it as quickly as it appeared, forcing the little girl out of his thoughts.

But it made him hesitate.

It threw him off his game.

The young kid smiled up at him, a warm gesture despite her foul mood. He smiled back, more to act normal rather than display genuine emotion. Internally he found himself panicking, even though the girl meant nothing in the grand scheme of things. All he had to do was walk straight past her and carry on with the plan.

But a spanner had been thrown in his wheel, grinding his momentum to a sudden halt. He reconsidered everything, shifting from foot to foot.

You can't spend much time in one spot, he told himself. *It looks suspicious. Make a decision.*

Begrudgingly, he went through a pre-determined set of mannerisms. He shook his head in apparent foolishness, as if scolding himself for forgetting something. He shrugged at the little girl, smiled again, and stepped straight back into his apartment.

Breathing hard, he cursed himself under his breath.

What are you doing, you fool?

He dropped the backpack on the bed — exactly where it had last been resting — and opted to wait for the phone to ring. It might be hours, but he wasn't about to let his superiors down in the final stretch. He didn't know what had come over him to spur him into setting off early, but the appearance of the young kid had startled him back into a clinical mentality.

He would wait.

Another couple of hours wouldn't hurt.

Besides, apparently dusk was the best time to strike...

37

S later burst into the grounds of the mansion with his senses thrumming, charged with a crackling energy that always came to him in the raging throes of combat.

He shot his gaze from left to right, soaking in all the sights at once. A blurred shape in his peripheral vision seized his attention, and he swung the AK-15 around to meet a tribesman scrambling frantically for his weapon. Slater noted the grenade in the man's left hand — he dropped it as he snatched for his rifle, letting it fall to the ground between his feet.

The pin still rested inside the device.

He had been in the process of removing the pin and hurling it through the open gate when Slater had charged into the compound.

Slater capitalised on the confusion, putting two rounds into the man's chest. He had considered targeting the head, but there was a sizeable margin for error when aiming at such a specific point. He considered himself accurate, but there was no time to miss.

He would die if the bullets didn't slam home.

Thankfully, the torso provided a bulky target, and the tribesman took both bullets in his upper chest, shredding muscle and sinew and penetrating deep into vital organs. He dropped, losing all control of his limbs.

No threat.

Slater ducked instinctively, anticipating gunshots from anywhere. Things were moving too fast to fully process his surroundings. He eyed the cluster of battered pick-up trucks parked at random angles across the courtyard, and slid behind one of them — just in case anyone else had a beat on him.

Numbers and patterns and sequences rolled through his mind, butting against each other in a desperate bid to seize the forefront of his thoughts. He recalled what Abu had told him.

A few in the courtyard itself.

A few.

He hazarded a guess that there were two left outside the mansion. A panicked shot rang off the other side of the pick-up truck he cowered behind. Slater noted its position, ejected the half-empty magazine, and rammed a fresh one home, reloading the AK-15 in one practiced motion.

He sprung out of cover and fired a precise volley of rounds in a dotted cluster at the last place he'd heard the nearest hostile. Time seemed to slow down — Slater analysed every inch of the robe-clad silhouette darting for cover behind an empty fountain in the centre of the court-yard, overwhelmed by the sudden explosion of pinpoint-accurate gunfire.

Slater adjusted, re-aligned, and fired once.

The guy had already been on the way down, so when the

round laced through the soft tissue directly behind his ear and shut his lights out forever, he sprawled on his front into the fountain itself. There was no water in the centrepiece — it was nothing more than a giant concrete bowl — so the tribesman slumped unceremoniously onto the fountain floor, surrounded by loose sand and a collection of weeds.

Slater saw the *jambiyah* whistling toward his head at the last second, shockingly close.

He let his legs go slack and dropped underneath the path of the curved dagger, missing it by inches. Another half-second of hesitation and the edge of the blade would have taken the top half of his head off. Still sprawling to the ground, he shot out a hand reflexively and seized hold of the last remaining tribesman's ankle. For some reason, the man had decided to bull rush Slater's position, opting to use a close-quarters weapon instead of attempting to pick him off from a distance.

The ankle pick takedown was a common staple of wrestling, taught in grappling schools across the world. It took considerable dexterity and strength to time perfectly, but it helped when one's adversary had zero professional martial arts training whatsoever.

Slater wrenched the man's ankle off the ground, throwing him entirely off-balance. Before the guy could launch a second swing of the *jambiyah,* Slater had effectively yanked his legs out from underneath him.

The man sprawled into the dust, landing hard enough on his back to omit an audible gasp.

From there, it was like clockwork.

Slater had lost his grip on the AK-15 in the scramble, but that didn't matter. He pounced on the man like a boa constrictor, squashing him into the sand with his full bodyweight. The man panicked and rolled onto his back, intent on making his way to his feet from there.

Just like they all did.

Slater sliced an arm underneath his throat and locked the choke tight, wrenching his forearm back with his other hand. Poised behind the tribesman like a human backpack, the result was inevitable. The tribesman heaved with exertion, managing to stumble upright for a split second. He had put all his effort into getting his legs underneath him, but when he made it to his feet he realised that Slater wasn't going anywhere.

What now? Slater thought.

Now, the blood supply to his brain shut off. The man's legs went limp, creating a result more disastrous than if he'd simply stayed put on the ground. The man pitched forward, losing all control of his bodily functions, and face-planted the sand hard enough to rattle his brain within its skull. Coupled with the choke hold, it put him out for the near future.

He'd wake up later.

Confused, disoriented, but alive.

Slater slid off the motionless body, collected his weapon, and slunk toward the house.

The man had got lucky.

He would live to see another day.

The mansion dwarfed everything else in sight, hovering in the centre of the compound like an ominous checkpoint. Slater knew that his only hope of ending the madness rested within. He had no idea what to expect. He had no idea what was waiting for him within the walls.

He shrugged and pressed forward.

Close-quarters carnage had always been preferable to open warfare. He favoured the madness of tight spaces. It leant greater weight on reaction speed — something he had in spades.

He stepped up onto the porch. Despite the intense ringing in his ears, an uneasy silence had descended over the entire compound. The atmosphere was as familiar to Slater as an absence of combat. So much of his life had been spent battling to merely survive that he had learnt to control his emotions, even in the most difficult of circumstances. As a result, his veins had turned to ice by the time he crossed to the double doors, shut firmly like a warning not to enter.

He had never obeyed warnings.

Thinking of Abu and the family the man had waiting for him to return home, Slater set into action. He thrust a shoulder into one of the doors, hard enough to rattle the entire thing on its hinges but possessing enough restraint to keep it locked in place.

By the time the noise of the impact had echoed into the building, creating a retaliatory wave of gunfire that shredded through the thick wood, Slater had already taken off at a sprint along the porch. He aimed for one of the broad windows running along the front of the property, all of them bolted shut.

He had come to learn that, no matter what precautionary measures were in place, a two-hundred pound dead-weight could break through all kinds of barriers.

He took the hit across his upper back, throwing himself backwards into the window to prevent any life-threatening injuries to his face or neck.

The windowpane detonated in a shower of glass.

Slater followed it through, slamming down onto the floor of a disused office.

He was inside.

38

T hree thoughts speared through Slater as he rolled expertly to his feet inside the massive room.

First — protect Abu.

The computer technician had become hopelessly embroiled in this conflict without argument, and Slater was eternally grateful for his assistance. He would fight until his dying breath to ensure the man made it home safe. It had been his call to keep him in the mansion, so the burden of responsibility rested solely on his shoulders to get him out.

Second — protect al-Mansur.

Despite the animosity leeching through his bones towards the Brigadier-General, Slater knew the consequences of letting the man get caught in the crossfire. Al-Mansur was integral to the terror plot, and Slater doubted that he had passed full details of the operation onto any of his underlings. The bulk of the knowledge on the matter rested inside al-Mansur's brain, and Slater needed to keep it functioning — at least until he had restrained the momentum and was able to stop and think for more than a few minutes at a time. When he had control over the situation, he would end al-Mansur's life without hesitation.

Third — kill everyone else in the damn building.

Slater had given up trying to be moralistic. Leaving the tribesman he'd just choked unconscious alive had been a grave error — he would more than likely have to deal with the man further down the line. The lives of thousands — if not hundreds of thousands — of people came down to what he could accomplish over the next couple of hours. It ate away at his insides, churning his gut even as he swept the room for any sign of hostiles.

A single wrong move now wouldn't just spell disaster for himself.

It would spell disaster for all of London.

Why the fuck is this happening? a voice hissed in his head as he hurried for the open doorway on the far side of the room.

He had no idea. Al-Mansur's motivations were as blurry as his own vision, pounding and wavering from the sheer dose of adrenalin in his veins.

He was simply doing as he always did.

Reacting. Rolling with the punches. Improvising.

From the precursory glance at the space outside the office, it seemed this room opened out into the main lobby, backed by the grand staircase spiralling up toward the second and third floor.

Wide open ground.

Slater cursed under his breath and pressed his back against the wall right near the doorway. He hated the unknown — he would have preferred the conflict to unfold in cramped hallways, with barely any room to move. He could use elbows and knees and sheer overwhelming force to turn those types of claustrophobic skirmishes into a nightmare for anyone he came across.

He hated high ceilings, and vast marble floors, and plenty of doorways to hide behind.

It was like a fatally dangerous game of hide-and-seek.

Reluctant to step out into the open, he opted to attune his hearing to the slightest disturbances in the mansion. It was difficult, given the beating his eardrums had taken over the course of the gunfighting. He settled his breathing and focused hard, squinting his gaze to narrow his focus. The rate at which his heart pounded in his chest was uncontrollable, but he could at least temporarily shut out the adrenalin.

A noise.

Close by.

Uncomfortably close.

Slater realised all at once that another breathing organism rested right around the doorway, standing opposite to him. When he became aware of the man, he could fine tune his own hearing, zoning in on the muffled, panicked breathing and the racking of a weapon's slide.

The guy had heard Slater crash into the office, but hadn't possessed the courage to charge in on his own.

Slater sensed the presence of death. It was a strange sensation — the knowledge that in the coming seconds one of them would die. He had shared it with many people in the past, and somehow always came out on top.

He moved like a wraith, first sending a couple of rounds into the wall itself. The walls were made of polished, panelled wood, thick enough to withstand a gunshot — but that had never been the intention. The sound of two unsuppressed AK-15 rounds at close range was deafening, drowning out all other senses, making the enemy recoil inward for that split second where their world went mad.

At that point, Slater rounded the edge of the doorway and swung the AK-15 double-handed, like a club, hard enough to break bones. The stock hit the tribesman square in the side of the head, bouncing off his skull with a noise similar to cracking open a coconut. The man went down instantly — if not dead, then flirting with the concept.

Slater moved his limbs like whips, rearing around to scout the rest of the lobby for any signs of life.

Too late.

He had no time to duck back behind the doorway before he glimpsed the two stationary figures, poised in the middle of the marble floor of the entranceway like silent statues. They seemingly hadn't moved in minutes, seeing that Slater hadn't heard a peep from them the entire time. They must have simultaneously frozen as they heard him dive into the adjoining office, aware that it would only be a matter of time before Slater came storming out.

Perhaps the man he'd just killed had been a decoy all along.

Al-Mansur stood side-by-side with the last remaining tribesman, a grizzled old man with a permanent scowl and a bulky Kalashnikov held between veiny forearms, its barrel locked rigid in the air.

Al-Mansur had a Jericho pistol pointed at Slater's head.

Slater didn't dare to bring his AK-15 around. It would take too long — a single vital second with which the two men in front of him would take the opportunity to tear him apart.

'Kill me,' he said, his voice hollow in the cavernous space.

Al-Mansur smiled grimly and shook his head. Then he spoke, his accent thick. 'Where is your friend?'

Slater paused, flabbergasted. 'You speak English?'

'Of course.'

'What was all that about before?'

'Gave your friend something to do. Threw you off-guard. Now where is he?'

'I don't know.'

'He fled with you,' al-Mansur said. 'Yet he did not return.'

Ah, Slater thought.

The Brigadier-General had been too disoriented by the previous conflict that he hadn't noticed Abu slink upstairs.

He didn't know the man was in the house.

What advantage that posed, Slater was unsure of.

Then he noticed the blur of movement at the top of his vision, flashing into sight on the second-floor landing. He could only see what was about to unfold due to al-Mansur's positioning — the two men were poised in front of the grand staircase leading up to the next storey.

A bulky shape burst into view, sprinting hard for the railing. Slater guessed that both al-Mansur and the sole tribesman were riding out waves of adrenalin — otherwise, they would have noticed the man coming. He imagined the pair didn't see true combat often.

It meant they had their gazes fixed firmly on Slater when Abu threw himself over the second-floor railing, hurling all caution to the wind. The man dropped unceremoniously, losing all control in the air, twisting once before falling like a two-hundred-pound dead weight onto the men standing before Slater.

At the last second, Slater scrambled out of the way, sensing a panicked burst of gunfire was imminent.

He was right.

Abu came down hard enough on the heads of al-Mansur and the tribesman to cause massive neurological damage to whoever took the brunt of the impact. The three men sprawled to the floor, limbs tangling and heads clattering off the marble. Al-Mansur's finger tensed around the trigger of his pistol and a shot blasted through the space Slater had occupied a moment previously.

Slater regained control of his course, getting his feet underneath him, and hurled himself at the trio — all three of whom were regaining their senses.

In one practiced motion, he soccer-kicked the tribesman's AK-47 out of harm's way. If he had missed, he would have wound up on his rear, vulnerable and exposed to a burst of unprotected gunfire.

Thankfully, the toe of his boot slammed home against the weapon's stock and it skittered away across the marble.

Slater exploded into action.

He crushed a fist into the tribesman's face with enough force to knock the man unconscious. For good measure, he thundered an extra shot into the guy's unprotected liver, adding insult to injury and giving him something to occupy his attention when he came to.

In the mad scramble, he rolled over on his back and came down on top of al-Mansur, crushing the man under his deadweight. The Brigadier-General squirmed for a decent grip on the IWI Jericho in his hand, but Slater smashed the gun away with a single strike.

He noted the proximity of their faces — only half a foot apart — and dropped his forehead into the bridge of al-Mansur's nose.

The man screamed, bucked, and rolled instinctively

onto his back to turn his face away from any subsequent blows.

Just as they all do.

Slater opted not to choke the life out of the man — or even the consciousness. He left al-Mansur's bodily functions intact, rolling off the body as soon as he sensed the man give up.

It took him a moment to process the stillness in the air.

In the space of three minutes, he had stormed a heavily-fortified compound and come away with nothing but a grazing bullet wound.

Sometimes, he surprised himself...

39

From across the room, Abu whimpered. The man had backed himself away from the conflict, resting against the banister running the length of the staircase. He had broken out in a cold sweat, and it took Slater a moment to realise why.

Abu's left ankle had twisted unnaturally, sticking out at an odd angle in grotesque fashion. On top of that, the man clutched his right shoulder in apparent agony, wincing as he rode out several waves of crippling shock.

He had landed hard.

Slater wasn't surprised that the fall had beat him half to death.

'What the fuck were you thinking?' Slater muttered, assessing the state of the computer technician.

'I wasn't,' Abu said. 'But I thought I'd try something that they wouldn't see coming.'

'You've likely torn your shoulder and broken your ankle. You're not going anywhere fast.'

'You might be dead if I did nothing.'

Slater nodded. 'Thank you.'

'What now?' Abu said, staring around the lobby at the smattering of corpses scattered across the room. 'What the hell have we got ourselves into?'

Slater exhaled, letting the cocktail of pulse-pounding neurotransmitters simmer down, controlling his breathing. His thoughts were muddied and scrambled. He couldn't focus on a single concept for more than a few seconds, instinctively reeling to something else.

Always moving.

Truth was — he didn't know.

'Our timeframe's far shorter than I thought it would be,' Slater said, vocalising everything running through his mind in an attempt to organise his thoughts. 'We've only got hours before something happens in London. There's three bomblets containing the Marburg virus in the hands of an unknown third party over there. I don't know if the package was stopped in transit, or if the guy responsible for setting it off has backed out. There's no way to know any of that.'

He turned his attention to al-Mansur, still cowering on the floor between them.

'But he does,' Slater said.

Things became clearer. Al-Mansur was the central node of this whole ordeal, the single man in charge of everything. It was more than likely that he had the capacity to call off the operation.

The Brigadier-General served as Slater's only link to the puzzle. It was all he had to work with.

I'll make it work.

He heaved al-Mansur up, charged with nervous energy, and hauled the man into a seated position on the marble floor. The confident demeanour had vanished, wiped out of al-Mansur as he came to the realisation that there was no more help on the way.

Slater had decimated the man's entire security detail.
Twice.

'Let's try this again,' Slater muttered.

Abu began to mirror the sentence in Arabic, but Slater held up a hand, abruptly cutting him off.

'The bastard speaks English,' he said.

'Oh,' Abu said.

Al-Mansur made eye contact with Slater for the first time since he'd re-entered the complex. Slater hesitated as he studied the man's gaze — it had changed significantly since his last visit. There was raw terror behind the eyes, something that couldn't easily be faked.

The next sentence that Slater was set to utter caught in his throat. He found himself thrown off by al-Mansur's panic, scrambling for words, breathing heavily.

Above everything else, the thought struck him that perhaps this man wasn't as all-powerful and all-knowing as he originally anticipated.

Despite his unease, he composed himself. He reached down and snatched up a handful of al-Mansur's shirt collar.

'You know that I won't stop,' he said, 'until you call this off.'

He studied the man's expression — besides the fear, there was intense confusion. Al-Mansur spent a long, drawn-out beat taking in what Slater had said. When he realised what the words meant, he shrugged, staring vacantly into the distance.

'He's concussed,' Abu muttered.

Slater nodded understandingly. All of Abu's weight had come down on top of the Brigadier-General's skull. Although he wasn't unconscious, his senses were rattled.

Slater realised he could use it to his own advantage.

Concussed individuals were highly suggestible.

Slater shook the man by the collar hard enough to cause a moan of despair — the action aggravated the pounding headache that had no doubt sprung to life behind al-Mansur's temple. He slumped forward, dejected.

Defeated.

'You're going to call your man in London and tell him to stand down,' Slater said. 'Understand? Then I might let you live.'

Al-Mansur said nothing.

He simply stared over Slater's shoulder, zoned out.

Slater yanked the man to his feet and dragged him through into the main office. The bank of digital screens were still tuned into CCTV feeds of central London — it was late afternoon in the U.K. and the streets were congesting with office workers getting off early. Slater kept his gaze fixed on the screens for an ominous moment before tearing it away to focus on al-Mansur.

He dumped the Brigadier-General down in one of the swivel chairs, oddly mirroring the last time he'd entered the mansion.

This time, there was no help on the way.

That was clear through al-Mansur's body language.

The confidence was gone.

'You're going to call your man in London,' Slater repeated. 'And tell him to stand down.'

He wouldn't say it a third time.

The AK-15 in his right hand hung by his side, poised. He was ready to use it. A single round through the top of the kneecap caused more pain than anyone could possibly imagine.

He would blow both al-Mansur's joints to shards, and then get to work on the rest of him.

Whatever it takes.

The Brigadier-General maintained his strange vow of silence, his vacant stare unfazed by the threats.

Slater clenched his teeth as desperation set in. He jammed the barrel of the AK-15 against al-Mansur's trouser leg. 'Did you hear me?'

'I heard you.'

The three syllables came out pathetically, as if every last option in the world had been exhausted.

Which they had.

Slater could taste the defeat in the air.

'And?' he said, leaning closer to al-Mansur, steadily applying more pressure with the AK-15, just a couple of ounces of resistance away from blowing the man's kneecap to pieces.

'Isn't it obvious?' al-Mansur said, refusing to take his eyes off the empty space over Slater's shoulder.

'What?'

'It's not my man in London. It never was.'

40

'Bullshit,' Slater hissed, leaning all his weight on the barrel of the AK-15.

The automatic rifle dug into the top of al-Mansur's kneecap, making him squirm. He rode out the pain without protest, refusing to change his demeanour.

'The cameras,' Slater said. 'You really think you'll convince me you have nothing to do with it? Not for a second.'

'Of course I have something to do with it,' al-Mansur said. 'I have everything to do with it. But it's not my man in London.'

'You'd better get talking before I put a bullet through your head.'

'Do it,' al-Mansur said. 'I have nothing left to live for.'

'What?'

'I'm not going to explain myself to you,' al-Mansur said. 'But my life is over already. No matter what happens from this point. The operation's been compromised. That's on me.'

'You co-operate with me and I'll give you a chance to get

out of here alive,' Slater said. 'It's not a great option, but it's the only one you've got.'

Al-Mansur smiled grimly. 'You think I care about myself? Please...'

'I won't keep this game up much longer,' Slater said. 'Spit it out or you're guaranteed to die. You never know — maybe I can help you.'

Al-Mansur scowled and spat on the ground beside Slater. 'You cannot do a thing. You will not do a thing.'

Slater tensed his finger against the AK-15's trigger. 'Talk.'

'Sayyid has my daughter,' al-Mansur said, blurting it out before he could stop himself. 'I have been forced to co-operate.'

Slater hesitated, rapidly putting the pieces together. Behind him, he sensed Abu recoil, realising all at once what was going on. Slater turned to see the man leaning against the doorway, resting on one leg, his face contorted in pain but paling as new realisations dawned.

'The tribesman?' Slater said, turning back to al-Mansur.

'The leader,' Abu whispered from behind. 'You ran into him in the mountains above Qasam. I told you this man does not associate himself with those savages.'

'You think I am willingly working with the tribes?' al-Mansur said. 'You do not know enough about me. I despise them.'

'I said as much yesterday,' Abu said.

'It could be a ruse,' Slater said.

'What business do you think I have in London?' al-Mansur said. 'You think I am bothered by what's going on halfway across the world? I care about my child. I care about keeping her alive by any means necessary. That's what bothers me.'

'Why?' Slater said, keeping his grip tight on the AK-15,

ensuring al-Mansur didn't budge an inch. 'Why the fuck is any of this happening? When did it begin?'

'Months ago. Something like this does not unfold quickly. It has been brewing in Sayyid's mind for years. Decades, even.'

'There's considerable risks involved,' Slater said. 'I don't see the reason for any of this.'

'I see,' al-Mansur said. 'Trust me, I see. Sayyid has ranted and raved to me for hours on end about why he is doing this.'

'Care to explain?'

'It's complicated.'

'I need to know,' Slater said. 'I need to know if I can stop it.'

'It is not a pleasant tale.'

'My life doesn't revolve around pleasant tales. Tell me.'

'What do you know about the history of Yemen?'

'Very little,' Slater admitted.

'Sayyid's ancestors have led the northern highland tribes for generations. His father was leader when the conflict with the British reached its apex, in the 1960s. Sayyid was a young boy at the time. For years the northern tribes had fantasised about their independence, so it was only natural that Sayyid's father took up arms against the British forces in Yemen at the first opportunity. It came in the form of the National Liberation Front, an organisation that encouraged violence against the British. I won't get into the finer details — we have a long and complicated history.

'As fate would have it, the conflict heightened. Sayyid's father and his fellow tribesman carried out many attacks on British forces down in Aden. They favoured the use of hand grenades. Their strikes were vicious and unrelenting. It took a certain Lieutenant-Colonel to bring about a crackdown on the tribes.'

'Mad Mitch?' Abu said, interrupting.

Al-Mansur nodded. 'You have heard of him.'

Slater wheeled around, studying Abu's expression. 'Who is he?'

'A well-known figure around these parts,' al-Mansur said. 'A Lieutenant Colonel in the British army, stationed in Yemen in the late 1960s. He didn't cause much damage himself, but the men under his command were brutal. Anonymous, nameless troops. They hit back at the tribes harder than anyone thought possible, trying to re-impose order.'

'Understandable,' Slater said, grimly anticipating what would come next.

'I'm afraid a collection of his men took it too far when Sayyid was just ten years old.'

'They were carrying out grenade attacks on British troops...' Slater said.

'I am not saying anything is justified,' al-Mansur said, shrugging. 'I'm merely explaining what happened. A collection of British troops stormed into Sayyid's encampment in the dead of night. They raped his mother over and over again, and beheaded her in front of her ten-year-old child. They forced her father to watch. A couple of them raped him, too. Then they sat Sayyid down, inches away from his own father, and slit the man's throat. Sayyid still tells me of the memories he has. His father's blood running all over him. And then they left Sayyid to process those events for the rest of his life. They left him alive. To stew. And plot. And retaliate.'

'Jesus Christ,' Slater said, wincing involuntarily.

'Now you see why he might hold a grudge.'

'It's been fifty years,' Slater said. 'He didn't care to try something sooner?'

Al-Mansur shrugged. 'It's half that. The other half is to send a message.'

'To who?'

'Who do you think?'

'What does he have against the Brits — besides the obvious?'

'He is displeased with many things,' al-Mansur said. 'We all are. Your friend here can confirm that.'

Slater turned to Abu, who shrugged and nodded accordingly.

'I must say, none of us are willing to take a response to this level,' al-Mansur said. 'But there is significant dissatisfaction with what the British are doing. They are funding a Saudi invasion of our land — it has killed thousands. They supply the Saudis with weaponry — high-tech weaponry — which they use on our people at will. Billions of dollars of weapons. All funded by the British. Sayyid intends to send a stark message. Look what happens when your politicians go off the rails. Look what it does to your people. There are consequences for your actions.'

'And you think this kind of reaction is justified? Rivers of blood in the streets? The deaths of hundreds of thousands of innocent people?'

'I don't recall ever mentioning what I thought about it,' al-Mansur said. 'Truth is, it does not matter. Sayyid came to me. With my daughter's head on the chopping block. I had no choice but to comply.'

'You'd cause suffering like nothing anyone's ever seen before to protect her?'

'Of course,' al-Mansur said, his gaze icy.

'Hundreds of thousands of lives...'

'Do you have children?'

'No.'

'Then you cannot judge me on what I should or should not do when my only child is at risk of being raped, mutilated and murdered. You may despise me for it, but I would end the world to see her live another day.'

'How do I know you're telling the truth?'

'It is the truth,' al-Mansur said, and Slater could see the raw emotion behind his eyes, the kind of wordless pain that couldn't be easily masked. The kind of pain that came from spending months worrying over whether your child was suffering or not. 'I do not care if you don't believe me. It doesn't affect me either way.'

'How long have they had her?'

'Too long.'

'Do you know if she's still alive?'

'She was yesterday,' al-Mansur said, his tone suddenly wracked with grief. 'But it's just a waiting game. Sayyid is a savage. He will cast me aside as soon as he is done with me. My daughter too. I just hope it is painless for her.'

'So you're powerless to stop this?'

Al-Mansur shrugged. 'Sayyid controls everything. But I would not lie to you. Even if I had the choice to stop this, I would not. For a number of reasons.'

Slater nodded. 'I thought as much.'

'Even if they didn't have your daughter?' Abu said.

Al-Mansur looked past Slater to make eye contact with the computer technician for the first time. 'I can't say for sure.'

'Where is Sayyid?'

'He doesn't leave his encampment. It's in the mountains above—'

'Qasam.'

Al-Mansur cocked his head. 'Yes. How did you...?'

'I've seen it. I've met the man. Did you know they carried out tests up there?'

'I heard they tested it on a live subject.'

'A wolf. I saw that too.'

Al-Mansur paused, and furrowed his brow. 'No. One of their own.'

Slater gulped back the gravity of the statement, realising that the infected animal must have been tucked into an alcove within the cave, contracting the lethal infection by chance alone.

A by-product of a horrific bioweapon test.

That explains Sayyid's reaction when he entered the cave, he thought.

He hadn't anticipated another infected subject.

Not on his mountain.

'This is happening tonight, isn't it?' Slater said.

He watched the expression on al-Mansur's face change. Now the man was being asked to divulge sensitive information that could pose a threat to the operation being carried out.

A threat to his daughter.

'Give me everything I need to know,' Slater said, 'and I'll personally assure that your daughter makes it off the mountain alive.'

'She's not on the mountain. I don't know where she is. It's indoors. I've seen videos.'

'I'll find her.'

'How do you propose to do that?'

'Because if you tell me what I need to know, I'll have the necessary information to put a stop to this. Then I'll have all the time in the world to go hunting for your child. I'm a man of my word. But this is beyond anything you could have imagined, al-Mansur. This is a cataclysmic event, judging by what I've seen and heard. It needs to end.'

The man said nothing.

'You have no allegiance to Sayyid.'

'I have no allegiance to you, either.'

'I'm the one standing here, with a gun trained on you. What do you think they'll do with your daughter if you wind up dead — killed in your own house? What kind of incompetence will that show? You think they'll let her go free?'

Al-Mansur paled, the blood steadily draining from his face with each passing question. He opened his mouth like a gaping fish and shuddered involuntarily.

It didn't take much longer than that.

'So?' Slater said.

'It's happening this evening.'

'What's the protocol?'

'Sayyid is set in his ways,' al-Mansur said. 'And they're fairly primitive. He wants to be the one to send the final orders. He's been fantasising about this day for decades, I imagine. He wants to be the one to drop the hammer.'

'Via satellite phone?'

'Yes. It's the only way they can communicate up there. He has a direct line to the man in London.'

'What are the orders?'

'He changed them yesterday. I wondered why, but now it makes sense. Maybe he thinks the animal was a divine sign.'

Slater understood.

'*Dhi'b?*' Abu said, putting the pieces together simultaneously.

Al-Mansur nodded.

'What does it mean?' Slater said, but he already knew.

'Wolf.'

Slater grimaced, remembering the trauma the wild animal had suffered. He couldn't fathom extrapolating that anguish to a city of eight million people.

'There's no way you can contact the bomber yourself?' he said.

Al-Mansur shook his head. 'Not a chance. Sayyid wouldn't hand over that kind of control. I've been the brains and the brawn, but never the leader. I do as he bids.'

'You can guarantee he's up there?' Slater said. 'If I make it to the encampment, and it's deserted, and the operation carries out as planned, and I find out you've deceived me — what do you think I'll do?'

Al-Mansur shrugged. 'I don't know.'

'I'll spend every waking breath tracking down one of the members of the tribes,' Slater said, leaning in, venom in his tone. 'I'll tell them you tried to give them up. I'm very convincing when I try. I'll make sure they tear your daughter to pieces. Understood?'

Al-Mansur stiffened, his expression ghost-like. 'Understood. They are on the mountain. I swear it.'

Slater nodded. He backed away from the chair and rested the AK-15 in Abu's hands. 'Tie him up, and stay here. You'll be no use if you come along. I don't think that ankle's going to heal for months.'

Abu glanced down at his mangled limb, looking queasy. 'Nor do I.'

'See what you can do with that set-up.' Slater motioned to the row of computer screens. 'Feed me any information you can. It's not a quick drive to Qasam.'

'You're going alone?'

'You see another option?'

Abu shrugged.

Slater turned to al-Mansur. 'If you had to bet the life of

your child on exactly when Sayyid is going to set this thing into motion, what would you say?'

'He was adamant about dusk for some reason,' al-Mansur said. 'So — dusk in the U.K.'

'Two hours,' Abu muttered. 'And counting.'

'Fuck,' Slater breathed. 'I need to go. Right now.'

Suddenly nauseous at the ramifications of failure, he steadied himself against the doorway. Before he left he scrutinised al-Mansur, a complicated man to decipher in any situation. The Brigadier-General had sounded sincere when he spoke of his daughter, but now he sat in the swivel chair with a certain aura of relief surrounding him.

He was pleased that he had been spared.

It set Slater off.

Hands free of weapons, he walked right up to al-Mansur, bending down so that their faces were inches apart.

'Have you seen what the virus does?' Slater said, menace in his tone.

'I've heard reports,' al-Mansur said.

'But have you seen it? Up close. In the flesh.'

'No.'

'Have you tasted the air around something that's bleeding from every orifice? It has a certain scent.'

'No,' al-Mansur said, suddenly reserved, as if he knew where the conversation was headed.

'You don't understand what you've done. You're passing it off like it's nothing. If it was your manpower and your political influence and your resources that enabled this to go ahead, then you're the lowest of human filth on this goddamn planet.'

'I had no choice.'

'You always have a choice,' Slater said. 'You could have directed those resources into getting your daughter back. I believe it was my friend here who told me you control half the north-western military sector.'

'He does,' Abu said.

'Don't you think you might have been able to put up a decent fight against the tribes with that kind of manpower?'

'They would have killed her.'

'I'm afraid I don't buy it.'

'Believe what you want.'

'You want this to happen, don't you?'

'I...'

'Say it.'

Al-Mansur shrugged. 'Somewhat.'

'Why?'

'Life gets boring out here. Sometimes you've got to spice things up. Besides, I agree with Sayyid. It's time to send a message.'

Slater withdrew the IWI Jericho he'd pocketed off one of the dead tribesmen and tucked into his waistband outside the mansion.

'You said...' al-Mansur hissed.

'I'm a man of my word,' Slater said. 'I'll find your daughter. But that doesn't mean she has to come home to a monster.'

He seized a handful of the man's straggly hair, holding his skull in place, so that al-Mansur was useless to resist. He pressed the cool barrel of the Jericho to the man's temple.

He pulled the trigger.

41

1800 hours Yemen time
1600 hours London time
Two hours until discharge

Slater and Abu stood side by side on the sweeping front terrace of the mansion, looking out over a sea of devastation in the courtyard before them. Beyond the front gates, the sun melted seamlessly into the opposite horizon, lowering the temperature to a pleasant warmth. Already the sky had begun to darken, fingers of dark blue snaking their way across the heavens.

Slater battled a sudden chill.

Night was falling.

It was all or nothing.

'The drive will take you just over an hour,' Abu said, keeping his voice low.

'You can speak up,' Slater said. 'Everyone here is dead.'

He studied the motionless corpses sprawled across the mansion's grounds, including the fresh addition directly in front of them. Just as he had suspected, the tribesman he'd choked unconscious had come to his senses and lay in wait for Slater to emerge from the giant building. Thankfully, the brief dance with the darkness had dulled his senses.

It had taken a simple reversal of the *jambiyah* in his hand to gain control of the dagger and slice the blade across the arteries in the man's throat.

Then it had been over quickly.

'I'm struggling to process everything right now,' Abu admitted.

'So am I,' Slater said. 'I keep thinking I'm going to wake up from this. But it just keeps getting worse.'

'How's the shoulder?'

Slater grimaced and adjusted his jacket over the blood-stained wound. 'It'll be fine.'

'You need medical attention.'

Slater scoffed. 'You should see what I've had to deal with in the past. Besides, you're worse off.'

Abu nodded, unable to protest that. He kept all the weight leaning against the nearest column, refusing to glance down at his disgustingly twisted ankle. There were certainly bones broken in the foot. His right arm had begun to swell beyond comprehension. Slater guessed he had torn muscles.

'I will manage,' he whispered. 'What if more reinforcements come?'

Slater kept his eyes on the bodies. 'I'd say that was as many reinforcements as al-Mansur was going to get. If there's more, just hide. It's more effective than fighting.'

'I can't even fight in perfect condition,' Abu said. 'What do you think I'll be able to manage now?'

'Like I said. Hide.'

Slater looked down at the two most important objects for the coming conflict.

The AK-15, reloaded with a full magazine, held poised and at the ready in his right hand.

The satellite phone he'd used to contact Abu in his left.

'If you fail,' Abu said, 'how will I know? It'll be radio silence.'

'You have access to the Internet through those computers,' Slater said. 'You'll know.'

'What if you drop the satellite phone along the way?'

'If you don't hear from me, then I'm dead. I won't let this go ahead — no matter what.'

'Were you telling the truth to al-Mansur?' Abu said, bowing his head. 'About his daughter?'

Slater paused and considered the question. 'I'm a man of my word. I'll do whatever I can to find her.'

'She didn't deserve to get wrapped up in this.'

'How do we even know he has a daughter?' Slater said. 'It could have all been a ploy to get me out of the house.'

'I caught a bulletin in the Yemeni newspapers close to a month ago. It was a press release from the Brigadier-General, informing the public that his child had been sent overseas to allies for a journey of self-discovery. I imagine he wanted to quash any rumours that his daughter had disappeared. It's likely Sayyid made him do it. She is real.'

'I want you to know that she's not my top priority,' Slater said. 'If you'd seen what this Marburg virus can do in person, you'd understand. Every ounce of my focus has to be locked onto stopping the attack from taking place. I hope you can accept that.'

'Of course.'

'I need to go.'

Slater tucked the satellite phone under his opposite armpit, freeing a hand to extend toward Abu. The man took it with a firm grip, and they shook for a long, drawn-out beat. Underneath the conversation, both of them recognised that this would likely be the last time they saw each other. The fallout from the chaos at al-Mansur's compound would be staggering. Slater imagined that attention would mount as soon as reinforcements entered the area.

For now, everyone appointed to protect the mansion had been cleaned out.

For now.

'Goodbye, my friend,' Abu said.

'See you around?' Slater said.

The man smiled wryly. 'I don't think so. You know that too.'

'If you didn't approach me in that courtyard,' Slater said, 'none of this would have happened. Everything would have unfolded for them as planned. If I manage to stop it, I owe it all to you.'

Abu shrugged. 'Let's not focus on who owes who. We both helped each other.'

'What will you do when this all blows over?'

'Return to my family. They'll be expecting me back from Hadhramaut shortly.'

'Will you tell them what you did?'

'Of course not.'

'No-one will ever know...'

Abu nodded. 'Best to keep it that way.'

The man raised the satellite phone in his hand. 'I'll be available on here for the next two hours. If you need anything. Then I'm gone. There'll be troops swarming this place by the morning.'

Slater nodded. 'Of course. Get home safe.'

Abu glanced down at his mangled foot and shrugged. 'I'll try my best. Now get going.'

'Yeah...'

Slater stepped down off the terrace and crossed the courtyard, his boots crunching against the gravel track. He selected a vehicle at random — they were all practically identical, complete with rusting rear trays and beat-up, dust-stained cabins. He threw open the door of the nearest ride and tossed the phone and rifle into the passenger seat. He noted that the rear window had shattered — all that was left was a giant gaping hole in the back of the cabin.

The keys were still in the ignition.

'You know this is suicide,' Abu called from the porch. 'He'll have every tribesman ready to die to protect him.'

Slater cast an arm in a wide semi-circle around the compound. 'You sure it's suicide?'

Abu noted the sea of corpses. 'Maybe not.'

'Take care of yourself, Abu,' Slater said. 'Safe travels back to your family.'

'Make sure this thing doesn't go off. You never know what might happen. What if it doesn't get quarantined in time? What if it spreads worldwide?'

'Exactly.'

Slater slammed the door shut and fired the pick-up truck to life. He navigated around a cluster of dead tribesmen near the front gates, and peeled straight through. He caught a final glimpse of Abu in the rear view mirror as he drove out of the compound, standing awkwardly on the front terrace, unmoving.

The man was scared.

Slater didn't blame him.

The suspension bounced and jolted as he made it onto the main track and set off in the direction of Qasam. A sweeping sheet of darkness had fallen over the Hadhramaut Valley, adding to the sheer isolation of the region. With dust rolling off the tyres on either side and a complete absence of human civilisation ahead, Slater shrugged off a sudden chill. He was heading into no man's land, an oppressive, empty plain as barren as an alien planet.

He rolled with the emotions and leant more weight on the accelerator.

He hoped to cut the drive to an hour.

He would need all the time he could get when he plunged into the mountains.

42

Diana hadn't moved from her seated position in the hallway for close to an hour now.

She had gone back inside, briefly. Both her mother and Steve had largely ignored her — it seemed like they had realised the slap had taken things too far. She didn't want to go back to reception, either — Beryl seemed too concerned with her living situation. Being thrust into foster care didn't appeal to her.

She just wanted to be alone.

The man from the flat at the end of the corridor had briefly emerged. He'd been sweating — Diana wondered why. He had seen her, and smiled again. She liked his smile. It reminded her of happier times, of she and her mother living on their own. There had been problems back then, but none of them had seemed daunting.

Now, everything about her situation terrified her.

She knew she couldn't carry on living in the same flat as Steve. Her mother's boyfriend had slowly shifted from annoying to downright abusive, and she hated the way his eyes lit up when he got angry.

It was like he enjoyed it when he hit her.

Diana didn't know much, but she knew a bad man when she saw one.

She wanted to get away, but she didn't know how.

Where to go.

What to do.

Who to trust.

The window at the very end of the hallway — right next to the stranger's front door — faced across the street to the opposite apartment building. Diana had watched the light steadily fade away as the sun hurried toward the horizon, slowly plunging the face of the other building into dusk.

She'd been told not to go outside when it got dark.

By who?

Her mother. She didn't particularly trust her mother right now. She was doing nothing to protect her little girl, simply standing back and letting Steve do as he pleased.

Diana hated that the most.

Steve was a bad person, but she had always thought favourably of her mother. Slowly, that trust had begun to slip away. She tucked her knees into her chest and began to rock back and forth as the corridor lights flickered on one by one.

Half of them didn't work, creating long shadows across the fetid carpet.

Above everything, she was confused.

She'd always had an anchor in her life, someone to tell her everything would be okay even when all was falling apart around her. Now she had nothing. Beryl meant well, but Diana didn't want to spend all her time down in reception. She was probably annoying the woman...

Inside her flat, the arguing started up again.

The raised voices floated out into the hallway, tinged

with venom and blame. Maybe her mother was finally standing up for herself, putting Steve in his place.

Diana scoffed under her breath.

Like that would ever happen.

Above that, she heard commotion from down the hallway.

Coming from the stranger's room.

Heavy footsteps.

As if he were nervous.

Diana thought about knocking on his door, asking if she could wait in his flat for a while as the tension died down in her own home, but a voice in the back of her head reminded her the dangers of being alone with strangers.

She decided to simply stay where she was, and wait for the man to re-appear.

He was bound to, at some point.

Then she would decide what to do from there.

43

1900 hours Yemen time
1700 hours London time
One hour until discharge

The dusty old pick-up truck rumbled up the steep mountainside track under the low blanket of dusk. Its sole occupant was invisible to the townspeople of Qasam, hidden in a veil of darkness behind the pair of piercing headlights that cut through the relative calm of the town.

Inside the cabin, Slater's stomach churned.

It wasn't the approaching chance of death that bothered him. Years ago he had come to accept his own mortality. It had been a strange shift in mindset, one that he had grappled with for some time, but when he eventually realised that the slightest change of trajectory could send a hollow-point round through his skull and bring his life to an abrupt end, it had almost carried a permanent calm along with it. He had lived each day like it was his last, because his line of work had demanded that he accept his inevitable demise.

Somehow, someway, he'd come out the other side unscathed.

The drive across the desert had given him time to think, something he'd rarely experienced over these past few days. Solitude had eluded him since he'd arrived in Qasam — there had always been something to do, some place to be, someone to confront.

There still was — but he had an hour to himself.

All to himself.

He had realised — after many attempts to skirt around the subject — that he'd come to Yemen as a method of assisted suicide. Much like how deranged civilians deliberately enticed law enforcement to gun them down — Slater had witnessed suicide by cop several times — he had entered the war-torn country expecting to bite off more than he could chew.

It had never seemed that way, but as the days dragged on it had become clear.

His career, and the way it had ended, had left him broken.

He didn't know what he wanted to do with his life. He had no family, no friends, no contacts of any kind. He had strolled into Yemen without even anticipating that he would leave.

This entire time, he had been trying to convince himself otherwise.

Now, he realised the truth.

And he realised what lay in the mountains dwarfed any of that, thrusting all his restless thoughts to the very back of his mind.

The concept of the Marburg virus truly rattled him. His hands were cold yet sweaty, his teeth chattered incessantly, and his left leg shifted restlessly against the footwell, shaking up and down like a jackhammer.

He wasn't afraid to die in the rocky caves above Qasam.

He was afraid to fail.

He felt he couldn't quite grasp the scale of what was set to occur.

Maybe he couldn't. Maybe it would take footage of blood in the streets, people screaming and flailing along the sidewalks, corpses littering central London.

Maybe then he'd fully understand.

It charged him with determination, icing his veins, carrying him through Qasam with his eyes locked firmly on the road ahead.

Unwavering.

There wasn't anything that would stop him spearing into the tribal encampment.

Whether that would result in success was anyone's guess.

But he would attempt a war all the same.

The pick-up truck passed through the town's limits and began the trek into the highlands. A warm coat of dim lighting that had washed through Qasam fell away, replaced by sheer darkness. Never had Slater felt so isolated. He gripped the steering wheel tight to combat his nerves and pressed into the swirling black, the headlights illuminating rocky outcrops and dark corners.

He checked the rear view mirror, glimpsing nothing but an ominous dust cloud trailing behind him.

He was on his own.

It had never been more apparent.

He wondered what kind of resistance he would face atop the mountain. Had he decimated the majority of Sayyid's forces at al-Mansur's mansion, or was there a hundred men waiting for any kind of interference?

Briefly, Slater considered the foolishness of his ploy.

What are you hoping to prevent?

If he killed Sayyid — and everyone stationed at the encampment — it would only serve to delay the bomber. The man wouldn't abandon ship simply because he didn't receive the orders from the leader himself. There were three bomblets on his person, and Slater fully expected the guy to use them.

Whoever he was.

One of the faceless millions trawling London's sidewalks.

Slater would never find him.

He could only target what he could feasibly achieve.

That was Sayyid.

So he shut all thoughts of failure and his own uselessness out of his mind and mashed the accelerator into the footwell, giving the vehicle everything it had. It surged up the slopes, taking the rugged track in stride, passing natural lookouts sweeping over the Hadhramaut Valley.

Anyone scared of heights would have blanched and turned back long ago.

He rounded a bend in the track and noticed a steep incline arching up into the darkness. There were dozens of potholes littering the track, each worse than the last.

And something else.

A foreign object, laid across the ground, masked by loose sand.

Something Slater didn't see until it was far too late.

Then all hell broke loose.

Both front tyres exploded simultaneously with a noise akin to a pair of gunshots, shredded to pieces by the spike strip laid across the mountain trail. Slater struggled to process what was happening — he recognised the sound, but the sheer force of the noise shocked him deeply.

The steel of the front wheels bit into the sand, screeching with a horrific whine, unprotected by the rubber tyres. The wheel leapt in Slater's hands, shuddering against the force. He wrestled for control. The pick-up truck's headlights dropped toward the trail floor, masking the view of what lay ahead.

Blinded, shaken, out of control, he wrestled for his own survival.

Fresh headlights flared on the trail ahead, appearing out of nowhere. An oncoming vehicle roared toward him, materialising out of the gloom like a screaming beacon. He guessed the car had been lying in wait just ahead, anticipating a new arrival.

Word must have spread of the events at al-Mansur's mansion.

Perhaps the tribesmen stationed at the Brigadier-General's compound had been expected to return by nightfall.

In the end, it didn't change a thing.

The oncoming pick-up truck surged into range before Slater could act. All his thoughts were preoccupied with keeping his own vehicle on course. To his right, the trail dropped off sharply, transforming into a sheer cliff-face that descended hundreds of feet to the valley floor far below.

In a cerebral chain of events, the oncoming truck sliced to Slater's left, shepherding him toward the edge.

He refused to budge on his trajectory.

Next a concussive blast rattled the cabin, accompanied by the horrendous groan of twisting metal. The sound only lasted a second, but Slater was coherent enough to connect the dots.

He had been rammed.

The oncoming vehicle had swerved at the last second, crumpling one side of his hood.

Smashing his truck off the road with sheer, unadulterated force.

It was the laws of nature. Kinetic energy. Unstoppable momentum. With shredded rags for front tyres, Slater was helpless to stop it. His vehicle buckled, twisted to the right...

... and dipped straight off the trail.

44

He moved with explosive precision. Every millisecond counted.

Even as the steering wheel left his hands and the cabin began to swing toward the drop, Slater had burst into motion. He vaulted out of his seat, twisted in the air, and scrambled tooth-and-nail for the open rear window frame.

The material underneath him lurched. It dropped away. He felt the sudden tug of inertia in the pit of his stomach, pulling him down, sucking him into a gaping abyss.

Into darkness and free-fall and a grisly demise.

He sliced both palms open on the window frame, still dotted with flecks of glass from where it had shattered. The wounds didn't even register in his mind. His entire being willed toward survival, toward that narrow window of opportunity to break free of the cabin — and certain death.

His upper body made it out through the frame as the vehicle's front wheels plunged into open space. The truck tilted and groaned underneath him.

The rear tray began to follow suit.

Slater ripped both legs out of the cabin, one by one, and they smashed down onto the flimsy tray. He almost toppled over whilst scrambling for purchase, an error that would have killed him. He found grip with a single foot and burst off the mark, hurrying along the back of the truck.

It tilted further.

He had less than a second. The rear tray had turned into an increasingly insurmountable ramp, arching up toward flat ground.

Only the rear tyres were left on the mountainside.

In an instant they would follow the rest of the vehicle and it would plunge into a chasm.

With Slater on top of it.

He snatched at the ridge attached to the very back of the vehicle. His hands were slick with blood, but he hurled himself over the back of the tray all the same.

Into thin air.

If he had miscalculated, if the vehicle had already plunged into open space, he would have leapt to his death.

Instead, he hit the ground like a freight train, missing the edge of the mountain by inches, rolling to safety in a spray of sand and blood. The truck groaned and disappeared from sight, whisked off the trail by the forces of gravity.

Slater lay on his back in the sand, bleeding profusely from both hands, his shoulder tinged with crimson warmth as the bullet wound re-opened. He couldn't believe what had just happened.

Then the icy fog set in.

He forgot all about the horrifying near-death experience, because it had nothing to do with the present moment. There were hostiles on this mountainside, likely armed and dangerous, hunting for Slater's head. They wouldn't stop until they were able to return it to their leader.

His concentration shifted to the truck screeching to a halt a hundred feet down the trail.

It had veered wildly off-course after ramming Slater's vehicle, having sacrificed its own stability to thrust him off the edge of the cliff. Now it kicked up torrential geysers of sand as it drifted to a halt, resting sideways across the trail.

Its twin headlights — now facing off the mountain's edge — were the only source of artificial light for miles in any direction.

The rest of the mountainside plunged instantly into darkness.

Slater rose off the ground like a man possessed, his gaze locked on the enemy vehicle. The pick-up truck had screeched to a standstill in an awkward position. To its rear, a wall of rock jutted into the night sky, blocking off any room to reverse. Straight in front of them, the trailside dipped away into nothingness. They were positioned horizontally across the track. It would take at least a ten-point-turn, moving one inch at a time, to get them back on track.

Slater would reach them before that.

Unarmed — with all his weapons sitting in the vehicle now resting at the bottom of the mountain — he set off slowly down the trail.

Taking his time.

Refusing to rush.

They would never hear him coming.

As he drew closer to the truck he was able to study the occupants who rested within. The pair were in the midst of a mad panic, leaning out each window to judge their position on the trail. They realised the extent of their situation, and began to grumble back and forth regarding what to do.

Slater couldn't speak Arabic, but he concluded that the men had agreed to ditch the ride and make the trek up to the encampment on foot. They seemed to be almost ready to set off.

There was no stress in their tone. Merely inconvenience.

They didn't know that Slater had made it out of the vehicle.

They didn't know they weren't alone on the mountainside.

The driver opened his door and began to step out of the cabin when Slater closed the distance and delivered a staggering uppercut into the underside of the guy's jaw. With a *crack* of breaking bone the man slumped back against the side of his vehicle, horrified by the development. Slater wrestled the weapon out of the man's hands — another Kalashnikov, this one a brutish, unsuppressed AK-47 — and fired it straight through the cabin.

Bullets shredded through the passenger's upper back, catching him off-guard as he clambered out of his own side. The guy disappeared from sight in a staccato of rifle fire and mortal grunts of agony.

Despite the shattered jaw, the driver made a move to retaliate. He burst off the mark like he intended to bull-rush Slater. If Slater failed to react the man would tackle him into the sand.

He sidestepped, smashed a boot into the man's groin, and watched the driver fall.

The wind torn from his sails.

Slater had transitioned into something darker, an entity hell-bent on stopping this madness. He didn't even consider showing the driver mercy. The man had just rammed his immobilised truck off a cliff...

As the man slumped into the sand, clutching his mauled

privates, hunching over in defeat, Slater pressed the tip of the AK-47's barrel to the back of his skull and fired a single shot through the guy's brain, stripping him of life in the blink of an eye.

His work complete, he turned and set off up the trail at a maddening pace.

Sprinting full-pelt.

Fury in his eyes.

Rage in his blood.

'Tick tock,' he muttered under his breath as he surged for the tribal encampment.

45

1930 hours Yemen time
1730 hours London time
Thirty minutes until discharge

The hollow silence permeating through the empty mansion set Abu's nerves on edge.

He had never experienced a quiet like this before. He knew what it meant. There were dozens of people here — yet they were all corpses. He refused to turn his eyes to the bodies as he hobbled aimlessly through the giant hallways, instead opting to peer up at the decadent ceilings above his head.

They were much more pleasant to look at.

There had been no sign of further reinforcements. The storm of tribesmen that had infiltrated the compound in an attempt to protect it from Slater had failed dismally — Abu didn't imagine that more men were on their way.

Not until the morning, when one of the Brigadier-General's detachments paid a visit to the mansion and found it in ruin.

By then, Abu expected to be long gone.

He finished his short lap of the ground floor, still in excruciating pain, and returned to the office where al-Mansur's body lay in a deep pool of arterial blood. The vast puddle appeared in his peripheral vision, but he didn't dare focus on it. Instead he crossed to the only swivel chair without blood stains splattered across its seat and dropped back into it. Sweat dotted his brow, even though the chill of night had settled over the desert compound.

He got back to work.

He left all the lights in the building switched off, letting the harsh light coming from the bank of screens bathe him in a pale blue glow. He navigated through directories and mulled over locked archives, attempting to piece together an elaborate puzzle that al-Mansur and his forces had no intention of letting outsiders decipher.

At the moment, everything was draped in a cloud of confusion. He could tangibly feel the cogs in his brain turning, struggling to decipher the cryptic files. Al-Mansur had somehow tapped into the hive mind of London's surveillance system — and there was no evidence of how he had done so. He must have employed the best of the best, or had inside connections.

There was no way to know for sure.

The answers were buried in a brain that was currently splattered over the far wall.

It didn't matter precisely how they had done it. What mattered was locating information that could be of use to Slater.

Briefly, Abu wondered how the strange American had fared on the mountainside.

He had never met anyone quite like Will Slater.

Abu tapped into an unnamed program embedded deep

in the most isolated directories, and a strange screen flashed into existence. He cast his gaze over thousands of lines of code — processing, analysing, narrowing his eyes at the strange requests.

He couldn't understand it.

Despite being one of the only computer technicians in the Hadhramaut Valley, Abu was the first to admit that he had a certain, unwavering skill set. He could tweak and repair almost any technical difficulty with the machinery required to run the mechanical drills and fuel pumps dotting the khat farms across the region. Those abilities were held in high regard, largely due to the fact that the drug was responsible for the employment of half of rural Yemen. He knew information regarding the sinking water table underneath Hadhramaut like the back of his hand.

Back-channels into confidential CCTV programs were an entirely different ballgame.

It should have been simple to decipher the text that lay in front of him.

But a crippling amalgamation of mind-numbing injuries, brain fog, and general ineptitude left Abu sitting in the swivel chair with his lips flapping like a dying fish.

He had nothing.

He could help with nothing.

He leant back in the chair and stared vacantly at the ceiling, angered by his own uselessness.

It would all come down to what Slater could manage.

Just as it seemingly had for the entire time he'd known the man.

Hopefully, Slater's relentless pursuit of forward motion would pay off.

Again.

46

1945 hours Yemen time
1745 hours London time
Fifteen minutes until discharge

S later made it to the top of the rise with his lungs burning in his chest, breath fogging in front of his face in the sudden chill. Despite everything, the drastic change in temperature didn't fail to amaze him. He struggled to process how it could go from blisteringly hot to painfully cold in the space of an hour.

As he continued to ascend the mountainside, fixated on what lay ahead, it only grew colder.

As the altitude rose, the temperature plummeted.

He recognised certain landmarks from the previous day — the rock formations dotting the sides of the trail activated certain memories, images that had been etched into his mind.

He didn't think he would forget them anytime soon.

He passed the same stretch of track that had burned the brightest imprint on his psyche the day before. He knew what he would find if he turned his attention to the shallow ditch on the side of the track, but he made sure to keep his eyes fixed directly ahead.

It would do him no good to study the headless corpse of the small child.

It would only serve to anger him further.

He had adrenalin and cortisol and sheer willpower flooding his mind. Any more of a spark and he would fall entirely off the rails. He had struggled in the past to keep control of his anger — and now it was threatening to bubble its way to the surface.

What Sayyid was attempting to do — as well as his own closeness to death moments before — had activated something deep inside of him.

Something primal.

A cluster of silhouettes materialised at the top of the track. Slater could make out their forms in the darkness — the three of them were backlit by the night sky. Looking up at them posed an advantage.

They wouldn't see him.

Not until it was too late.

They were obviously sentries, deployed to ensure that no-one made it into the encampment in the final hour. Despite the pessimistic thoughts coursing through Slater's head — the knowledge that nothing he achieved here would make a notable impact on the outcome — he pushed on regardless.

He could at least try.

Still racing forward, he raised the AK-15 and fired relentlessly up the trail, selecting his targets carefully, moving from one tribesman to the next. The shapes twisted and jerked in the night sky, thumping to the sand in pools of blood. Slater didn't pause to assess the damage he had caused.

He pushed straight through into the encampment.

He gazed out across the same rocky promontory he'd chanced upon the previous day — at night, it looked different. The shadows were accentuated, the cave entrances drowning in darkness and terror. It left room for the imagination to conjure all kinds of horrors.

Thankfully, Slater barely had time to think.

He kept sprinting, leapfrogging the three dead bodies — men who had never even posed a threat. Their weapons lay useless at their feet. On the way past, Slater reached down and snatched up a fresh magazine, recognising one of the firearms as an identical AK-15. To save time rummaging around in his pockets for spares, he ejected the magazine in his own rifle and chambered the fresh one home.

He noticed the shift in the air, the crackling electricity charging the atmosphere all around him.

He had become unstoppable.

Bedlam erupted inside the encampment. Harsh artificial light illuminated the collection of huts, plunging out of pre-installed floodlights. There were only a handful of the devices scattered across the wide space, casting elongated shadows across the rocky ground.

Vehicles surrounded the huts — the same battered pick-up trucks that seemed to be an extension of the land itself around these parts. Slater noted Toyota Land Cruisers sprawled at random across the plateau, parked in haste.

Already, men were piling into the vehicles, screaming obscenities in their native tongue.

Gunfire ripped across the stretch of flat land.

Muzzles flared.

Slater threw himself into a narrow crevice between two

sweeping plains of rock, a natural alcove that blocked three-quarters of his torso from the line of fire. He took the chance to survey the scene before him, breathing hard, sweating from every pore at once despite the night chill.

Shadows moved through the huts like wraiths — it was chaos. Slater couldn't determine who was armed and who wasn't. He counted five or six silhouettes ghosting across the promontory, fanning out.

He swallowed a ball of apprehension.

The longer he waited, the more chances these men had to capitalise on the situation. They had reacted faster than he anticipated, beginning to form a rudimentary semi-circle in an attempt to close him off.

Through the muzzle flashes and the deafening staccato of gunfire and the harsh blinding glare of the floodlights, Slater spotted something.

A solitary figure, hustling through the encampment.

Limping uncomfortably on one leg.

Moving as fast as his ageing, broken body would allow.

Slater recognised the attire. It was the same outfit the man had worn yesterday.

Sayyid.

Hauling ass for one of the pick-up trucks on the outskirts of the encampment.

Slater glanced at the vehicle itself and realised there was a man in the driver's seat. He had his neck craned behind him, watching Sayyid approach.

Waiting for his leader.

Slater put two and two together. He realised that Sayyid would be away in less than a minute if he didn't act. He couldn't afford to waste another second. He started to tense himself, preparing to burst across the stretch of no man's land like a coiled spring releasing all at once. That was the only opportunity he would have to make it to the pick-up truck in time.

And then what?

He had no time to consider what would happen next.

First he had to make sure not to get caught in the crossfire.

He lowered the AK-15 and placed one bloody palm on the rock, at chest-height, ready to explode.

Then he heard it.

A relentless barrage of screaming, hurling phrases into the air, coming from his left. He tore his attention away from Sayyid to ascertain the source of the madness.

A drug-addled tribesman came sprinting out of the darkness. The man must have located Slater amidst the promontory and thrown himself into a suicidal dash, sacrificing his life to spare his leader.

Slater noted the crazed look in the man's eyes, and the fragmentation grenade clutched between the white knuckles of his left hand.

His heart dropped.

47

Slater had seconds to act.

He assessed the distance between them and concluded that the bomber had built up such momentum on his mad dash that if Slater gunned him down, the sheer kinetic energy would carry him and the live grenade into the alcove.

There was little he could do to avoid it.

With a dozen feet between them, Slater realised the tribesman was going to hurl himself into the crevice at the last second, releasing his hold on the grenade in the process. The subsequent explosion would blast them both to shreds.

He held his breath for a moment too long, paralysed by indecision. There was nothing he could do.

The tribesman — a young man with hollow cheekbones and a thin frame — covered the last stretch between them.

Slater changed direction in an instant and hurled himself out of the crevice, using both arms to carry himself onto flat ground. The bomber realised the change of direction and moved to slow down — his intention was to bearhug Slater, nullifying the distance between them and assuring he was caught in the blast.

Slater dropped low and lashed out with a heavy combat boot, putting every ounce of strength in his frame into the move.

The toe of his boot connected with the tribesman's shin, splitting the bone in two. His leg caved unnaturally, folding in on itself, and the man lost all control of his body. He tumbled awkwardly over the top of Slater, pitching forward, cascading into the alcove.

One second! a voice in Slater's head screamed.

He rolled like his life depended on it — which it did. He hauled himself away from the thin slit in the plateau, at the same time as the tribesman tumbled into it.

The grenade slipped out of the man's grip, detonating on the floor of the alcove.

Slater had put a dozen feet between himself and the crevice by the time the fragmentation grenade went off, but it knocked every scrap of breath from his lungs all the same.

The world swam.

The concussive blast hit him like a gut punch, rendering him immobile for a spell. The walls of the crevice had shielded most of the force of the detonation — if they hadn't, he would have been flung across the promontory like a rag doll, his internal organs crushed and broken.

A mind-numbing *crack* flooded his senses, deafening him. His eardrums screamed in protest, ringing from the sheer decibel levels of the explosion.

There was little heat or fire. Grenade blasts seldom unfolded like the movies — they roared into existence with traumatic force and destruction, horrendously loud and packing an unrivalled punch. Slater made it to his feet, stumbled once, and shook his head from side to side in an attempt to get his wits about him. The blast had rattled him, but it hadn't put him out.

That was all he needed to know.

He was on the move before his hearing had even returned, ducking instinctively as Kalashnikov rounds sliced through the air around him. The gunfire came in precise bursts, sending pieces of the rocky promontory floor flying in all directions.

Slater made for the same vehicle Sayyid had almost reached — deaf to the world, but determined not to stop.

If he paused, he died.

He was closer to the encampment than he originally thought — he reached the outermost tents within seconds. A bullet shredded the canvas of the nearest wall, and he recoiled away from the impact site, ducking amidst the giant tents.

He had just managed a brief sigh of relief when a round shredded through his right calf.

He still couldn't hear anything, so the bullet wound presented itself in the form of a crippling wave of pain. Blood and flesh sprayed out of his lower leg, and he buckled temporarily under the horrendous stabbing sensation.

Eyes throbbing, ears thrumming, lungs burning for relief, his leg screaming for mercy, he wobbled.

The concept of surrender forged in his mind all at once, presenting itself on a frighteningly tantalising platter. It would simply take a single beat of hesitation to cave into his brain's desperate plea for relief. He would collapse in the encampment, succumbing to the pain and the agony and the nausea.

Instead, he ignored everything and closed the last few feet of ground between himself and the vehicle with animalistic determination.

His right leg barely functioned. He dragged it along the ground like a crippled dog, willing himself forward with every fibre of his being. Ahead, Sayyid finished scrambling into the rear tray of the vehicle — another Land Cruiser. The man had taken his time — his old, frail body could only move so fast.

The rear tyres spun on the dusty rock and the vehicle began to accelerate as soon as Sayyid was onboard.

Slater hurled himself at the back of the vehicle, clenching his teeth hard enough to grind them down in an effort to combat the pain. He snatched onto the lip of the rear tray with crimson-stained fingers, sinking his flesh into the corrugated metal.

As soon as he had the slightest semblance of a grip on the Toyota, he hurled himself onboard. Athleticism lent a helping hand and he came down in a bloody, sweaty pile on the rear tray of the vehicle, gasping for breath, not daring to look at his leg.

All at once, the gunfire abruptly ceased.

Slater understood.

He had dived into close proximity of Sayyid, and none of the remaining tribesmen would dare fire on their leader. Slater sensed the man lying right next to him.

He wondered if the driver would slam on the brakes, bringing the vehicle to a halt in the middle of the plateau.

There, Slater would become a sitting duck.

Instead, the driver panicked. No-one could be reliant to always make the tactically sound choice in a high-intensity combat situation — and the man commandeering the Land Cruiser certainly didn't react as he should have. Slater had seen it a thousand times before.

The driver registered that the precious cargo — Sayyid — had made it onto the vehicle. Maybe his senses were flooding with adrenalin, and he didn't even recognise that Slater had also hurled himself onboard.

Whatever the case, the man kept his foot mashed against the accelerator.

The Land Cruiser shot across the promontory, bucking and jolting underneath the uneven ground.

Slater's hearing began to return, accompanied by the distant screams of tribesmen scattered across the mountainside. All pleading with the driver to come to his senses and slow down. If he would just stop ... Slater would have exhausted all his options.

Instead, Slater used the opportunity to grab two handfuls of Sayyid's traditional *futa,* dragging the old man into range. He managed a glimpse at the man's hands and saw one of them clutching a high-tech satellite phone, its tiny screen glowing dimly in the night.

'Fuck,' Slater whispered, snatching at the phone.

Sayyid sneered, exposing rotting teeth, and rolled away with surprising dexterity.

That phone is everything, Slater told himself.

Secure it.

As Sayyid scrambled away across the tray, Slater became reckless, diving after the old man. As he lifted his head above the tray's lip, gunfire exploded across the promontory, bullets whistling through the air all around him.

He ducked back underneath the line of sight, protected by cover.

The barrage of shots only spurred the driver on. He quickened his pace, and both men in the rear tray were thrown around as the Land Cruiser gunned it toward the mountain trail.

The side of Slater's head smashed into the lip of the tray, and he grimaced as a wave of disorientation rolled over him.

When he regained his senses, he twisted on the spot to see Sayyid poised on the other side of the tray, his back pressed against the driver's cabin.

The man had lost his weapon in the confusion — an IWI Jericho 941, the same sidearm all the tribesmen were armed with.

It rested in the space between them, free for the taking.

Sayyid didn't care.

He pressed a button on the face of the satellite phone, dialling a number.

The man's face twisted into a sneer as the call was answered.

48

Searing waves of fire coursed through Slater's calf — he could tell from the extent of the pain that the muscle was horrifically damaged — but all of that fell away as he watched Sayyid make the call.

In one fluid motion, he hurled himself across the tray, battling resistance as the vehicle accelerated. One blood-soaked palm came down on the Jericho pistol and he snatched it up, slotting his finger inside the trigger guard as he flattened himself out on his stomach, lengthways across the rear tray.

The call connected, Sayyid opened his mouth to speak...

... and Slater fired, a single bullet that spat out of the barrel like a screaming heat-seeking missile and blasted Sayyid's face apart, tearing into the soft cartilage between his eyes and sinking straight through, pulverising his brain in a harrowing spray of gore.

The tribal leader slumped back against the rear window of the cabin, all his limbs going limp at once.

The satellite phone cascaded out of his hands.

It bounced off the lip of the tray.

The device disappeared from sight, falling out of the Land Cruiser.

Slater remained on his stomach, breathing hard, shocked by how close he had come to failure. He pictured the driver stamping on the brakes as the shot rang out, recognising that all was not as it seemed. The deceleration would give Slater a chance to leap out of the rear tray and secure the satellite phone — wherever it had landed amidst the promontory.

Instead, Sayyid's faceless corpse slumped over, revealing the shattered rear window of the cabin...

... and what lay beyond.

'Oh, Jesus,' Slater whispered.

By sheer dumb coincidence, the Jericho round had been powerful enough at such close-range to blast straight through the back of Sayyid's head, slicing inside the cabin. It had finished its short but catastrophic existence embedded deep in the back of the driver's neck. The man was now slumped motionless over the steering wheel, bleeding uncontrollably down the back of his shirt.

Slater swore again and scrambled to his knees as he realised the Land Cruiser wasn't slowing down anytime soon.

His eyes went wide as he ran through the list of options in his head.

There were few.

To make things worse, he looked over his shoulder to see one of the tribesman sprinting wildly for the area where the satellite phone had skittered to a halt. The man had abandoned his own vehicle a few dozen feet from the impact zone, descending on the site with rabid intensity.

'Shit, shit, shit.'

Slater spat curses as his pulse quickened. The Toyota

picked up speed, now travelling at close to fifty miles an hour across the promontory. It had set itself on a direct collision course with one of the rock formations surrounding the plateau. The impact was inevitable.

Slater had to jump.

It was the only option.

Not quite convinced that the fall wouldn't kill him, he sucked up every ounce of nerve in his body and stuffed it down, suppressing his natural instincts to remain in the tray.

You have to go.

Now.

He blanched, paling as his limbs failed him. The ground on either side of the Land Cruiser raced by at an unbelievable rate, blurring as the driver's body leant further on the accelerator.

GO!

He threw himself off the tray, into open space.

For a second he fell, blissfully suspended in the air, letting the wind buffet against his clothes, stinging the wound in his calf where a chunk of flesh had been torn clean off.

Then he smashed into the hard rock with enough concussive force to blast him into temporary unconsciousness, an impact that shook him all the way through to the core. His brain turned to a stutter-like effect, flashing in and out of experience. He felt his legs slapping the ground, then his back, then his arms, and finally his head, bouncing off the promontory floor like a watermelon cracking open.

He had rolled with the impact, taking most of the trauma out of the landing.

But it shut him down all the same.

He came to rest in a seated position, hunched over in

sheer crippling agony as the Land Cruiser sped away behind him. A few seconds later, he heard the screeching of metal and the thunderous *boom* as the truck crunched into a jagged outcrop of rocks, crumpling in on itself.

He simply sat, and squeezed his eyes shut, and panted like a dying dog.

The Jericho was nowhere to be found. He had lost it at some point during the brutal barrel roll. He rested both hands in his lap and blinked back a strange, nauseating sensation.

Something had broken within him.

It was an odd dynamic. He had never experienced such determination coursing through him, desperate beyond measure to secure that *fucking satellite phone,* but his body refused to respond. It had taken the beating of a lifetime, a series of succeeding injuries, each more grim than the last. Now he floated in a strange semi-conscious state, his mind screaming at his limbs to function but finding no response.

Barely able to string a cohesive thought together, he lifted his gaze.

He was powerless to stop it.

The tribesman who he'd seen hauling ass across the flat expanse screeched to a halt fifty feet away. The man stared around in a wide semi-circle, searching for the soft subtle glow of the satellite phone's screen. He didn't know where it had fallen, and neither did Slater.

Move, Slater told himself. *Get up.*

Nothing worked.

A pulsing, searing heat worked its way up his right leg, beginning in his damaged calf and snaking its way into his hip. He winced as the pain threatened to put him to sleep, but all that melted away when he saw what came next.

The tribesman reached down, plucked the satellite

phone out of a narrow crack in the baked plateau, and stared at the screen. He pressed the same button that Sayyid had utilised in the Land Cruiser and lifted the device to his ear as the call re-connected.

'*Dhi'b,*' the man said, loud and clear.

His voice echoed across the promontory, and even though Slater's hearing was operating at a fifth of its normal capacity, he picked up on every inflection in the man's tone.

The single syllable was laced with finality.

Wolf.

Slater went pale and bowed his head. Above the horrific pain, above all else, depression washed over him.

He had failed.

Dismally.

He sunk down into unconsciousness, suddenly power-less to resist its seductive lure.

The world faded away.

49

Inside the Brigadier-General's mansion, Abu hunched his back as he leant toward the screen, bathed in its glow. With his nose inches away from the pixels, he studied the lines of code appearing and disappearing across the screen.

They meant nothing to him.

Squinting, trying to filter out the mind-crushing pain emanating from his broken ankle, he noticed each line of code ended with a set of coordinates.

Longitude and latitude.

Abu highlighted one of the newest arrivals on the screen. With nothing else to do, he set to work attempting to figure out what it meant. He drew the keyboard closer to his face and tapped out a couple of basic commands, tweaking the cryptic message in question.

Suddenly, the speakers on either side of the monitors barked into life, jolting Abu in his seat.

'Be there in twenty minutes,' a voice said in Arabic.

'Okay,' another man said. 'I'll wait.'

'When's your shift end?'

'An hour.'

'Okay.'

An audible click echoed through the empty office.

The code disappeared.

Abu widened his eyes. The program monitored calls...?

Another line of code materialised out of thin air. Abu executed the same commands, and once again audio tore through the otherwise-silent office.

This time, he sat up straight in his seat.

His pulse shot through the roof.

He heard muffled sounds, none of them pleasant. The revving of an engine, the jolting of suspension. Then a distorted gunshot. A clatter, like the device itself had been dropped.

Silence.

Abu sat in the darkened office, rocking back and forth in his seat, plucking at loose strands of hair atop his head. He had never experienced a silence so uncomfortable.

What the hell was going on?

Then a new voice appeared. On the other end of the line.

'Hello?' the voice said, speaking Arabic. It was deep. 'Hello?'

No-one answered.

The other end of the line hung up also.

Abu froze.

Could it be?

He hastily brought up a satellite map of the Earth by flicking to an empty tab on the computer's internet browser. He copied the co-ordinates from the line of code before it disappeared, and inputted them into the program as fast as possible.

They brought up a location.

Abu froze in panic.

A red arrow dropped into the mountainside above Qasam, revealing the source of the call. He leapt out of his seat, sweating hard, scrambling to work out what to do.

No-one had said anything...

Maybe Slater had got to the phone in time...

He stood awkwardly on one leg for what felt like an eternity, hunched over the bank of screens, chewing at a fingernail.

'What do I do?' he muttered. 'What do I—?'

Suddenly, it made sense why a program like this would exist on al-Mansur's computer. It monitored all satellite calls in the region, able to anonymously tap into anything within proximity. Al-Mansur must have been using it to keep tabs on the tribes — to make sure his daughter was still alive...

If he had the capability to infiltrate London's CCTV systems, he surely had the capability to monitor a primitive collection of highlanders...

A new line of code appeared, this one identical to the previous one that Abu had intercepted.

The same device.

Sweating over the keyboard, he executed the same commands as fast as his fingers would allow, his hands shaking as he did so. Paling, wondering what he might find, the audio burst into life.

Vacant ringing.

The call hadn't been answered yet.

Then the ringing cut off, replaced by a voice.

'Hello?'

The same deep voice that Abu had heard before.

The bomber.

Awaiting instruction.

They're going to give the go ahead, a voice in Abu's head screamed.

Cut it off!

He keyed over to the line of code, executing a kill command with a rapid outburst of typing. He smashed the ENTER button, wondering if it would work.

The other end of the line went dead.

Abu felt like passing out from sheer relief. He slumped back into the chair, wiping sweat from his forehead.

Then a voice boomed out of the speakers.

The bomber's voice.

Abu had only muted the satellite phone on the mountainside.

He hadn't killed the call itself.

'Hello?' the voice repeated. Then the tone changed. 'Look, I'm going to assume this is the all-clear. I haven't heard you both times. There must be connection problems. I'm going ahead with it. Insha'Allah.'

'Oh, fuck,' Abu whispered in English.

The bomber hung up the phone.

50

H ussein lifted the backpack over both shoulders, even going so far as to connect the two chest straps, forming a barricade across his upper torso.

Men far smarter than himself had concluded that Kingston would serve as the most virulent suburb to unleash the Marburg virus. With the discharge of the viral spores concealed under the panic of a general suicide bombing, nosy civilians leaving their offices would flock to the scene of the incident, desperate for a look at the small-scale terror attack.

Little did they know that the real thing would begin days or weeks later — and by then, it would have spread through most of London.

The headaches would begin, all at once, crippling most of the population.

Then the nausea.

Then all hell would break loose.

Hussein wouldn't be around to see it. He had visualised it for months, though. Suddenly calm, he triple checked that the backpack was secure before making for the door for the final time. He knew the direction he was to head. There was a tube station at the end of this street, a central node for all residents of Kingston to funnel through, either to make their way further into London or return home from work.

At six in the evening, the streets would be full with activity.

Hussein could barely wait.

Soon, the three months of tension would be in the past.

Replaced with bliss.

He had managed to get the sweating under control — or perhaps he had nothing left to perspire. In any case, he threw open the door and stepped out into the hallway, silently bidding farewell to the tiny flat that had acted as his home for the past three months.

Soon, his home would rest in the heavens.

The little girl hadn't moved for the past hour. Unnerved by her presence, he didn't make eye contact with her this time. There was no need for pleasantries — he had no further need to blend into the millions of other residents of London.

Now, emotionless, expressionless, he locked the door to his flat — he wasn't sure why exactly — and strode purposefully down the corridor toward the stairwell.

He could feel the child's eyes boring into him.

He ignored her gaze. As he passed her by, he thought he heard a muffled sob. An anguished outcry. He didn't respond.

When he made it past her, he breathed a sigh of relief.

Again, he wasn't sure why. Maybe she was a bad omen. When he made it to the stairs and descended rapidly, he forgot all about her. Instead he listened to his shoes ringing off the walls of the stairwell, feeling the weight of the device on his back.

Inside was enough plastic explosive to take out a couple of civilians — those closest to him when he set the thing off.

But — unbeknownst to London when chaos erupted — the steel bomblets had been primed, ready to release the weaponised strain of the Marburg virus into the atmosphere as soon as the traditional explosives detonated. Everything had been crammed into the backpack in such a way that the spores were guaranteed to leak into the street, protected from incineration by the blast itself.

Once again — men far smarter than himself.

He was simply the trigger man.

Reaching the bottom of the stairwell, he took a deep breath and prepared himself for the last act of his short life.

In ten minutes, he would unleash something not even he could fathom.

51

Diana couldn't take it anymore.

She had slipped back inside half an hour earlier. Briefly.

It had culminated in another verbal assault from Steve, lambasting her for fleeing and worrying her mother. Diana told Steve where to stick his criticism, and returned hastily to the hallway to stew over what had transpired.

This time, the tears didn't stop.

She sniffled and wiped her eyes and choked back sadness, but nothing seemed to stem the pain. Her home had been torn from her, and she had been forced out here to try and deal with it. She was too young to handle any of this — she wanted to simply get away, as far away from Steve and her mother as she possibly could.

She wanted new parents.

She wanted a new home.

She wanted a new life.

When the quiet man from the end of the hallway materialised again, Diana tried to make eye contact with him. She pleaded for attention — anything to take her mind off her home life. She pined for a conversation with an ordinary human being. The man seemed entirely different though — it puzzled Diana. He had affixed her with a kind look every time they'd seen each other for as long as she could remember.

It had been months since the man had moved in.

Even though they had never spoken, Diana had always felt that the man silently cared about her. Now his actions seemed robotic. His stare had turned vacant. All the colour had drained from his face and his eyes flicked off the walls incessantly, never hovering in one place for too long.

Never coming to rest on Diana herself.

It seemed like he was both nervous and excited for something. He was still wearing the same enormous backpack — she had never seen him with it before today.

He moved straight past her, almost deliberately ignoring her. Diana watched the backpack shift up and down as he continued to stride down the corridor, laser-focused.

The bitter voices flared up again, emanating from underneath the gap at the bottom of her front door. She listened to the venomous tone of her mother's voice, then the overwhelming rage of a deeper male voice — Steve at his most furious.

No more.

Diana got tentatively to her feet and shuffled from foot to foot, still hesitant.

The stranger from down the hall disappeared into the stairwell. He was moving fast. With purpose.

She wondered why.

The past six months of her life rose to a boiling point inside her. She felt every scrap of sadness and anguish. The tears refused to stop flowing. She couldn't take another day

— even another minute — hanging around this hole. It didn't feel like home.

It hadn't for quite some time.

Without realising the ramifications of what she was doing, Diana trotted after the stranger.

She had never actually spoken to him before.

She wanted to change that.

52

S later came screaming back to reality in a cacophony of noise and light.

For a moment he thought the world was ending, but he quickly realised it was all in his head. Needles of strobe-like lighting seared across his vision, as if deliberately waking him from the dead. His heartbeat roared in his ears, drowning out all other sounds — of which there were plenty. As the thrumming of his pulse became muted, he heard rabid screaming echoing across the promontory.

He looked up and blanched at what he saw.

Confusion still reigned across the plateau — multiple silhouettes ghosted across the flat ground, their features plunged into darkness by the night. They were tribesmen, and there were plenty of them. Slater had enough common sense to recognise that he didn't stand a chance against them. In optimal health, he would have torn through the remaining forces without breaking a sweat.

Now, though...

He didn't want to assess his injuries. He knew he would pass out if he did. He could barely feel his right leg — the bullet wound was no doubt horrific, having ripped a chunk of his calf clean off. Briefly he wondered why he hadn't passed out from blood loss yet. If the wound had cut his fibular artery, he wouldn't have lasted a minute.

He was lucky in that regard.

Then he saw the distant pale glow of the satellite phone, still clutched in the grip of the tribesman who had single-handedly cast a major city into something out of the apocalypse, and his memories came screaming back.

Nausea twisted his gut.

He had failed.

The reminder hammered home, just as he locked eyes with the tribesman. The man noticed him, sitting there helplessly near the mouth of the mountain trail, unable to mount any kind of decent resistance.

The man's face twisted into a sinister grin.

Not only had he succeeded at carrying out his leader's plan — now the man had the opportunity to avenge Sayyid's death.

Slater watched him duck into the pick-up truck he had used to cross the promontory and fire up the engine.

The headlights flared, blinding Slater to what came next. He squinted in the glare, his head pounding, his brain pleading for rest.

The pick-up truck shot towards him.

He willed himself to move, to do anything to stop the resulting impact, but his legs refused to work. They had turned to jelly, just as the majority of his body had, shutting itself down to combat the pain rolling over him like an invisible ghoul tweaking all his nerve endings at once.

The pick-up truck surged forward, its hood aimed straight at Slater's motionless form.

Slater bowed his head to shield his eyes from the

approaching lights. He didn't have the willpower to move — what was the point?

As he sat there, London would be reeling from one of the most devastating attacks in human history.

He didn't deserve to live to see the aftermath.

It was his fault.

As he drooped his head to face the dusty rock beneath his feet, he noticed a man-made object resting at the very edge of his blurred vision. He rolled his head to study it, using what little energy he had left.

The Jericho.

The pistol had clattered to rest just a foot away from him — in the darkness, he hadn't seen it before. Charged with a final spark of determination, he reached over and snatched it off the ground, coating the grip in his own blood.

The pick-up truck bore down on him, engine screaming.

Fuck this.

You don't need to die here.

He unloaded the remaining contents of the magazine, losing count of how many times he fired. In his lucid state, he had no idea where he was aiming or how accurate his shots were.

He simply pointed into the light, and unleashed everything he had left.

Yet his motor reflexes must have held up.

The decade of training he'd undergone must have channelled itself into his subconscious over time.

Because — even as the driver stamped on the brakes to shield himself from the barrage of gunfire — Slater heard the windshield shatter. Above the din of the burning rubber and the throaty engine and the wind whistling across the promontory, his ears picked up a pathetic wheeze, followed by the gargling of blood and gore.

He knew exactly what the sound meant.

One of the rounds had blasted straight through the man's throat, undeniably fatal. Without being able to see the extent of the damage, Slater capitalised on a surge of momentum and ignored his instincts, climbing to his feet in one fluid motion. He stumbled, wobbled, but remained standing.

The pick-up truck screeched to a halt alongside him, and he stared into the cabin to see the driver pawing half-heartedly at the gaping wound underneath his chin.

He would be dead in seconds.

Slater heard outcries from across the promontory — the remaining tribesmen must have thought the conflict was over. He was the first to admit that he was one tough son-of-a-bitch, but his better judgment took control.

He wouldn't win a fight against them.

He could barely keep himself conscious.

With his limbs moving like they were being dragged through mud, he opened the driver's door and yanked the dying tribesman out of the crimson-stained seat. The man offered no resistance — he had barely any time left. He toppled out of the cabin, pitching forward, face planting the promontory floor and lying still.

Slater collapsed into the driver's seat, blinking hard.

Somehow, he found the strength to lean on the accelerator and droop one bloody hand onto the top of the steering wheel.

The pick-up truck lurched forward, the engine drowning out the screams of the remaining tribesmen.

One glance in the side mirror and he could tell they were giving pursuit.

He tuned out everything else and plunged onto the mountain trail, the suspension groaning under the exertion.

Run.

53

Each time Slater gained ground on the convoy of vehicles hot on his heels, a wave of misery made him lag.

Every foot of ground he covered as the pick-up truck twisted and roared down the track only compounded the nausea.

You failed.

The thought roiled through his mind, drowning out everything else. It didn't matter that there were three identical pick-up trucks in his rear view mirror, keeping pace with him, desperate not to let him escape. In fact, he didn't give a shit if they caught up to him and put a bullet through his brain.

He would almost welcome it.

As the hood of the truck bounced and rattled over the uneven ground, he asked himself why he was bothering to flee.

How will you live with yourself — watching the news, seeing the trauma inflicted upon hundreds of thousands of people — knowing that you could have stopped it?

The memory of the tribesman speaking the "go-ahead" word seared his mind.

Dhi'b.

Wolf.

You failed.

Rivers of blood in the streets.

The vehicle went airborne as it shot off a particularly steep patch of disturbed rock. Slater's stomach dropped into his feet. When the front wheels smashed back to earth and he jolted painfully in the driver's seat, the headlights flickered out for a brief instant.

In the total darkness, Slater noticed a soft glow coming from the passenger footwell.

The headlights burst back into life and he corrected course, continuing his rapid descent of the mountainside.

He searched for the source of the artificial light, and his gaze came to rest on the satellite phone that had been used to make the call. The tribesman had discarded it into the passenger footwell when he'd leapt into the vehicle.

His work complete.

His attention resting solely on Slater.

Slater reached down and snatched it up, keeping one hand on the wheel. Flicking his eyes between the treacherous road ahead and the satellite phone's screen, his heart skipped a beat as he registered what the device said.

The text was in Arabic — indecipherable to Slater — but there was no mistaking the symbol displayed harshly on the digital screen.

An exclamation mark inside a triangle.

Error.

'Oh my God,' he whispered.

The call hadn't gone through.

But why?

Abu.

Frantically, Slater exited the warning screen and brought up the keypad, ripping his attention from focal point to focal point as he smashed digits into the phone. He couldn't take his eyes off the trail for more than a couple of seconds — any more than that and he would find himself spearing off the edge of the mountain.

Finishing the string of numbers, he dialled.

He pressed the phone to his ear, smearing his own blood across his cheek.

Abu answered almost instantaneously.

The man muttered some kind of greeting in Arabic — unsure about the unknown number.

'Abu, it's—' Slater began.

'*Will!*' the man screamed. 'I thought you were dead.'

'I'm—'

'Shut up,' Abu said, suddenly dangerously serious. Slater had never heard him like this. 'There's no time. I have details about the bomber.'

'What?'

'The man in London. I know where he is.'

'How—?'

'The call didn't go through, but the guy's going through with it anyway. We have minutes.'

'Fuck.'

'I could track the co-ordinates of where the call was answered from,' Abu said. 'It's an apartment building on Brook Street, in a suburb called Kingston. Very busy. It'll be hell if the device goes off.'

Slater twisted the wheel sharply to guide the pick-up truck along a steep bend in the trail. For a moment the rear wheels skidded out, jolting his heart in his chest. He corrected course and surged forward, fleeing from the remaining tribesmen.

'I...' he started, trying to compose his thoughts.

Everything was moving too fast.

'There's nothing I can do,' he admitted.

'You were military?' Abu said. 'You can make calls? If we know where he is...'

'Uh...'

Slater hadn't considered anything of the sort. He hadn't been anticipating that he would learn of the bomber's exact location — it opened a wide range of possibilities he hadn't had time to consider.

He *didn't* have time.

He had minutes.

Less than that.

Just a few hundred feet down the trail, he glimpsed the soft glow of Qasam, resting peacefully in its alcove on the mountainside. He would roar into town in seconds. Battling for control of the wheel, he suppressed a mind-crushing headache and considered his options.

'Okay,' he said. 'It'll get me killed, but I can do that.'

'Get you killed?'

'I didn't exactly part amicably with my old employers.'

'You have to stop this, Will.'

'I know.'

'It might be too late.'

'I know.'

He made to hang up the phone, but Abu interrupted. 'And one last thing...'

'What?'

'I found al-Mansur's daughter.'

Slater paused. 'You *found* her?'

'Hanging in a closet, in a spare room. Sayyid must have left her there, for al-Mansur to find. Sadistic bastard.'

'Fucking hell,' Slater said. 'Maybe it's best he never knew her fate.'

'Yeah...'

'Brook Street. Kingston. Apartment complex. Middle-Eastern male. That's what I have to work with?'

'You got it,' Abu said.

'Whatever happens,' Slater said. 'I won't ever speak to you again.'

'I'm leaving the mansion now. I've done all I can.'

'Thank you. If it wasn't for you...'

'I know,' Abu said. 'Good luck, my friend.'

The line went dead.

Slater gripped the wheel tight, his knuckles turning white, attempting to compartmentalise his emotions while struggling to control a battered old truck that was one good impact away from structurally disintegrating. He covered the last stretch of the mountain trail and shot through into the streets of Qasam.

Residential buildings flashed by on either side.

This late in the evening, civilians were in their homes, evident by the warm glow emanating from the windows Slater screamed past. He narrowed his eyes at the road ahead, vision blurred and head pounding. At the same time he moved to dial a number into the satellite phone, a number he never thought he would have to use again.

He took a deep breath.

Making the call was a death sentence.

But all other options had been exhausted.

He finished entering the digits and moved to dial...

...when his attention was torn away from the device as the road opened out ahead.

There were at least a dozen military vehicles parked across the street, forming a rudimentary blockade to prevent any kind of civilian traffic passing through. Slater counted a small army of uniformed soldiers wielding automatic weapons — he couldn't tell if they were private mercenaries or official forces.

His judgment came down on the latter.

There was no other reason for them to be here — they were al-Mansur's forces, called in to eliminate a hostile in the encampment. Slater could tell by their mannerisms that they were milling around, preparing for a targeted offensive.

They were ready for war.

Thankfully, he had commandeered a tribesman's vehicle, which made them hesitate. They weren't sure exactly what to make of the Land Cruiser that came roaring into sight, its front windscreen shot out and its chassis littered with bullet holes.

Slater checked his rearview mirror — sure enough, the four vehicles in pursuit were less than a hundred feet from his rear, closing in fast.

They weren't going to slow down.

It would take mere seconds for the remaining tribesmen to communicate with the soldiers and unite against him.

He was bottlenecked into a fatal trap.

Activating the brakes, he screeched to a halt in the middle of the deserted laneway. The soldiers watched him wordlessly, draped in shadow, confused as to what was unfolding.

Slater took a deep breath, hurled open the driver's door, and ran with everything he had left into an adjacent alleyway, keeping the phone locked tight in his grip.

54

Chaos broke out.

The soldiers screamed at him in Arabic, urging him to stop. His right leg threatened to give out, an act that would be a death sentence in every sense. He pictured himself sprawling to the pavement, help-less to resist the storm of bullets that would shred his back apart and kill him in seconds.

But he stumbled, righted himself, and ducked into the lip of the alleyway just as a chunk of the mud-brick wall directly alongside him exploded, showering him in debris.

They were firing on him.

They knew.

For a single, terrifying moment, his consciousness became detached from what lay ahead. The dark alleyway pitched and yawned, twisting in his vision. He paused, reel-ing, wondering if he had lost his mind.

Then he realised exactly what kind of condition he was in.

With his brain rattled by the impact with the ground back on the mountainside, his senses were beginning to fail themselves. He afforded himself a single moment to rest a hand against the mud-brick wall beside him. He sucked in air, regaining his balance.

Then he set off again.

He was the last chance for this plot to be foiled.

Maybe he was trying in vain.

Maybe the Marburg virus had already spewed forth from the bomblets, invisible to the naked eye, worming its way down the throats of civilians craning to get a look at the aftermath of a standard suicide-bombing.

That's how they'd do it, Slater realised.

Disguise it as something else.

Something more ordinary.

Something guaranteed to capture the attention and headlines of the first world until the real onslaught revealed itself in all its blood and gore.

A shiver ran down Slater's spine, invigorating him.

He heard soldiers and tribesman alike converging on the mouth of the alleyway. With no cover to hide behind, he was a sitting duck if he stayed put. He ran straight by a nondescript wooden door leading into a residential building, this structure also made of mud-brick. Unable to use his feet due to the crippling hole in his calf, he shouldered the door inwards, snapping the lock with a single shove.

The power of adrenalin.

He hurried into a cramped, claustrophobic hallway with minimal lighting and horrendous air filtration. The atmosphere was heavy and thick with humidity. Slater felt the sweat leeching from his pores as he hobbled frantically deeper into the building, sinking down the rabbit hole.

He didn't know where he was headed.

He just needed a few minutes alone.

That was all it would take.

Finding a derelict door at the end of the hallway, he smashed it open with another heavy blow and limped into an empty, low-ceilinged room containing a toilet and shower in the far corner.

There were no windows, and the tiny uninhabited living quarters stank of dilapidation.

Slater slammed the door shut behind him and slumped to the floor, sweating and bleeding and breathing hard.

He rested his back against the door, panting restlessly, attuning his ears to the sound of approaching combatants.

He could hear them milling around in the alleyway, their voices harsh and discordant. Their yells and barks filtered through into the room, floating under the doorway.

It would only be a matter of time before they found him.

There was no escape.

Squeezing his eyes shut to combat the various sensations washing over him — pain, resignation, acceptance — he finally dialled the number resting on the satellite phone's screen.

The call went through straight away.

Slater lifted the device to his ear and waited for the line to connect.

It was answered with total silence. Just as it always had been.

'It's Will Slater,' he said, speaking fast, his tone charged with purpose. 'You might think I'm dead, but that's something to discuss later. Get me Williams as fast as you possibly can.'

'What's this about?' a voice said.

'Get me Williams,' Slater repeated.

'Sir, I don't think—'

'If you don't put me through to Williams, I'll have you thrown in a black prison. You're just a dispatcher, but you've heard of them. Off-the-grid locations. I used to work for Black Force and I can have you dragged into one of those for the rest of your life for disobeying orders. Get me Russell Williams, right fucking now.'

'One moment.'

There was a pause at the other end of the line. Slater knew it would only drag out for a second or two, maximum. His old life had been gruelling and unrelenting, but he'd be damned if his superiors weren't efficient with their time.

They had to be.

Their line of work demanded it.

Then a familiar voice presented itself, incredulous, laced with disbelief. 'Slater?'

'Hey, Williams.'

'What the fuck are you doing? You know we have to come for you now.'

'I understand.'

'The way things went down ... you really expect us to just leave you alone? You should have kept your head buried in the sand.'

'Listen to me,' Slater said. 'This isn't about me. There is a man on Brook Street, in a suburb of London called Kingston, and he has three bomblets packed with a weaponised strain of the Marburg virus. He's going to set them off in the next few minutes. Middle-Eastern complexion. He'll have a backpack. They can't miss him.'

Williams had known Slater for long enough to understand that he was deadly serious. Whatever was unfolding, it was bad. 'Can you get to him?'

'I'm in Yemen,' Slater said.

'What the hell are you doing in—?'

'Russell!' Slater barked. 'Minutes. Get onto your contacts

in London. You need to prevent this. Pull out all the stops. I can't stress how goddamn serious this is.'

Slater could tell there were a million questions rolling through the man's mind, each on the tip of his tongue, but Williams recognised a dire situation when he saw one. He kept his response succinct. 'On it. Stay where you are. You know we need to bring you in.'

'There won't be anything to bring in.'

'Will...'

Slater ended the call and tossed the phone across the room, where it shattered against the opposite wall, its screen disintegrating into shards of glass.

There was nothing left to say. He had done everything he possibly could. It was out of his hands. Inside a grungy, darkened mud-brick room buried in the depths of a building in a remote mountain town, Will Slater let out the tension he'd been holding in ever since he'd caught sight of the infected desert wolf.

The fate of hundreds of thousands of people rested upon the reaction speed of the organisation that had exiled Slater only weeks earlier. Now, it all came down to how fast his superiors were.

And they were *fast*.

The commotion in the exterior hallway amplified. Slater heard the bodies rushing along the corridor, heading straight for the door he had his back against.

A thunderous crash jolted him on his rear — a body running straight into the door. There was a sharp pause as the man on the other side of the door understood what the resistance meant.

Someone was holding it shut.

They had their man.

Slater heard sharp commands resonate through the

building, and the activity heightened. Another impact against the flimsy frame sent him skittering across the floor again. He scrambled to his feet and threw a shoulder against his own side, keeping it shut.

For now.

It wouldn't be long before they fired straight through the wood, gunning him down where he stood. Panicked breathing and grunts of exertion trickled underneath the door frame. There were at least five men in the corridor now.

More would follow suit.

Slater had nowhere to go. He heard the racking of a slide — it spelled certain death if he stayed where he was. His options exhausted, his brain aching, he longed for rest.

Briefly, for a shadow of a moment, he started to succumb to his wounds and slid tentatively down the door frame.

Waiting for it to crash down on top of him.

Waiting for the end.

Then raging hot fire ignited inside his chest, charging him with a fight-or-flight assault of sensory overload. He felt the lightning crackle on his fingertips, invisible yet overwhelming. He ignored the pounding headache, the mangled lower leg, the bleeding palms, the battered torso, the bullet wound in his shoulder.

None of that mattered.

Because he was Will Slater, and Will Slater *didn't fucking quit.*

Gnashing his teeth together like a bat out of hell, he charged forward, yanked the door open, and launched himself into the corridor with nothing but his bare hands and a decade of experience as a black-operations warrior to rely on.

55

Russell Williams sat on one side of the sweeping oak desk that filled the majority of the room. Various official military personnel were powering their way in, awaiting the arrival of the President of the United States. Williams bore no official insignia on his neatly-pressed uniform — in fact, he had no idea what his rank was in the first place. Over the last few weeks he had been thrust from position to position like it was nothing. A career in black operations had muddied his official status, and now it had been entirely thrown out the window.

The chaos that had unfolded in the wake of Will Slater's departure had shaken up the ranks significantly.

Now, things had escalated considerably more.

The President barged into the Situation Room, his composure faltering. It was one-thirty in the afternoon in Washington D.C., and the man had been torn from a lunch meeting to deal with one of the more volatile situations the White House had ever seen.

'How long since you got the call?' the President said, dumping himself down at the head of the table.

'Just over two minutes,' Williams said.

'You sure it was Slater?'

'Certain.'

'Brook Street. Kingston. London.'

Williams nodded. One of the underlings must have informed him of the details on the way over.

'When is this set to happen?' the President said.

'Right now.'

The man paused for a single moment, mulling over the options. 'What's the likelihood Slater's messing with us?'

'He wouldn't. I know when he's serious.'

'Where is he?'

'Yemen.'

'Why is—?'

'No time,' Williams said. 'Do we make the call or not?'

'Do it,' the President said. 'Right now. Marburg ... my God.'

Military personnel scrambled for phones, carrying out procedures that had been run through time and time again in preparation drills. Amidst the chaos, Williams sat rigid, staring blankly across the table at the opposite wall.

The President noticed.

'Russell.'

Williams looked up. 'If this thing is already out there ... it's going to spread faster than we can quarantine it. We can't lock down a city. It's dusk in London, too. It'll spread like wildfire.'

The President nodded. It was the first time Williams had seen the man vulnerable — the usual icy glare that he sported in volatile situations had given way to something close to panic.

'Do you know what Marburg does to its victims?' Williams said.

'Not fully.'

'You don't want to.'

'Before I forget,' the President said, 'tell me. Did you trace Slater's call?'

Williams nodded. 'He's in a village in Yemen. In the Hadhramaut Valley.'

'Send a team in,' the President said. 'I want him extracted. Whatever it takes. We've been looking for him for too long.'

'What about the other guy?' Williams said.

Jason King.

The President shook his head. 'He's smarter. He left a United States military officer dead in Dubai. He won't show his face ever again. Slater's more reckless. He'll keep getting wrapped up in situations like these until we catch him.'

'Who do you want me to send into Yemen? Who can detain him?'

'Did he sound hurt?'

'Yes.'

'Send in a SEAL team. I want him back.'

Williams nodded. 'Understood.'

The conversation faded out, replaced by the urgent babbling of a cluster of military personnel, all barking orders and instructions into receivers at once. Williams stayed motionless amidst the carnage and pressed two fingers into his eyelids, riding out a sudden wave of nausea.

His mind turned to images of the Marburg virus in the streets of London.

The sheer trauma that would result...

He didn't want to think about it. He leant back in his chair, ran a hand through his hair, and wondered if Slater had managed to make the call in time.

56

London
England

At almost six in the evening in Kingston upon Thames, the streets had begun to fill with shift workers heading home from their offices. The sun had melted into the horizon, casting a tinged orange glow across the narrow laneways, adding a translucent quality to the hordes of civilians flocking back to their residences.

Hussein stood idly on the busiest corner of Brook Street, watching the passers-by with a curious gaze. He had pulled to a stop on the pavement seconds earlier, opting to glance intermittently down the road as if waiting for a bus.

He had been told to behave that way.

He judged the distance between himself and the swarming crowd of pedestrians to his rear. The foot traffic didn't cease, almost amplifying as he paused to ascertain the level of damage he would cause. From this position, he estimated that the initial blast would kill close to a dozen of the closest civilians.

Panic would erupt. Pedestrians would scatter.

And then, influenced by the anguished cries of those who were wounded, they would return in flocks to either lend assistance or simply gawk at what had unfolded.

Hundreds of people would inhale the spores before the police cordoned off the scene.

The authorities themselves would contract the virus, returning home to their families before they displayed any symptoms.

Hussein decided to cause as many casualties as he possibly could in the initial blast. The more collateral damage he could cause, the greater the interest amongst the general population.

He wanted all the eyes in the country on this location come tomorrow.

You never know, he thought. Maybe residents of other cities would venture to London in a naive attempt to lend a helping hand to those affected by the blast.

Little did they know...

With that thought in the back of his mind, he opted to get closer to the twin channels of pedestrians heading in different directions on the jam-packed sidewalk. He shuffled his way through the crowd, leaving the edge of the gutter, coming to rest with his back against a wrought-iron fence bordering a park.

This is it.

He would turn his back, slip his hand into his pocket, extract the detonator, and depress the small grey button on the side of the device.

Just as he had been instructed.

The uncontrollable sweating had started up again. Despite the evening chill, it was unavoidable. Hussein recognised that he was coming to the final stages of his short existence. He struggled to control his breathing, but decided that it didn't matter.

Who cares if they see me panicking?

They'll all be dead before they can do anything about it.

Fingers slick with perspiration, he slipped his hand into the pocket of his trousers and came out with the tiny device that would spell suffering for hundreds of thousands of lives.

Perhaps millions.

The thought charged him with nervous energy.

He whispered a silent prayer, closed his eyes, turned his back to the crowd...

...and pressed down.

His grip slipped, the thin coat of perspiration between his skin and the button enough to slide his index finger off it. Frustrated, thrown into disarray, Hussein swore at himself under his breath and wiped his palm on the side of his trousers.

He caught a few dirty looks, as passers-by noticed the agitated man with the backpack in their midst, but no-one cared enough to do anything about it. No-one gave him a second look. No-one wanted to appear overly paranoid. They went about their business, carrying on with their lives.

Hussein reached for the button again.

A small prodding sensation against his leg startled him, freezing him in his tracks. He looked down and noticed the girl from the block of flats standing there, directly alongside him, peering up at him with eyes brimming with tears.

He faltered, just for a moment.

'Excuse me, mister,' the girl said. 'What are you doing?'

She had no idea. Hussein realised that the incident was an almighty coincidence — the girl must have been suffering at home and latched onto whoever passed her by.

She had no knowledge of the contraption strapped to his back. He breathed a sigh of relief.

Hussein didn't answer her.

He couldn't.

He could understand a few key phrases in English, but he couldn't speak the language itself. He babbled, unsure of what to do.

What are you waiting for? a voice hissed in his head.

He composed himself. Maybe he'd considered the girl a bad omen back in the hallway, or maybe he hadn't anticipated seeing a familiar face in the crowd, or maybe he had to briefly grapple with the idea that she would be killed in the blast, her tiny body torn to shreds by the force of the plastic explosive. In the end, he concluded that it was inconsequential — if the girl wasn't killed by the initial explosion, choosing to remain in her flat, she would have succumbed to the Marburg virus anyway.

A fate worse than death itself.

Whatever the case, the sudden interruption made him hesitate.

And that was what did it.

By the time he reached for the detonator, watching the little girl's face twist into a grotesque mask of abject horror as she realised what was about to happen, he had allowed the plain-clothed police officer to sprint into range.

He never saw the man coming.

The officer — a fifty-something man hardened by decades of experience in the force — came tearing across the road, weaving between traffic, his gaze fixed on Hussein. Hussein noticed a flash of movement out of the corner of his eye, but his gaze in turn was affixed to the little girl. He knew he was about to kill her, but it didn't bother him anymore. Something far worse was in store for everyone who survived the initial blast.

The short, stocky officer hit him so hard that for a moment he blacked out on his feet, utterly stunned by the force of the impact. The man had opted to dive across the sidewalk, covering the last couple of feet in a single instant, crashing shoulder-first into Hussein with enough momentum to send the two sprawling back across the sidewalk.

As he was falling, Hussein stabbed with a sweaty finger at the detonator, which had already begun to slip from his grasp.

He missed.

The last thing he saw — reeling off-balance in the air — was the little girl standing frozen in the midst of the foot traffic, mouth agape, shocked by what she was seeing.

Hussein couldn't believe it either.

A single moment of hesitation had cost him and his commanders three months of painstaking preparation.

And it was all because she had poked him inquisitively.

Unbeknownst to the little girl, she had inadvertently prevented an apocalypse.

Fuck, was the last thing Hussein thought.

He came down awkwardly against the wrought-iron fence, his temple cracking against one of the rusting posts with enough weight and momentum behind it to cave his skull in. He experienced a horrifying explosion of seared nerve endings, a blinding flash of white light as his senses shut down...

...and then nothing at all.

57

Russell Williams had devolved into a nervous wreck by the time the call came through.

He sat in near-silence within the Situation Room for the entire duration of the wait, surrounded by the most important men and women on the planet, each of them battling their own emotions as to what a weaponised virus in central London might spawn.

He couldn't quite grasp the consequences.

When the President was informed that the British Prime Minister was waiting for him on the line, the silence in the soundproof room became deafening. The conversation was brief, and perhaps the most important in human history.

It would either spell relief, a reprise from a full hour of horrific worry and trepidation, or disaster. Williams baulked at the ramifications of failure — they would do their best to contain the spores to a certain section of the city, yet it would be near-impossible. It would take expertise and a plan that they didn't have the framework for.

It would fail.

When the President let out the breath that had caught in his throat and dropped his head gratefully to the table in front of him, a collective sigh of relief spread through the Situation Room.

'Fuck me,' Williams whispered, wiping his forehead with a shirt sleeve. 'You did it, Slater.'

Nobody spoke for what felt like forever. Details would come through later, but the present moment was reserved for letting the tension of what might have transpired dissipate, fade away into nothingness.

Finally, Williams spoke. 'What did they say?'

'The call went out to every officer in the city at the same time,' the President said. 'Fifty seconds later the bomber was tackled. A plain-clothed cop got him on a street corner. He was talking to a young girl.'

'Jesus...' Williams said. 'Was it close?'

'Down to the second.'

'And the girl?'

'Nothing to do with him. She appeared to be distracting him, although it seems she was just curious. Whatever the case, she's been brought in. She'll be labelled a national hero, I assume. Prevented a suicide bombing.'

'That's all this is being treated as?'

'Anything more and the world would lose its collective mind,' the President said. 'Best we keep it under wraps. For obvious reasons.'

Williams sighed and leant back in his seat. He stared up at the ceiling, his heart still racing. He didn't think the adrenalin in his system would fade for quite some time.

'Where do we go from here?' he said.

One of the Army officers piped up. 'At this level, the fallout is going to be grim. We'll be dealing with this for months. But the threat's over. Now we can pick up the pieces and work out what the hell happened.'

'Something tells me you'll find what you're looking for in Yemen,' Williams said.

'The SEAL team...?' the President said.

'En route,' Williams said. 'It's a volatile place, but they should be in and out before the day's over.'

'Slater knows about this. I want him brought in as fast as possible.'

'I don't know...'

'What?'

'The way he was talking,' Williams said, staring at the table in front of him, tugging intermittently at the short beard he'd begun to grow out. 'I don't know if we'll find him in one piece.'

'Well, let's hope we do,' the President said. 'Otherwise this will be one confusing mess for quite some time.'

The man rose out of his chair, ushered to the doorway by an aide.

Williams stayed where he was, thinking hard.

No-one would ever know the gravity of what had been prevented.

Except a select handful in the upper echelons of government...

...and an exiled Special Forces operative in war-torn Yemen.

HOURS LATER, resting in one of the unused offices buried in the depths of the White House, Williams was startled into action by a knock at the door.

He shifted from his position on the broad leather couch,

adjusting his suit and straightening his posture as a military official stepped into the room. He had sunk into a state of shock as the time ticked by, awaiting news from Yemen. Outside, the sky had begun to darken.

Soon, night would fall.

'Sir,' the man said. 'We've heard from the SEALs.'

'What did they say?'

'They entered a small village named Qasam quietly, at four in the morning, Yemen time. They found bodies.'

Williams bowed his head. 'Fuck. Slater was a good man.'

'Not Slater.'

Williams widened his gaze. 'What?'

'Five men in official military uniform. We believe they were soldiers under the command of Brigadier-General Abdel al-Mansur. And four more bodies, covered in traditional dress. These are just preliminary estimates, but we believe them to be members of the northern highland tribes.'

'How did they die?'

'A combination of methods. It seems a handful were beaten into submission in a rundown apartment building in the centre of the town, then the rest were picked off with their own weapons.'

'Consistent with a single hostile?'

'At this point, yes.'

'Jesus Christ.'

'We can't find Slater. The SEALs will keep looking, but they can't be around for long. I'm sure you can understand that our time in-country has to be kept to a minimum. We're not supposed to be there.'

'Pull them out,' Williams said.

'Sir?'

'Extract them. You won't find Slater. I don't know why I expected you to in the first place.'

'Sir, if he's there...'

'He won't be. I don't think you people understand what you're dealing with here. He's been in service to our government for the last ten years. He's killed hundreds — thousands, even — of our enemies. If you didn't find his body, you won't find him.'

'Why is he no longer in service?'

'That's above your pay grade. And it's the reason you haven't heard of him.'

'I'll give the orders,' the man said, exiting the room with a quick nod.

Williams slumped back against the couch, a wry smile spreading over his face. He had heard something in Slater's voice during their brief conversation that had convinced him that the man could be found. He quickly realised how foolish of a thought that had been. Perhaps a brief moment of hesitation on Slater's part, but nothing permanent. That iron will that had become the stuff of legend throughout the halls of the White House must have come roaring back.

As it had for years.

Williams rose off the couch and crossed to the nearest window as darkness fell over the grounds of the White House. He stared out over the Ellipse, fifty acres of well-maintained grounds to the rear of the massive building in which he stood.

He wondered if it was beneficial to the world to have a man as talented and relentlessly driven as Will Slater out there, roaming the globe.

He wondered where Slater was now.

Then he gave up on that train of thought and turned back to face the room, crossing to the doors that led through to the interior of the White House. There was work to be done.

He would leave Slater to his personal crusade.

Employed or not, Slater would carry on.

As he always had.

As he always would.

WILL SLATER WILL RETURN.

MORE BOOKS BY MATT ROGERS

Join the Reader's Group and get a free 200-page book by Matt Rogers!

Sign up for a free copy of '**HARD IMPACT**'.
Meet Jason King — another member of Black Force, the shadowy organisation that Slater dedicated his career to.

Experience King's most dangerous mission — action-packed insanity in the heart of the Amazon Rainforest.

No spam guaranteed.

Just click here.

ABOUT THE AUTHOR

Matt Rogers grew up in Melbourne, Australia as a voracious reader, relentlessly devouring thrillers and mysteries in his spare time. Now, he writes full-time. His novels are action-packed and fast-paced. Dive into the Jason King Series to get started with his collection.

Visit his website:

www.mattrogersbooks.com

Visit his Amazon page:

amazon.com/author/mattrogers23

Made in United States
North Haven, CT
30 May 2022

19670704R00203